Unforgettable in Love

~ The Maverick Billionaires ~

Book 7

Bella Andre &

Jennifer Skully

UNFORGETTABLE IN LOVE

~ The Maverick Billionaires, Book 7 ~

Meet the Maverick Billionaires—sexy, self-made men from the wrong side of town who survived hell together and now have everything they ever wanted. But when a Maverick falls head over heels for an incredible woman he never saw coming, he will soon find that true love is the only thing he ever really needed...

Lyssa Spencer is the apple of the Mavericks' eyes, the little sister they adore and vow to protect. But Lyssa isn't a little girl anymore. More than anything, she wishes they could see she's a grown woman and perfectly able to take care of herself. Her new boss, Cal Danniger, certainly appreciates and respects her abilities. And she appreciates Cal...in every way possible. Yet she can't imagine he'd ever consider dating her, not when her brothers would rip him limb from limb if he so much as looked at her the wrong way. But boy, does she ever want him to look at her just that way.

The Mavericks are Cal Danniger's best friends as well as his business partners. So when they ask him to watch over Lyssa by giving her a job in the San Francisco Bay Area, of course he agrees. While she impresses him with how smart, dependable, hardworking, and dedicated she is, he's not at all prepared for the powerful, sizzling attraction that takes everything in him to fight. He needs to keep his hands off her no matter what, even as he dreams of all her sweet spots he desperately wants to touch.

After one passionate and unforgettable night in London that neither can resist, Cal vows never to let it happen again...if he could only stop thinking about Lyssa, or wanting so much more.

Between a secret Lyssa is keeping from him and the Maverick Billionaires hell-bent on protecting her at all costs, do they have any chance of finding a future together?

A note from Bella & Jennifer

When we began to write about the Maverick Billionaires, we both fell head over heels in love with our strong yet vulnerable heroes and hoped readers would too. But we never expected such an amazing outpouring of love for our books! It has been, and continues to be, one of our greatest pleasures to write about our Mavericks, the women they love, and the families they have built.

We are so pleased to let you know that the series will be continuing far beyond seven books—but before we say too much, we'll let you read more about the heroes and heroines you have to look forward to meeting in *Unforgettable in Love*. We hope you absolutely love Lyssa and Cal's story, which might very well be our most requested book to date!

Many of you may recall our reader letter in *Reckless in Love* in which we told you about two wonderful ladies, Doris Beach, Jennifer Skully's mother, and Judy Moffett, after whom we created Francine Ballard, Charlie's mom. Francine is heroic, suffering from debilitating arthritis, yet she never gives up, walking a mile a day despite her pain. And that's what Doris Beach and Judy Moffett did: They pushed through, kept going day after day, kept smiling, kept laughing, kept everyone around them laughing. So much more than just our inspiration for Francine, they inspired our lives. This past year we lost Doris and Judy, both at the age of ninety-five and within a month of each other. They will be greatly missed, but they will always be in our hearts and continue to inspire all the people whose lives they touched.

With love,
Bella Andre and Jennifer Skully

P.S. Please sign up for our New Release newsletters for more information on new books. http://www.Bella Andre.com/Newsletter and http://bit.ly/SkullyNews

Dedication

To Doris Beach, loving mother, and Judy Moffett,
dear friend.

Devoted friends for thirty-five years.

Chapter One

Lyssa Spencer had flown in sumptuous private jets before. But this was by far the nicest plane she'd ever been in. The carpet was plush, the seating was upholstered in the softest leather, and the onboard bathroom was so large and luxuriously appointed that she could have quite happily lived in it.

"Did one of my brothers get a new plane?" she asked Cal Danniger as she settled into a leather armchair, making herself comfortable for the long flight to London.

Across the cabin table, Cal shook his head. "No."

"I didn't realize any companies rented private jets this nice."

"As far as I know," he said in that deep voice that made all of her nerve endings come alive despite knowing he was *off-limits*, "none do."

It finally dawned on her. "*You* own this jet?"

He nodded.

She felt all kinds of embarrassed. As if she'd implied that Cal was nothing more than an administrative lackey for her brothers, rather than an incredibly successful businessman in his own right. Especially when she knew exactly how it felt to be undervalued in the shadow of her amazingly successful family.

Her whole life, she'd been seen as nothing more than an extension of the Mavericks. Most people didn't realize that, apart from Daniel, the Mavericks were actually her foster brothers. But blood ties didn't matter—they had grown up as family, which meant that she had five big brothers. Six, if you counted Gideon, who, upon entering the fray, had immediately treated her like a little sister he needed to protect.

"I didn't mean—"

She would have continued her apology, but the flight attendant stepped into the cabin. "Would you like coffee, Mr. Danniger?" The woman had zeroed in the entirety of her attention on Cal, and her gaze on him was like a caress.

And why not? Cal was an extremely attractive man. In his mid-forties, with a few strands of gray streaking his chestnut hair, he was tall and fit, his eyes a penetrating silvery shade that made Lyssa feel like he could see all of her secret hopes and dreams and longings.

This summer at Ari and Matt's wedding, Lyssa had drunk just enough wine to let her guard down with her girlfriends and voiced her appreciation of Cal's taut muscles and toned body. Unfortunately, Daniel had overheard and gone Neanderthal on her. Her brother's words still rankled: *He's not for you.*

It was precisely how the Mavericks had always taken care of her—by trying to make all of her big decisions for her while also dictating everything she could and couldn't do. She knew they loved her to pieces and would do anything for her. They had already done *so* much. They'd looked out for her growing up in Chicago and supported her in her choice of majors at college and then in her career as an accountant. And she loved them without reservation. Even if they too often treated her like she was still fourteen years old, rather than a twenty-six-year-old woman who was perfectly capable of taking care of herself and making her own decisions, big and small.

Cal smiled at the flight attendant. "I'd love some coffee. Thank you, Delilah."

"I'd love a cup, as well," Lyssa said, even as she wondered if he had any idea how sexy his smile was. Delilah had certainly noticed.

"It will be my *pleasure,*" the flight attendant said to Cal with absolutely no subtlety—and not even the slightest glance toward Lyssa—before she headed back to the galley, her hips swaying.

To Cal's credit, his eyes didn't follow the woman's movements, nor did he seem to be counting down the minutes until he could sneak away with her to make use of the onboard bedroom.

His behavior was consistent with what Lyssa knew

of him. While he definitely didn't lack for female company—some might even use the word *playboy* to describe him—at his core, he was an upstanding guy who would never take advantage of his wealth or position of power.

Cal had been her boss for six weeks. In September, she'd quit her job in Chicago, moved to San Francisco, and taken on the accounting activities for Gideon Jones's Lean on Us Foundation.

For years, Gideon had owned a painting given to him by Karmen Sanchez, a fellow comrade-in-arms who had been killed overseas. Little had Gideon known that the painting was worth sixty million dollars until his fiancée, Rosie, who had knowledge of the art world, had done some research and realized he was in possession of a rare masterpiece by famed eighteenth-century artist Miguel Fernando Correa. Instead of using the money on a lavish new lifestyle, he'd started a foundation to benefit foster children, returning veterans, and military families. As a veteran himself, Gideon understood the difficulties of assimilating back into civilian life. Rosie had gone through the foster care system along with his sister, Ari, so it was only natural for him to want to help. However, given that Gideon had neither the time nor the expertise to run a nonprofit foundation, Cal had offered to step in to manage it.

Cal's first move had been hiring Lyssa, and she absolutely loved her new job. Though a part of her wondered if her brothers had asked Cal to give her this job because they knew how unhappy she'd become at her previous company, it only made her more intent on proving to all of them that she had *earned* it.

As they waited for coffee, they got down to business, both opening their folders on their latest potential contributor, resort tycoon Dane Harrington. Dane had built a worldwide empire of health spas and resorts. Though his headquarters was in Northern California, he was currently in London launching a new resort. Dane was the reason for this trip—they hadn't wanted to wait for his return to the U.S. to make their pitch.

"I'd like to begin the presentation by explaining a bit about the programs we want to fund," Cal told her. "Once I'm done with the dog-and-pony show, it would be great if you stepped in with the budgets."

Lyssa almost gave herself whiplash looking up from the papers she'd been scanning. "You want *me* to detail the budgets to Dane?"

Cal smiled, seemingly unaware of just how sexy he looked—or how much he made her heart race. "You're the one who put the numbers together, so you're the best person for the job."

Lyssa was astounded. She'd figured he'd brought her along simply to run the presentation software and provide background data if he needed it, not to actually present her budget to a hugely valuable donor.

"Besides," he added, "I've never seen anyone do as

thorough a job as you."

His appreciation for her talent made her glow in a way she couldn't hide. In Chicago, she'd been relegated to collections despite having earned a degree in accounting with honors. She'd asked her boss for more responsibility, but he'd had no interest in finding out what she was capable of. Working for Lean on Us was a dream come true, even better because she'd moved to San Francisco, which she loved.

As soon as Lyssa had flown the coop, her parents had also decided it was finally time to go west and join the rest of the family in the Bay Area. Though she was pleased that her parents would be nearby, she had a niggling suspicion that one of the main reasons they were moving was so they could still watch over her.

Her brothers had found the perfect home for her folks in Portola Valley and were having a great time fixing it up. Her dad had taught them all about home repairs when they couldn't afford a repairman, so each of them not only knew their way around a tool belt, but after spending so many of their days behind a desk inside an office, they loved the hard, hands-on work of the house renovation project.

Delilah returned with their coffees. "There you go, Mr. Danniger. Your coffee, just the way you like it."

"Thanks, Delilah." Though he was polite, he was so focused on the document he was reading, he barely looked up.

"If there's anything I can get you, Mr. Danniger, just let me know." She paused before adding a husky, "*Anything* at all."

At last, Cal met the woman's gaze. "I'm good, thanks. But I'll let you know if I need anything later in the flight."

Delilah practically melted into a puddle of goo when his eyes met hers. She seemed distracted as she put Lyssa's mug down in the middle of a stack of papers, coffee slopping over the rim to leave a ring.

Lyssa sopped it up with a napkin as Cal opened another folder, saying, "Let's move on to the six-month forecast."

Her numbers were solid on their plans to purchase buildings, hire staff, and buy equipment. This was where new contributors came in. As huge an amount as sixty million sounded—and despite the fact that Cal was working *pro bono* for the foundation—when the money was spread across everything they hoped to accomplish, it was nowhere near enough.

Throughout the flight, Cal never wasted a moment. He was intelligent, diligent, incisive, and all business. And, she thought with a sigh she never gave voice to, sexier than any man she knew.

A few hours after takeoff, Lyssa's stomach growled, loudly.

"Was that your stomach?" Cal grinned. "Or is there a monster hiding in one of the closets?"

She gave him a lopsided grin. "While I can't guarantee there aren't any monsters hiding on your plane—which would make an awesome plot for a horror movie, by the way—I can tell you that I'm starved."

He pressed a button and spoke into the intercom. "Delilah, could you please take our orders for dinner?"

As if she had been waiting breathlessly just outside the lounge door for Cal to summon her, Delilah was immediately at his side. "What would you like, Mr. Danniger?"

It was obvious to Lyssa that she hoped his answer would be, *You.*

"I asked the chef to bring steak and lobster on board, along with fresh fruit and vegetables. Is that okay with you, Lyssa?"

"Better than okay," she said as her stomach grumbled even more loudly in anticipation of the delicious meal. Living on her own, she'd made cost-cutting measures because she wanted to manage her career without her brothers' handouts. She never wasted a leftover, always brought a bag lunch, didn't own a car, and walked to the foundation's headquarters. Steak and lobster would be a rare treat. If she had leftovers, maybe she could take them home.

"Please bring us some of everything, Delilah."

"With *pleasure*, sir."

Lyssa tried not to roll her eyes at how over the top the woman was behaving. But honestly, she shouldn't be too hard on Delilah. Cal was the kind of man who made women act a little breathless and crazy.

"Excuse me," Lyssa said, getting up.

The luxurious bathroom had both a shower and a jetted tub. Mirrors all around reflected her face, and the walls and floor were tiled in gold-flecked marble. Even the taps were gold.

This rivaled any of the jets her brothers owned. She suddenly wondered just how much money Cal had. Was he also a billionaire?

As she washed her hands, she looked into the mirror and realized her cheeks were a little flushed. This was how she always felt around Cal, like all of her senses were heightened simply by being near him.

Lyssa reminded herself for the thousandth time to stop being ridiculous. Not only was he her boss, he was also one of her brothers' closest friends and would never dare step over the line with her, even if he wanted to. Which he clearly didn't. She dried her hands on the plush towel and walked back toward the lounge.

She couldn't resist peeking through the door of the connecting bedroom, however. Yet again, her mind created fantasies she couldn't banish—silk sheets against her naked body, strong fingers caressing her skin. What kind of lover would Cal be? Standing in his bedroom, she could easily imagine his kisses, his lips on her body, and how easily the tub in the bathroom could fit two people who were desperately hungry for each other.

He'd never been married, didn't have kids. As far as she knew, he didn't date long term either. She'd seen him in plenty of gossip magazines, always with a different actress or celebrity. But in the pictures, Cal always seemed a bit bored. Thinking about it more, she realized he'd never brought a woman to any Maverick function and had gone stag to Ari and Matt's wedding.

Her brothers might know why Cal was still alone. Was there some big, dark secret in his past? Had his heart been broken, never to recover? Or was it simply that he'd never found anyone who made him want to give up his freedom?

She would never ask her brothers what they knew about Cal's single status. If she did, they'd surely get wigged out about *why* she wanted to know. No doubt Daniel would start that *he's not for you* business again.

Regardless, she wanted her job more than she wanted a glorious tumble with Cal on that big bed—a fantasy tumble that was as likely to happen as winning the lottery, which meant she had absolutely nothing to worry about. So once again, she forcefully shoved away all thoughts of attraction.

The steak and lobster were on the table by the time she returned, and her mouth watered at the delicious smell.

"Oh my God, this is so good," she said around the

first mouthful of butter-drenched lobster. Living off ramen and salads made her appreciate a hearty meal. Lyssa attacked every scrumptious bite with gusto. Looked like there would be no leftovers, after all.

"My chef will be pleased to hear you think so," Cal said, laughter in his voice at her reaction to the food. "James is one of the best chefs in the business. I feel lucky every day that he agreed to walk away from his other clients to work with me." Cal held up a bottle. "Would you like champagne?"

"We've still got a lot of work to do," she replied. "I'm afraid champagne will make me sleepy."

"Actually, it might be best if both of us rest after we eat. That way, we'll be fresh when we get to London. There's a bedroom in the back of the aircraft that you can use, if you'd like."

She tried to will her cheeks not to blush at his mention of the bedroom after all the fantasizing she'd done. Especially when she thought she saw a brief flash of heat in Cal's eyes. Talk about an active imagination. Why on earth would Cal ever look at her that way?

Whatever the look was, it disappeared in an instant. And it was enough to remind her that she was here to do a damned good job for the foundation, not to dream about kissing her boss.

"Actually, if it's okay with you, I'd prefer to use this time away from distractions—" Especially something as distracting as sleeping in his bed! "—to keep powering through our to-do list before we meet with Mr. Harrington."

"It's rare to meet someone who works even harder than I do," he noted with another smile. "I knew hiring you was a good decision."

"The best one you've ever made," she agreed with a cheeky grin.

With that, she settled back to eat her dinner, bound and determined to ignore her attraction to her boss. No. Matter. What.

Chapter Two

They closed their last research folder as his plane landed at Heathrow. Lyssa yawned, covering it with her hand. Having ventured all over the world on business trips for the past two decades, Cal was used to jet lag and dramatic time changes, but he figured Lyssa would need a little time to recover from the all-nighter they'd just pulled.

"You've gone above and beyond for the past eleven hours," Cal said. "Why don't you plan on hitting the sack for a few hours once we get to the hotel?"

"You went above and beyond too," she pointed out. "And actually, I'd prefer to stay up until at least nine tonight to acclimate to the time change. Otherwise, I'll probably be up in the middle of the night."

Yet again, it struck Cal just how much of a go-getter Lyssa was. She'd been running at full speed since the day she'd started working for him six weeks ago.

The truth was that he'd hired her as a favor to the Mavericks. Evan had mentioned how much Lyssa hated her job in Chicago. Sebastian had noted what a great job she'd done helping his fiancée, Charlie, with the accounting for her sculpture business. And Daniel had hinted that his parents would love to move west, but only if Lyssa were there too.

Before he'd hired her, Cal had only ever seen her in party mode—at backyard barbecues, weddings, birthdays, holidays. She was always laughing, always having fun. He'd wondered if he'd regret taking her on, if she had it in her to be serious and get work done.

He should have known better. Lyssa was a Maverick. During the past six weeks, even when Cal had thought he might be overloading her with half a dozen projects, she got through them all in record time, then asked for more. Thus far, she had brilliantly managed the office, while also putting together research portfolios on potential contributors, plus outlining their plans for the future in alignment with Gideon's vision for Lean on Us. Big plans that far outpaced the sixty million dollars he'd received for the painting. Cal had secured a few smaller contributions, along with funds from each of the Mavericks, but billionaire Dane Harrington was their first huge prospect.

Cal strongly believed in Gideon's vision of helping soldiers returning from active service, given that they often experienced a hard time. Add to that injuries or PTSD or even a soldier's death, help could be required for years by both veterans and families. Given Gideon's past, he understood the healing process more than most. Cal was also glad that they would be helping foster children, another cause very close to Gideon's and all the Mavericks' hearts.

It was midafternoon by the time they cleared Customs and hailed a taxi to the hotel. He'd booked a suite, charging it to his own company, not the foundation. They'd used his plane for the same reason. At this point in his life, Cal liked a certain amount of luxury, but he certainly didn't expect the foundation to pay for first-class accommodations or flights. Especially given that he was also planning to take care of his own business while he was here.

In the back of the cab, Lyssa smiled at him, looking a little bleary-eyed from staying up all night. He wasn't sure she'd manage to remain awake until nine p.m., no matter how determined she was to acclimate to the time change.

The bellman showed them to the suite, which consisted of two bedrooms with a sitting room between and a breakfast nook just inside a set of balcony doors.

Not wanting her to feel at all uncomfortable, he explained, "While this can be set up as a connected suite during the day so we have a place to work, at night you can completely lock off your side."

He couldn't quite read her expression as she said, "I'm sure there will be no need for that, but thanks for letting me know."

"Why don't you take that room?" Cal pointed to

the larger one. "It has a soaking tub."

"Are you sure you don't want the Jacuzzi?" she asked, a blush suddenly staining her cheeks.

"I prefer a shower."

Her rosy flush deepened. "But what about the tub on your jet? Don't you ever use it?"

Lyssa was beautiful, smart, funny, and she could hold her own in a conversation. Not to mention that the incredible sounds of pleasure she had made while eating her steak and lobster should be deemed illegal.

But there were two *massive* strikes against dating Lyssa Spencer. First, she was the Mavericks' younger sister, and his close friends and colleagues would kill him for even looking at her the wrong way, let alone touching or kissing her. And second, she was his employee.

"The tub was already there when I bought the plane," he replied as he shoved all thoughts of Lyssa naked and glistening in the bathtub out of his head. "I didn't feel like remodeling it."

His cell phone rang, and seeing it was Gideon, he answered on speaker. "Hello, Gideon. Lyssa and I just arrived in London. We'll be meeting with Dane Harrington tomorrow."

"That's great," Gideon replied, but he didn't sound at all pleased. Once he said, "We've got a problem with the IRS," Cal understood why.

Stepping into the sitting room, Cal put his phone

on the coffee table. He beckoned Lyssa to join him as he settled on the sofa. Whatever fatigue either of them had been feeling vanished at the anxiety in Gideon's voice.

"What's the problem?" Lyssa asked, looking seriously concerned, since the IRS was her purview.

"They're denying us nonprofit status." Gideon's voice was a harsh rasp.

Lyssa blanched. Given that their donors counted on the charitable tax deduction, being denied nonprofit status would be disastrous from a fundraising perspective.

"Could you please text a photo of the IRS letter to me so I can see exactly what they're objecting to?" Lyssa asked, keeping her voice calm despite her obvious anxiety. "Once I know what the issue is, I'll get in touch with them immediately to work on reversing their decision."

"I just sent it. I'd appreciate a call back as soon as you've interfaced with them."

"Will do." The smile in her voice died the moment the call ended.

The text had already pinged through to her phone, and Cal's arm brushed hers as he leaned over to read the letter with her. It looked like nothing more than a bunch of slightly threatening legalese to Cal, but he wasn't a tax specialist.

Then Lyssa pointed at one of the paragraphs toward the end of the letter. "They're denying the foundation nonprofit status because they think it's for the benefit of a private person. But that's not what I put on the form." She turned to look at him. "I can show it to you."

She was so close Cal could see the flecks of gold in her pretty brown eyes, and for a moment, he forgot about anything other than how lovely she was.

Damn it, he thought when he caught himself, he needed to stop doing that!

Forcing himself to get back to business—and *only* business—he told her, "I don't need you to show me anything. I trust that you filled out everything correctly."

"I did," she said. "Fortunately, I've got a contact at the IRS. Tasha's brother, Drew, gave the name to me when I helped him set up his nonprofit after their dad disappeared." Tasha was Daniel's significant other, and all of them assumed they'd be getting engaged in the near future. "I'm sure if you speak with him and explain what looks to have happened, he'll help sort things out for us."

He could step in now, act the heavy with the IRS agent to demand he fix things pronto. But this was Lyssa's show. "You should call. It's your paperwork, and you've already established a rapport with him."

When she smiled, he was surprised to see gratitude in her eyes. Still, she asked, "Are you sure you don't want to do it? Your name will carry a lot more weight than mine."

"I'm sure." He'd witnessed just how persuasive she could be many times over the past six weeks. Plus, the guy was her contact, not his.

Miracle of miracles, when she dialed the man's direct line, he answered. Cal walked to the large plate-glass window to look out at the view of Hyde Park, not wanting to hang over Lyssa's shoulder.

"Hi, Roger, this is Lyssa Spencer with the Lean on Us Foundation." Despite her concerns about the foundation, he could hear the smile in her voice as she said, "Yes, it's nice to speak with you again too. How is your daughter doing now that she's started preschool?" After listening to his reply, she said, "Oh, that's wonderful!" After a brief pause, she spoke again. "I'm enjoying San Francisco—thanks for asking. Although I'm reaching out today because we just got a letter denying us nonprofit status, which was a bit of a surprise. I know you're extremely busy, but if you wouldn't mind going through the paperwork with me so that we can iron this out, I'd really appreciate it."

Cal listened as they went through the form and confirmed that everything looked fine, until she finally got to the part with the problem. "Yes, Roger. I believe that might be the error right there. Could it have been keyed into the system incorrectly?" When Roger obviously agreed that was what must have happened, she asked, "Do we need to resubmit? Or can this be fixed right away? We're approaching donors, and we need to be able to confirm that any contributions will be charitable deductions."

Cal turned away from the London view in time to see her grin as she gave him the thumbs-up. "Thanks so much, Roger. I'll look for a revised letter. And if you wouldn't mind sending that as soon as possible, it will keep my boss from breathing down my neck and making my life absolutely miserable." She winked at Cal as Roger agreed on his end to help her any way he could. "Thank you, Roger. If I ever decide to quit this job, I'll certainly think of you and the IRS as an alternative."

"Yes!" Lyssa exclaimed after she'd hung up. Jumping off the couch, she bounded toward Cal, her right hand up for a high five. But when her foot caught on the rug, she stumbled into his arms instead.

Their impromptu hug lasted only a few seconds, yet it was far too long for his peace of mind. Silently swearing, he reminded himself yet again that he needed to stop thinking about how good she felt in his arms.

"I never thought I'd see the day when anyone could wrap an IRS agent around their little finger," Cal noted. "Am I right in assuming that he offered you a job too?"

She was laughing as she stepped out of his arms,

her color high. "He was a pussycat. And yes, he did invite me to come work at the IRS anytime." She clapped her hands. "I'm so pleased we got it all worked out."

"*You* got it all worked out." Cal gazed at her glowing features as she laughed, the rosy flush in her cheeks. "I never had a doubt."

* * *

I never had a doubt.

Lyssa let the compliment sink in.

Cal believed in her. And that hug… The feel of his arms around her was *so* good. But she couldn't fixate on that now—or ever.

Her email pinged a moment later. "Hopefully, that's from Roger."

"If it is," Cal said, "it will be the fastest IRS correction in history, and I'm going to give you a raise."

Indeed, when she clicked her email, the corrected letter had arrived. Her grin was huge. "I'll send it to Gideon immediately so he can stop worrying."

She forwarded the message and received an immediate happy-face emoji and a thumbs-up from Gideon.

"That settles it," Cal said, his approving smile going straight to her heart. "I'm raising your salary by five thousand a year."

"Five thousand?" She could hardly believe it. She wouldn't have to live on peanut butter and jelly sandwiches and an apple for lunch anymore. But since all she'd done was fix something that never should have been broken in the first place, she said, "You don't have to do that, Cal. Especially when I know we need every penny we can get for the foundation."

"I sure as hell do need to do it, Lyssa. I'm a man of my word. And," he teased, "do you think I want to lose a star employee who has an in with the IRS? This calls for a celebration. Something special to commemorate our first major victory."

She should have been exhausted after having been up for almost twenty-four hours. Instead, she felt energized. "Fabulous. What shall we do?"

"If you trust me, I might have a surprise up my sleeve that I think you'll like."

"Of course I trust you." Even if a part of her wished he was a little *less* trustworthy when it came to his unspoken vow to her brothers never to look at her as an attractive woman. "How long do I have to get ready?" By now, she was desperate for a shower and a change of clothes.

"How about an hour? That should give me time to make arrangements."

"How dressed up should I get?" She'd packed mostly business attire, plus jeans, a shirt, and one dress just in case.

"On the dressier side, if you've got something that will work."

"I do."

After unpacking and shaking the wrinkles out of her dress, she took a luxurious shower. She was back in the sitting room before the hour was up.

"You look nice," he said.

She might have blushed, even though it was nothing more than an ordinary compliment her brothers or parents might have given her. "Thank you." She ran her gaze over him. He looked dashing in a blue pinstripe suit. He always dressed well, his suits tailored and fitting to perfection. "So do you."

A cab was waiting outside, and Cal handed the driver a piece of paper with their destination. As they started a madcap race through town, she gazed at the crowded London streets flashing by, the double-decker buses, the tower of Westminster Cathedral. "I love London. It's always so full of life."

"Have you been here before?" Cal asked.

"Daniel took me during summer break once in high school when he had a conference to attend. I loved the way history comes to life in every nook and cranny. I've always longed to come back."

He looked confused by the idea that she'd never returned. "I'm sure your brothers could have sent you back anytime you wanted. If not on one of their private planes, then first class on a commercial airline."

Lyssa shook her head. "No, I hate the idea of sponging off them. I know they're billionaires, and sending me on another trip to London wouldn't have been so much as a drop in their bank bucket, but I decided a long time ago that I wanted to pay my own way as soon as I was able."

She felt spotlighted by Cal's gaze as he said, "I get it. I've always wanted to make my own way too."

The cabbie lurched to the left and stomped on the brakes right before he slammed into the curb. That was when she saw where they were.

"Are we going up on the London Eye?" When Cal nodded, she practically hugged him again, on purpose this time, rather than stumbling into his arms. "When I was here before, I did a tour of the Tower of London and a boat trip down the Thames to Greenwich, but I didn't have time to fit in a ride on the London Eye."

Cal's smile grew. "Then it will be my pleasure to take you on London's finest Ferris wheel."

Everything about London excited her, but going up in the London Eye would be amazing.

Especially because she'd be with Cal.

Chapter Three

Cal paid the cabbie as Lyssa climbed out to stand on the pavement and gaze up.

The London Eye dominated the skyline. She'd heard the pods could hold up to twenty people and had an amazing three-hundred-and-sixty-degree view of London. At the top, London would be a carpet of lights below them.

Lyssa clapped her hands in delight. "This is such a wonderful treat. Thank you."

She felt Cal close beside her, smelled his deliciously male scent she shouldn't have let herself notice. And yet she closed her eyes a moment to savor it.

"Thank *you* for solving a huge problem and making it look so easy."

"That's my job," she said with a smile. She felt giddy, a combination of happiness and probably sleep deprivation as well.

A tall attendant with bushy white eyebrows appeared. "Mr. Danniger?"

"Yes." Cal shook the man's hand. "Are you ready

for us?"

"Your capsule will be here in a few moments," he answered in a cultured British accent.

"We have a whole capsule to ourselves?" She turned to Cal, her heart rate tripping over itself at his kindness.

"We deserve a solo capsule." Cal smiled. "Especially after what you accomplished today."

She felt herself blush. *Aw shucks, it was nothing*, she wanted to say. But Cal made her feel important and needed, and she didn't want to diminish those feelings.

The attendant gestured for them to follow him. "Your private capsule has arrived."

Their reflections showed in the capsule's one-way-view windows as they bypassed the waiting queue. Whispers, along with the clicks of cameras, followed them as though they were celebrities.

The dress she wore was one of her favorites, the green fabric accentuating her dark hair, the cleavage just short of plunging, circumspect yet with a hint of skin.

The attendant opened the door with a flourish.

Stepping inside, Lyssa gasped. She twirled around the interior, taking in every detail as the door slid shut on their own private nightclub. "How did you arrange all this in an hour and a half?"

Cal smiled, a sparkle in his eye. "It's amazing what can be accomplished when you set your mind to a task.

But you already know that, don't you?"

In one corner, a string quartet played a pretty bal-
lad from the forties. In another corner, a lavish array of
appetizers was spread out on a long table. A parquet
dance floor lay in the center beneath fairy lights
crisscrossing the ceiling. Two leather chairs faced out
to maximize the view, a champagne bucket on a café
table between them.

With barely a jerk, the capsule moved, rising slowly, the lights of London filling the windows.

As wonderfully as her family treated her, no one
had ever done anything like this for her. Maybe it was
that Cal wasn't family, that he wasn't obligated, that
he'd simply appreciated what she'd done. Whatever
the reason, she wanted to relish every moment of this
London fairy tale he'd created for her.

* * *

Cal waved a hand at the table laden with appetizers.
"We ate such a small lunch before the plane landed
that you must be starving. I know I am." After handing
her a plate, he took one of his own, piling on hors
d'oeuvres.

"This all looks delicious," she agreed. "I have to try
one of each." She took a bruschetta, a lobster roll, a
shrimp puff, and a phyllo star.

Once her plate was full, she moved to the window
again, her smile lighting up the night sky. "It's gor-

geous, beautiful, fantabulous."

Then she took a bite and made a sound of such pleasure, it wound sensuously through him. He never should have let it affect him, but Lyssa experienced everything with so much wonder, so much passion. She'd been amazed by his plane, enchanted by the hotel suite, and now she was in awe of the city view from the London Eye.

Cal found it surprising and refreshing. After all, her brothers were as rich as Croesus. They could afford to give their sister anything she wanted. She could be lying on the beach in Saint-Tropez, living off the Mavericks. Instead, she worked for the foundation and put her whole heart into it.

He shouldn't find her attitude so surprising, though, not when he already knew what really mattered to her family. Though Daniel Spencer headed a huge home-improvement conglomerate, he was still passionate about making free how-to videos. Matt Tremont was an amazing inventor with robotics factories worldwide, yet the light of his life was one small boy and his new wife, Ari. Will Franconi's import-export empire circled the globe, but he'd drop anything and everything for Jeremy, his wife's sweet kid brother who'd been injured in a childhood accident and would always have the heart and mind of a seven-year-old. Evan Collins ran a multinational financial corporation, yet he'd welcomed his estranged mother back into his life, along with his long-lost twin siblings, Kelsey and Tony, never considering that they might want his billions. Now he and Paige, the love of his life, were expecting a child. And for Sebastian Montgomery, the most important thing in the world was his fiancée's career—and keeping a wide smile on Charlie's face.

Susan and Bob Spencer had raised the Mavericks to be loyal and loving. The Spencers had worked their entire lives at what many considered menial labor— Bob as a baggage handler at O'Hare and Susan as a waitress. Though they'd already had two children they could barely afford to feed and house, they'd happily welcomed four foster boys into their home because those kids had needed them desperately.

That was the stock from which Lyssa Spencer had sprung. Of course she worked hard and appreciated everything she was offered.

Cal popped the cork on the champagne. "You didn't get your champagne on the plane. Are you ready for a glass?"

A waiter bustled over from a darkened corner. "If you'll allow me to pour, Mr. Danniger."

Cal handed over the bottle. When a man had a job, no matter what it was, you had to let him take pride in it.

The man finished pouring, handing them each a glass. Then he disappeared again behind a potted plant, discreet and unobtrusive.

Lyssa pulled Cal to the window. "Look! There's Big Ben. And Tower Bridge. It's so wonderful seeing it all from the best vantage point in town."

He was used to jaded women who expected exotic trips and expensive treats as their due, women for whom the most scintillating topic was themselves. But then, he'd never dated a down-to-earth woman, had he? Someone who worked for a living, who had responsibilities. Someone to whom family was the most important thing. Those were the qualities that made the Maverick women extraordinary.

And Lyssa had all those qualities in spades.

"It's so beautiful up here," she said, her voice dreamy as the capsule moved in a slow upward glide.

"Shall I turn down the lights?" the waiter interrupted softly. "It makes the panorama even more spectacular."

"Yes, please," Lyssa said, gracing the young man with such a bright smile that his cheeks reddened in response.

After the fairy lights dimmed, Lyssa circled the capsule again, trailing her hand along the rail, besotted by the lights stretching out below them. "It's otherworldly."

Cal was mesmerized far more by her enjoyment and her delight than he was by the dazzling lights of London. And by her beauty, even as he told himself she was untouchable.

She picked up her champagne. "To the most amazing night ever."

He tapped his glass to hers, forcing back a vision of an even *more* amazing night in his bed. "Yes," he said instead, "to an amazing night."

"And the food is scrumptious." She was still working on the same plate, nibbling on the appetizers.

The darkness was broken only by the dimmed fairy lights. Even the band lay in darkness except for the discreet lights on their music stands, the music drifting over the two of them like something from heaven.

"It's magical," she whispered.

He was suddenly afraid to look at her. The setting was too enchanting, too enticing. Too seductive. Perfect for romance...and a prelude to a sizzling-hot night of sex.

The quartet ended one song and began another. Lyssa set down her champagne and her plate. "I love this song."

Though hauntingly familiar, he couldn't place the tune.

"'Unforgettable,'" she said in response to the question in his eyes. "It's perfect for this unforgettable night." She waited a beat. "Nat King Cole? From the fifties?"

The sweetness of her smile dazzled him. Then he finally understood what she was hinting at. "Would you care to dance?" He held out his hand, even though a voice in his head was telling him that dancing with her would be playing with fire.

"Why, I'd love to, Mr. Danniger." Her hand in his, she let him lead her to the dance floor.

The capsule wasn't large, and dancing seemed too incredibly intimate as he took her in his arms. He'd danced with her at Matt and Ari's wedding, but those had been fast, fun dances and included two young boys and the rest of the single women. Even then, he'd felt Daniel's evil eye on him, and it had made him laugh to think that his friend could ever be worried that Cal would dare touch his sister.

But as he twirled Lyssa in his arms tonight, Cal realized Daniel's evil eye wasn't far off the mark. She felt so sweet in his arms.

Too sweet.

"Where'd you learn to dance?" he asked as she followed his steps gracefully.

She laughed, and the honeyed sound vibrated through him. Whenever she laughed at the office, he lost his train of thought for a few moments. "I used to make my brothers dance with me when I was little. You should've seen them, hauling me around while I stood on their toes and bossed them around." She giggled. "They'd turn beet red, but Mom told them that someday, when they got married, they'd have to know how to dance. I danced to this song when we played it on Dad's old record player," she added softly. "And where did you learn?"

"After the first charity function I attended, I realized I'd better master ballroom dancing."

Her eyebrows went up. "You took lessons?"

He shook his head. "I watched and analyzed."

Her smile almost brought him to his knees. "Of course. That's how you do everything, isn't it? You watch and learn."

"You do the same thing," he noted as they executed another perfect glide around the capsule.

They were at the very top of the wheel now, the sight of London spread out in a dizzying panorama before them. Or maybe it was simply that the feel of her in his arms made his brain fuzzy.

He hadn't wanted to admit it. Hadn't wanted to face the truth. But with Lyssa in his arms, there could be no more hiding from the fact that he'd noticed her all along. Noticed her skill at work, her ability with people, her sweetness, her confidence, her willingness to do anything he asked. She soaked up knowledge and responsibility like a sponge. He'd noticed how beautiful she was at Matt and Ari's wedding. If he was honest, he hadn't truly taken his eyes off her since then.

That was the real reason for Daniel's evil eye. Daniel must have suspected what was really going on inside Cal's head, even when Cal refused to admit it to himself.

Just then, Lyssa missed a step, and when she stumbled, he held her tighter, full against his body.

The voice inside his head—the one warning him to take a step away from her, rather than toward her—had been right. He never should have taken her in his arms, never let the waiter dim the lights, never given her champagne, never watched her lips move as she devoured the appetizers, never danced with her to a song that would always make him think of her from this day forward. If he'd been thinking straight, he would have seen the temptation in bringing her to the London Eye, where nothing could possibly remain "just business" up high in the night sky. Especially when she was wearing a dress that hugged her curves and hinted at the gorgeous skin beneath. Hell, if he could do it all over, he wouldn't have taken her on this trip and shared a suite with her at all.

He respected her brains and her wondrous ability to bring the people they worked with on board their team. But now, he also had to admit how beautiful she was. How good she smelled.

And how damned perfect she felt in his arms.

He was drunk on her smile, on her laughter, on the feel of her skin. Drunk on her hypnotic scent.

There had never been a woman he'd wanted more than he wanted her in this moment.

Yet there had never been a woman more off-limits than Lyssa Spencer.

★ ★ ★

God, dancing with him felt good. Lyssa had danced with Cal at the wedding. But those had been fun and flirty dances.

This was so much more. Her hand on his shoulder, his muscles beneath her fingertips—he was so incredibly sexy. For a few moments, it didn't matter that he was so much older than she, that he was her boss, that he was a close friend of her brothers. All that mattered was breathing in his scent while they floated around the dance floor in each other's arms.

The scrumptious food, the delicious champagne, the beautiful music, the magical city lights far below them was the fairy tale.

And she was dancing with the handsome prince.

The song ended before she was ready to let him go. When he drew away, she had the oddest urge to hang on, when she'd never been a clingy woman before.

"One more dance?" she asked as the quartet began to play another classic song she loved.

She saw the hesitation on his face, the slight frown on his brow, the downward curve of his mouth, and her spirits started to plummet. But then, as if he'd been debating with himself and had lost the argument, he pulled her close again and twirled her around the floor.

Lyssa gave herself up to the romance of the night and the feel of Cal's arms around her.

★ ★ ★

They danced the night away. Or rather, until nine o'clock, when the lack of sleep, the champagne, the rich food, and all the dancing had Lyssa drooping on her feet. Cal had reserved the capsule for two hours, and as they came to rest at the bottom, the timing was perfect to head back to the hotel and get some sleep. Lyssa thanked the waiter and the musicians profusely. Then Cal flagged down a cab and bundled her into the back.

She laid her head against the seat. "Thank you, thank you, thank you," she said, though her eyes were already closed. Her profile was exquisite as the city lights flashed through the window. "Best night ever."

"It was a very good night," he agreed, even as he worked like hell to shove away an extremely sexy vision of giving her a spectacular night in their hotel room.

As it was, holding her in his arms while they danced had been exquisite torture. He'd wanted to tangle his fingers in her hair, tip her head back, and kiss her until she moaned. Hell, right here in the back of the cab, he could still feel the imprint of her body against his. How soft. How sweet. How warm. How perfect.

Her breathing slowed and steadied as she fell asleep. He took in the delicate slope of her nose, the smoothness of her high cheekbones, the brush of her long lashes, and he swore there would never be another night like the one they'd just shared. He couldn't risk it. Not when holding her in his arms made it nearly impossible to remember that she was the Mavericks' younger sister, that she was his employee. And that he was much too old for her. Not when he still ached with the need to touch her, to feel her skin beneath his fingertips, to taste the sweetness of her lips.

Lyssa is untouchable. No other woman in the history of the world has been more off-limits. And he damned well better remember that.

As the cabbie took a turn, she shifted closer to him, mesmerizing him with her sweet scent as she instinctively curled up against him in sleep. With her soft body so temptingly near, Cal realized just how much trouble he was in.

One twirl around the dance floor, one breath of her, one forbidden night dancing above the London skyline was all it had taken to condemn him to a future full of unquenchable, unrequited desire for this exquisite woman he could never have.

The taxi pulled up in front of the hotel, the attendant rushing to open their door. As Cal paid the cabbie, Lyssa's eyelids fluttered open.

"I fell asleep, didn't I?" she said dreamily.

"Just for a few moments."

He backed out of the cab, letting the hotel attendant help her. He could never put his hands on Lyssa Spencer again. Not when he was afraid his control would crumble at the barest touch.

The hotel lobby was brightly lit, filled with couples in evening dress heading out for a late dinner or a show or dancing. The elevator emptied, and he somehow managed to usher Lyssa inside without touching her. A mirrored hotel wall reflected her beauty, her sweetness. Along with his utter fascination with her.

Her lids half closed, she leaned against the wall and glanced at her watch. "Right on time. I'll be in bed just after nine."

"Sleep in tomorrow," he said, even as he tried not to think about how good it would be to crawl into bed beside her, inside her. "We don't meet with Dane Harrington until eleven."

At their floor, he felt like carrying her in his arms over the threshold of their room. But he wouldn't. Couldn't.

"Thank you again," she murmured. "You're too good to me."

What he wanted to do with her was anything but *good*. He wanted wicked and reckless. All. Night. Long.

At her doorway, she turned to face him again, a dreamy smile on her lips.

"Is there anything else you need?" Careful politeness was his only weapon against his own desire.

"You," she whispered just as her eyelids began to

close.

You.

She couldn't possibly have said that.

Or meant it.

Pushing his self-control further past the limit than he'd ever gone, he stepped closer to her, but only to reach for her doorknob. "I've got an early meeting, but I'll pick you up at ten thirty tomorrow. Why don't you go to bed now?"

"Okay." She fluttered her fingers at him over her shoulder. "Good night, Cal."

"Good night, Lyssa." He closed the door and leaned against it, still hearing her voice.

You.

If she'd been any another beautiful woman, he could have dealt with his desire, either by getting it out of his system or by ignoring it. But Lyssa was impossible to ignore. He didn't think he'd ever get her out of his system.

She was intelligent, funny, dedicated, caring. All he'd ever asked for in a woman.

She was also Lyssa Spencer, the Mavericks' younger sister.

She worked for him.

And he was too old for her.

Off.

Limits.

Forever.

Chapter Four

Lyssa woke refreshed from last night's adventure. Her body still remembered just how good it felt to be in Cal's arms. *So* good.

Something else played in the back of her mind. A conversation they'd had before she'd crawled into bed. But she figured it couldn't be all that important if she couldn't remember it.

She glanced at the clock. Nine thirty in the morning. She'd slept for twelve hours. But she remembered every one of her *very* sexy dreams about Cal.

She had no illusions that he would fall madly in love with her. He was her boss. He was years older. And he was also her brothers' friend, which made him as off-limits as they came. But, she thought with a smile, that didn't mean her subconscious couldn't have some fun dreaming about him.

She bounded out of bed when the phone rang on the bedside table. When she picked up, a man from the front desk told her, "Your breakfast has arrived."

Realizing Cal must have ordered for her, she threw

on a robe and opened her door. The waiter rolled in a trolley, and she tipped him as he left.

Her mouth watered as she uncovered poached eggs and toast, coffee, and juice. The toast was English style, stacked upright in a rack. The coffee was hot and the egg yolks perfect for dipping her toast into.

She'd been too tired last night to put away her clothes, so between bites of toast and egg, she cleaned up the room. After drinking a second cup of coffee and munching on another piece of toast slathered in jelly, she got into the shower. By ten twenty-five, she was heading down to the lobby to meet Cal.

As always, the sight of him sent a jolt through her, especially when she remembered his arms around her and the feel of his body as they danced. She wouldn't allow herself to get all dreamy about it, however.

Only a fool would dream of romance with her off-limits-in-every-way boss.

They sped across London in a taxi, neither of them speaking much—apart from her thanking him for sending up breakfast—as they reviewed their presentation one last time.

They pulled up in front of a townhouse on a street that looked like something out of a Jane Austen novel—a pale sandstone façade with a wrought-iron railing and wide front steps flanked by red, white, and pink geraniums that were still blooming despite the October chill.

Cal pressed the bell, a gong reverberating inside the house. The door was opened by a stiff-necked butler, his jowls fleshy, his eyes rheumy, and his bearing haughty.

"Miss Spencer, Mr. Danniger. Mr. Harrington is expecting you." His low baritone was soft with solemnity as he opened the door and signaled them to enter.

The foyer was as big as a hotel lobby, the marble floor intricately laid with a mosaic of prancing peacocks. A grand staircase led to a landing adorned by a huge painting of an eighteenth-century noblewoman fluttering a fan of peacock feathers.

"Mr. Harrington will see you in the parlor," the butler said as he led them through double doors to the right. "Please take a seat while I bring refreshments. As Americans, I assume you prefer coffee."

"Either coffee or tea would be fine, thank you," Cal replied as the man backed out, closing the doors behind him.

The parlor was magnificent, with old-fashioned chintz furniture that, while pretty, looked as unyielding as a park bench. The carpet was a plush Aubusson that Lyssa recognized because Will had imported several similar rugs from France. A chef could have roasted an entire cow in the fireplace, while the mantel was marble, and the lion-shaped andirons looked like bronze. All around were delicate figurines on tables, some with skirts that looked as if the lace had been dipped in porcelain. Lyssa was afraid to sit or even move in case she broke something.

When the doors opened, she expected the butler returning with their coffee, but the man entering was much taller and much younger, his short hair very dark, his eyes very blue, his features aristocratic.

Dane Harrington looked as though he could have stepped out of a Jane Austen novel too, apart from the fact that he was wearing jeans and a sweater.

The two men shook hands first. "It's great to meet you, Cal." Then Dane turned to her. "And you must be Lyssa Spencer. I appreciate both of you flying to meet me here, as we're two weeks away from opening my latest resort at Dunston Castle, just outside London, and I couldn't have gotten away until the launch was over." He waved a hand at the sofa and chairs. "Please have a seat."

Cal chose the nearest chair, while Lyssa looked nervously at the various antique options, terrified the delicate sofa would crack beneath her. Once Dane Harrington sprawled his long body in that creaky chair and it didn't even strain, Lyssa finally relaxed.

The butler entered with a coffeepot, cups and saucers, and a plate of English tarts.

Dane smiled at the man. "Thank you, Fernsby."

Fernsby set the tray on the delicately painted coffee table, pouring the coffee, then pointing to the plate of treats. "Butter tarts and Bakewell tarts. Both delicacies here in England."

Dane laughed. "According to Fernsby, no one bakes as well as the British."

Fernsby gazed down his nose at his employer. "There is a reason we have *The Great British Bake Off*, sir." Then he turned on his heel and marched out of the room.

Dane was still laughing as he said, "Don't let him know I said this, but I think he's right." He lowered his voice as if he were confiding a secret. "Bakewell tarts are the best."

"Your house is amazing too," Lyssa said. She'd pored over brochures and magazine shots of his resorts when she was researching, but this place, with its period furniture—not to mention a butler right out of the Victorian era—was a far cry from his contemporary resorts.

"When I first saw it after buying it with all the furnishings, I originally intended to redecorate." He smiled. "But it's growing on me. It feels like a stepping stone back in time."

"There's a special charm to it," Lyssa agreed. "I wonder if altering it might extinguish some of its magic?"

"You've said exactly what I've been feeling but couldn't put a name to," Dane said. "This place is *magic*."

Cal nodded. "Lyssa knows magic when she sees it."

And she did. Last night had been magic. And maybe she was still under its spell.

Then Dane waved his hand. "On that note, let's skip the small talk. Talk to me about the foundation."

Lyssa got out her laptop, putting it on the table next to the coffee service. "We've put together a presentation—"

"Please," he said, "no presentation." He looked at her, then Cal. "Just give it to me from the heart."

Cal didn't miss a beat. "Gideon Jones is the most honorable man I know. Instead of pocketing the money he received for the Miguel Fernando Correa painting, he's putting it to work for foster care children, like his fiancée once was, and for veterans like him. He's seen PTSD firsthand. He lost comrades and witnessed the aftermath of what their families endure. He's seen the struggles of those who were injured, their lives radically changed. While Veterans Affairs does what it can, this foundation can do so much more."

Dane raised one dark eyebrow. "He got sixty million for that painting, and it's not enough?"

Lyssa couldn't keep from jumping in. "Honestly, no. Not for what we want to do. We envision rehab facilities, social groups for veterans' kids, aid for widowed families. We can't expect people to come to us. We have to bring these services to them in cities throughout the U.S. Can you imagine what one facility costs?" She rattled off a number, and Dane's eyes widened. "If we want to put one in every major city, sixty million is like a dandelion in the wind." She blew on her fingers as if she were blowing away dandelion fluff.

"I see your point, Lyssa. Tell me more."

"As you know from our brochure, Gideon Jones was a veteran himself. He lost a whole squad in Afghanistan. He joined the army to take care of his little sister, Ari, and his mother. But it was hell over there, and when he returned stateside, he couldn't find his sister. He didn't know she'd gone into the foster care system. And he also couldn't face himself due to suffering through his own fair share of PTSD from what he'd been through."

She knew Gideon wouldn't mind her revealing this. He wanted his story out there. He wanted donors to know how necessary their contributions were.

"It took Ari ten years to find him. She tried through the army, sent letters everywhere, did searches. In the end, my brother Matt helped her, and that's when they finally found Gideon. He was a man who couldn't let go of his guilt. That's what PTSD can do to you, leaving you with guilt for the things you didn't do, the comrades you couldn't save."

Her emotions were rising, but it was impossible not to let the story move her.

"A friend of his over in the war zone gave Gideon

the painting, and a week later, she was killed right in front of him. The foundation is dedicated to her— Karmen Sanchez."

Gideon hadn't told her the story, but she knew it from Rosie, who had fallen in love with Gideon with all her heart, and his sister, Ari, who had loved him all her life.

"It was a long journey back for him. But he found his family, Ari and the Mavericks, my brothers. All of this is why Gideon wants to help soldiers who returned with terrible scars, both inside and out, and help the families of men and women who will never return. That's what Gideon's Lean on Us Foundation is all about—helping people who gave their all for their country, as well as children in foster care. Both his sister and his fiancée were in that system. And Gideon knows how much those kids need scholarships, job training, education. But we can only continue the work with generous donations from people like you."

For several moments, Dane was silent. And she worried that maybe she'd been too emotional, that she'd veered too far from cold, hard facts.

Finally, he spoke. "My grandfather came back from the Second World War a changed man." His voice was soft, infused with reverence. "I never knew the man he used to be before he went away. But my grandmother claimed he could make her laugh so hard she'd nearly wet herself. After the First World War, they called it shell shock. After the Second World War, he was never the same. He jumped at loud noises. He woke in the middle of the night screaming from terrible night-mares. He never talked about his experiences over there. But he was at the liberation of Auschwitz."

Lyssa swallowed hard, holding back tears. Just the thought of it was tragic.

"He was an old man when I was a kid, but he had me watch this movie with him, *The Best Years of Our Lives*, about veterans returning from World War Two. A young guy who lost his arms. An older man, a banker, who couldn't find his place in the world again. A pilot who'd flown fighters and screamed out in nightmares. I once asked my grandfather if it was like that for him. He said no." Dane paused. "It was so much worse."

The three of them sat in silence a long moment, the pain and the anguish of both Dane's grandfather's story and Gideon's story swirling around them.

"Maybe if my grandfather had an organization like yours to turn to," Dane said in a low voice, "he could have healed. I'd like to hope so." His words tugged at her heartstrings as he added, "I wanted to hear what both of you had to say. I wanted to make sure your foundation is legit." He rose. "I have something to show you."

They followed him out of the parlor, up the grand staircase, taking the left fork past the painted noblewoman. The rugs were lush, the hardwood dark, the walls highlighted with carved moldings. And yes, there was definitely magic here.

He opened the door to a study at the front of the house. The paneling was an ancient wood polished to a shine, with a desk against the wall, and while the rolltop was an antique, the laptop was state-of-the-art, including two monitors.

Above the desk hung a twelve-by-twelve painting of two angels, one light, one dark, their fingertips touching as if they were bringing the world together with peace and prosperity for all.

"It's Gideon's painting," Lyssa said with reverence—and surprise.

"Yes," he said, turning to both of them with a wide smile. "I'm the anonymous buyer."

★ ★ ★

The artist was Miguel Fernando Correa, who'd created the magnificent piece in the mid-1770s. The tale was that he'd also painted a portrait of Karmen Sanchez's great-great-great-something-grandparents, and Karmen's mother, Ernestina Sanchez, had provided authentication papers for the painting Dane had purchased.

Amazingly, Mrs. Sanchez had never tried to claim the painting, saying that Karmen had given it to the person who was supposed to have it. And Gideon had used it only for good.

"I suppose you could say I brought you here under false pretenses," Dane said. "But I have a proposition for you both. And for Gideon Jones." He pulled out the desk chair, pointing to the two leather chairs in the room. "Please, sit and let me explain. When I heard how Gideon Jones planned to use the money, I immediately wanted to be a part of it. After I've enjoyed the painting for a time—" He waved a hand at the wall. "—I intend to have it displayed, making the rounds of museums or maybe art galleries. Everyone should enjoy it. I find it amazing that Gideon Jones would use the money to start a foundation. But I still wanted to meet you because I needed to be certain that the foundation wasn't created simply for financial gain. You know the kind of thing I'm talking about, don't you? Paying huge salaries, making purchases in the foundation's name, like private planes and retreat homes."

"I do know," Cal said, "but that's not what Gideon—or Lyssa and myself—are about."

Dane nodded. "I understand that, after listening to the two of you. You both believe wholeheartedly in what you're doing. And you believe in Gideon Jones."

"If you met Gideon and his fiancée, Rosie, and her son, Jorge, there wouldn't be a doubt in your mind," Lyssa told him with the same passion that had infused her words down in the parlor. "He's one of the most selfless men I know."

"I'd like to be a part of this in whatever way I can," Dane informed them. "You need more funding. I have contacts. I even have a few contributors in mind. I can pave the way. And together, the two of you can bring in the money you need. You make a great team."

"Thank you," Lyssa said, "but I'm just the account-ant."

Why was she downplaying herself? Cal wondered. Didn't she realize that it had been her impassioned tale, every word straight from her heart, that had won over Harrington?

"And don't worry, I'm still giving you the addition-al donation. Like I said, I wish to God my grandfather had received the kind of help you're offering. My brothers and sisters feel the same way."

The information Lyssa had found on the Harring-tons showed a close-knit family, three brothers and two sisters, all highly successful. Dane was the eldest.

"I'll be back in the States in a couple of weeks. I'd like to meet Gideon and his family then, if possible."

"I'm sure Gideon will be thrilled to meet the man who made all this possible," Cal said. "And I can say without reservation that your offer of help and contacts is beyond our wildest dreams. With you on board, I have no doubt that we will accomplish everything Gideon envisions."

They returned to the parlor and discussed logistics.

Then Harrington said, "Fernsby will be offended if you don't try at least one of his Bakewell tarts. He truly is an amazing baker."

"I would know if he'd appeared on *The Great British Bake Off,*" Lyssa said, "because I've binge-watched every season." She put two of the treats on a plate and handed it to Cal.

Harrington chuckled. "It's not for want of trying. I have a feeling he'll get on the show one day soon."

"Mmmm," she said, her eyes closing with pleasure after she took a bite. "This is amazing."

"Fernsby will be very happy to know you feel that way."

While Lyssa and Dane shared a smile over Fernsby's dreams of baking on TV, Cal felt the unwarranted bite of jealousy. Dane was a good-looking guy, late thirties and closer to Lyssa's age. The two of them would be a perfect fit.

Cal knew he had no right to be jealous. Even getting to hold Lyssa in his arms for an hour of dancing was far more of her than he should ever have. And it didn't bear thinking about any longer, damn it.

When the meeting came to a conclusion, Fernsby packed up the remaining tarts in a box for Lyssa. Her smile was like a sun shower. "Thank you so much. These are the best tarts I've ever tasted."

"Flattery will get you everywhere," Fernsby said in an elongated British drawl.

Once they'd said their good-byes, Cal asked, "Do you mind walking a bit? Or will it be difficult in heels?"

"No problem at all." At the end of the block, once they were out of sight of Dane's home, she did an impromptu little dance on the sidewalk. "That was the best pitch meeting *ever!*"

"I agree," he said, even while steeling his body not to react to the way her curves moved beneath her clothes as she danced in place. "Gideon is going to be thrilled." He hoped his voice didn't sound strained; he was having a hell of a time breathing naturally at the moment.

The homes in Dane's neighborhood were magnificent structures, most taking up at least half a block, with grand entrances and long, perfectly manicured hedges. The sun was out, a pretty fall day, a little cool but no rain.

They had turned a corner and headed out to the main road to find a taxi when Cal realized something. "We have the foundation set up wrong."

She shot him a startled glance. "Wrong how?"

"*You* were the one who sold Dane Harrington, Lyssa. *You* made him believe in the foundation." He paused to look into her eyes. "You shouldn't be working for me—we should be partners. Dane Harrington saw that right away, and I should have realized it earlier."

Wonder and disbelief and gratitude shone in her

eyes. "Do you really mean that?"

"Wholeheartedly." He stopped in the middle of the sidewalk, a lady walking a Pekingese forced to skirt around them as he held out his hand. "Are we in agreement, partner?"

Chapter Five

Lyssa stared at his outstretched hand. *Partners?*

Of course she was proud of how well things had gone. But the truth was that Dane Harrington had already planned to donate to the foundation. All she and Cal had needed to do was pass his honesty test. So it hadn't been much of a challenge.

Which was why, although a big part of her wanted to put her hand in Cal's to shake on the deal he was offering, she didn't. Instead, she laid her palm on her chest and said, "Thank you. From the bottom of my heart. You can't know how much your faith in my abilities means to me. One day, hopefully soon, I will happily accept your offer to be partners. But I'm not quite ready for that yet. I want to be the best I can be, and to get there, I need to learn so much more from you."

Though he looked surprised by her response, she could see respect in his eyes too. "Okay, I'll accept your no for now. But I won't wait too long for you to feel that you're ready. Especially when I think you're far closer than you know."

Yet again, his words filled her with a glow. She adored her brothers and parents. But Cal was the first person who believed she'd already accomplished huge things, rather than seeing her as someone who needed taking care of. Her brothers never disrespected her, and she knew they loved her unconditionally. But the Mavericks had never truly seen her as a capable woman.

"Tell me the truth." After a deep breath, she asked the question that had been hanging over her for weeks. "Did my brothers put pressure on you to give me this job?"

She could see the answer on Cal's face even before he replied. "It was more of a heavy-duty suggestion, rather than pressure." He shoved his hands in his pockets, clearly uncomfortable with what he'd told her. "They're just concerned about you. They want you to be happy. I hope you won't be angry with them for that."

"No, I'm not angry." Disappointed, but not angry. "You must have worried you'd been saddled with a slacker."

He laughed. A genuine laugh, thankfully, that lifted the mood again. "The foundation needed an account-ant. You wanted to leave Chicago. I hoped it would be a good fit, which it clearly is." He gave her a sideways look. "But if you didn't work out, I was willing to give you the boot."

She laughed too. "I'm so glad you didn't."

"I am too, Lyssa." The smile in his eyes warmed her from the inside out. "Really glad."

★ ★ ★

When Lyssa looked at him that way, her eyes so bright and intelligent and sweet all at the same time, his brain turned to mush. Which was why, instead of hurrying off to bury himself in work and keep his distance, he found himself saying, "Whenever I have a massive victory at one of my companies, I like to make a point of celebrating. What do you say to the rest of the day off to enjoy London?" He had meetings planned for his own business, but suddenly none of them seemed particularly important.

"Are you sure?" she asked. "Now that Dane is on board and has given us a list of wealthy associates to contact, there's even more work we can dig into."

"I'm sure," he said. Even though he wasn't the slightest bit sure how to stop wanting to be near the loveliest woman he'd ever known. "Now we just need to figure out what we want to do. A museum, maybe? Or we could hunt down a tearoom and get the full works?"

"Actually," she said, "there's something I found online when I was getting ready for the trip that looks like it could be a lot of fun. Only I didn't think we'd have time…and even if we did, I wasn't sure you'd be interested."

"Try me."

"It's a London street art tour."

"You mean like graffiti?" He frowned, feeling like the fuddy-duddy she probably thought he was.

"It's art," she told him. "And it's all over the city, but particularly in the East End. Evidently, some of it is really famous, and huge careers have come from the walls of London."

Before last night, he couldn't remember the last time he'd done something just for fun, apart from attending Maverick barbecues when he was in the Bay Area. If he went to a function, there was always business—a customer, a donor, a potential investment.

It occurred to him how boring his life had become.

"I'm in."

The way her eyes lit up made him more ecstatic than when Dane had darn near begged to join forces with the foundation.

* * *

An hour later, dressed in jeans, T-shirts, sneakers, and light jackets, they took the Tube to meet up with a free guided tour. It was an eclectic group, with an older couple from Scotland, a couple of Scandinavians, and two middle-aged women who hadn't seen each other since high school and were clearly thrilled to be together again. Their tour guide had turned his body into an art form. Every square inch of visible skin, except his face, was covered with tattoos, from mythical creatures to skulls to jungle animals.

"Call me Delic," their guide said, "short for Psychedelic. This place used to be dodgy. You wouldn't walk in here without a weapon. But when Banksy had the idea in 2008 for a mural celebrating graffiti as art, life in this tunnel changed entirely. No one was allowed to enter while he worked, until the day he unveiled it. Since then, the city has allowed graffiti here with no penalties. You won't find much of Banksy's original art left. In fact, you can come here every couple of days and see something brand new."

"This is going to be amazing," Lyssa said softly to Cal.

The problem was that being with her felt amazing. And he was starting to crave it—the chance to see one more smile, to hear her laugh, to breathe in her sweet perfume, to watch her walk across a room toward him.

Delic led them into the tunnel, naming some of the artists as if they were international stars, none of whom Cal had heard of. But even he had to admit the art was remarkable. It covered the walls, the curved ceiling, the overhead beams. There was word art, flower art, bird art, psychedelic art, people art, animal art. He and Lyssa stood before a ferocious wolf.

"It should be in a museum." She was as enthralled

as he was.

Delic stopped next to Lyssa. "Take pictures," he advised. "It'll be gone in two or three days. I wish we could preserve them, but that's the nature of street art. Here one day, gone the next."

"I thought graffiti was just for gangs or hoodlums. But it's truly art," Cal observed.

Delic's mouth curved in a wolfish smile that reminded Cal of the painting on the wall. "There's big money in street art now. People get commissions." He waved an arm encompassing the entire tunnel. "It's also a venue for up-and-coming artists to show off their style." He moved three murals down, Lyssa and Cal following. "Look at this one."

Cal could make out the words DO OR DIE in mesmerizing colors. A figure was built into each letter, an old man, a young Black woman, an Asian teenager, a middle-aged Russian wearing a babushka, an Indian woman in a sari, a bearded man with a turban.

"You see how it brings all the peoples of the world together, young and old, whatever ethnicity."

"It's beautiful," Lyssa said on a breath of wonder.

"I've been all over the streets, and this is the first time I've seen this guy. I'm telling you, he's going to be huge. Take a picture," he ordered. "Remember the name—Han Solo."

"Like Han Solo from *Star Wars*?" Lyssa asked as she snapped a picture.

Delic snorted. "You think anybody uses their real name?" Said the man who called himself Psychedelic. "No one knows who Banksy is."

Cal felt a surprising excitement running through him. He'd be looking for this Han Solo. And he wanted to find out more about Banksy too.

They walked from there, sometimes getting on the Tube, then getting off at another station to view the side of a building or a long wall covered in fantastic murals, until they ended up in the East End.

Delic gathered the group around him. "More than anyone else in London, East Enders love their street art. Prepare to be dazzled."

And the street art dazzled Cal. But Lyssa shone even brighter.

She took pictures of everything, asked great questions about the artists and what the graffiti meant. The art wasn't just paint on walls; there were statues plopped down in the middle of a sidewalk, even a man standing on a plinth, his clothes painted exactly like the building behind him. At certain angles, he disappeared into the background. There were even little dragon statues glued to the tops of light poles, hidden gems everywhere you looked.

They wandered among ramshackle buildings now reinvented with mind-blowing murals, the colors bright against the sky. The art changed as the clouds passed overhead, took on different hues, the shifting light bringing out new facets.

"Come back in a week, and the place will be entire-ly different." Delic shrugged. "It's transient, like people are." Then he shot them all with two finger guns. "And I guarantee you will be back."

At the end of the block, he waved in his flock. "We've arrived at the moment you've all been waiting for." He held up his hands like a maestro. "Now you create your own street art."

Cal looked at Lyssa. "Did you know about this?"

She grinned. "I thought it might be best if I let you discover the full extent of our day out once you'd been enraptured by the street art we've seen."

"I'll watch you do it," he said.

She batted his arm. "Oh no, you won't. You're go-ing to create some magnificent graffiti today, or I'll tell my brothers you chickened out."

She made some *bawk-bawk* sounds, and without thinking, he reached out to cover her mouth with his hand.

Her eyes went wide as his palm touched her lips, and he quickly pulled away, but not before he had to acknowledge the bolt of lightning that jolted through him.

Working to focus his attention on the art, he real-ized that for the first time in a very long time, this tour had made him feel truly excited about something that had nothing to do with work. He'd never sowed wild oats. Instead, he'd gone to college, then to work, built his assets, grown his company. But today, with Lyssa, he felt young and carefree.

"Okay," he said in a voice he hoped sounded relaxed, "I'll do it." Then he teased her. "Although there's a chance a graffiti chicken who bears a striking resemblance to you might make an appearance…"

She was rolling her eyes with a grin as Delic spoke again. "Let me give you a few basics about making street art. First, nothing is off-limits." Then he gave them a brief review of street art techniques.

Cal hadn't realized there *were* techniques. Though he had to admit that much of the work he'd seen today was true artistry.

With dramatic flair, Delic's voice boomed out their final instructions. "Now, put on your masks and goggles, grab a spray can, and start painting."

The beige wall where they were standing had obviously been painted over for the workshop. Lyssa was the first to choose her space on the end.

Cal grabbed the spot next to hers. "What are you going to paint?"

"Word art. Good luck with your Lyssa-faced chicken," she joked.

As she retrieved a can from the rolling table a couple of paces behind them, Cal stared at his section of blank wall. He was forty-six years old, a businessman who knew spreadsheets and recognized business opportunities. He didn't actually *want* to paint a chicken that looked like her, but he had no clue what to paint instead.

As if she saw his dilemma, she murmured, "Remember what Delic said—nothing is off-limits. Just relax."

If she only knew just how much was completely off-limits, starting and ending with *her*.

Relax. Lyssa was right. He never relaxed. Except last night, when he'd held her in his arms.

A word suddenly formed on the wall beneath his paint can. That was one of Delic's techniques: *Let your hand spray instead of your mind controlling*. Cal's hand started with yellow. When he'd sprayed the word, he picked up a green can and hit the wall with the same word, off-kilter from the first.

He didn't forget Lyssa, but he no longer looked at her, allowing his hand to spray while his mind wandered. Next was red, once again off-kilter, the word seeming to slide down the wall.

He thought about his life, which had been all about work from the day he'd graduated from college. He'd long ago thought about being a lawyer like his dad. But that hadn't happened. He'd once dreamed of having a family. It hadn't happened either. There'd always been reasons why the time wasn't right for marriage. Always a way for him to justify that his career was more important.

But was that true? Or was there something else going on? Something that Cal didn't want to face?

Pushing the questions from his head, he found blue and purple and orange. Color after color, he sprayed the same word until Delic clapped his hands.

"Put down your paint cans. And let's see what you've done." He made his way down the line of artists, giving kudos, making comments.

At last, Cal stepped back to see what he'd painted.

* * *

Lyssa tilted her head to look at her art. It wasn't anywhere near the quality they'd seen on the tour, but it said exactly what she'd wanted to say, and she was pleased with her first-ever attempt at street art.

Then she stepped back to view Cal's art.

"Wow." She turned to face him, beyond stunned by what he'd produced. "Way to play me like you're a street art novice."

"I *am* a novice. I've never even thought about spray paint art until today." Cal frowned at what he'd done. "Anyway, the colors are all jumbled together. You can barely read the word."

"Are you crazy? This is a freaking *masterpiece*. It's like you threw everything that's inside you into that word you sprayed on the wall. And turned it into art."

It was simple yet elegant, the word *relax* over and over in all the colors of the spectrum, every paint can that had been on the rolling table behind Cal and some of her colors too.

But he didn't seem as pleased by it as she was. "Do you even know what it says?"

She fished her phone out of her pocket and played the song for him, "Relax" by Frankie Goes to Hollywood, feeling its beat in her core. "Your painting has the same kind of beat as the song. It just keeps playing over and over in your head." She opened her arms to encompass the whole thing. "It's like those colors were trapped until they spewed out of you onto the wall."

Though he shrugged, his eyes, usually gray, had softened to silver, and she knew he was pleased by her comment.

"It must be subliminal," she had to note. "It must be what you really want to do. *Relax.*"

"It's nothing more than the last word you said to me. I couldn't think of anything else to paint."

She folded her arms and shot him a look. "I don't believe you."

He pointed at her painting. "Even though 'believe' was the word you sprayed on the wall?"

She glanced at her word art, which she'd done in simple blue and white. "I like what I did. I'll even probably put a picture of it online. Hashtag HavingFuninLondon and all that. But I was *thinking* while I put it up there." She pointed at his art. "You were *feeling.*"

Something flared in his eyes. He almost seemed to sway into her for one brief moment.

Then, just as quickly, he stepped back. Almost as if he'd been about to commit a crime.

Chapter Six

Relax.

Didn't she know that song was about sex?

Looking at his crazy, mixed-up piece of the wall, it somehow symbolized all his crazy, mixed-up feelings about her.

"It's garbage." He was embarrassed by how he'd let himself go. Bending down, he grabbed the first can of paint he could reach. Orange.

Lyssa, guessing his intention, threw herself in front of the wall. "You are *not* going to paint over that."

Seeing her spread-eagled against the wall, all he could think about was that song again. And sex. And Lyssa in that position, in a bed, naked.

Damn it! He needed to erase that vision from his brain and never, ever think anything like it again.

"If you don't get out of the way," he said, "I'll have to paint over you too."

Laughter bubbled out of her. "I dare you."

Again, he didn't think before acting, even though that kept getting him into trouble with Lyssa. Before she could leap away, he aimed for her stomach and painted her white T-shirt orange.

She looked down at herself, clearly stunned. "I can't believe you did that."

Despite his inner war over his completely unauthorized feelings for her, he couldn't hold back his grin. "I warned you."

Then she grabbed a paint can and sprayed his T-shirt before he could react. She was covered in orange, he was splashed in teal. He grabbed for the can she was holding, but she darted away. And he took aim at his wall.

Again, she jumped in front of it at the last moment, so he covered her back in paint instead.

"Now you match back and front," he teased.

Laughing, she turned on him to try to grab his can. As he held it out of her reach, she stretched for the spray paint in his hand, her body plastered to his. She squirmed against him, pulling his arm, trying to get the can.

Just that quickly, everything shifted inside him, making him forget all the things he shouldn't do. Everything he'd sworn to himself he wouldn't even *think* about, let alone act on.

But one touch was all it took, her heat against his wet shirt, spreading through him. His arm snaked around her as if it had a mind of its own, anchoring her to him. The scent of her hair, some fruity shampoo, stronger than the smell of paint, mesmerized him.

Relax.

And he felt himself relaxing into her, wanting her.

Delic's booming voice broke the spell. "Hey, you two, no spray-paint fights."

Cal loosened his grip.

Even as he wanted to hold on to her forever.

* * *

They took the Tube back to the hotel. No taxi driver would allow their paint-splattered bodies on his seats.

"If we put ultraviolet light on you, you'd be psychedelic," she said with a laugh.

Cal's hair and face where he hadn't been covered by the goggles and mask were a spray of color, as was his T-shirt.

He put a hand to her forehead, leaving a streak of heat from his touch. "You look like a blue-and-white fairy. Except for the orange." Smiling, he laid his palm against her stomach.

She almost gasped at the contact. She was right back there on the street, her body plastered against his as she struggled to get the paint can, the feel of his arm across her back like a brand. Right back at the moment where she'd been unable to think about anything except kissing him. Right back at that moment when she'd forgotten all the reasons why she shouldn't, even if his touch had been purely accidental.

All too soon, he held up his hand. "You're already dry."

She put her hand on the teal splotch she'd sprayed on his chest. She could feel his heart thundering. "You're dry too." Her voice was too husky, too sultry, and she broke the tension with a smile. "You look like a kid with those goggle marks."

He traced the goggle lines around her eyes. "So do you."

The train lurched to a stop at a station, jostling them together. People crowded on, and she pressed against him. She relished the crowded train. It gave her an excuse to once again feel his body along the length of hers.

Far more quickly than she wanted, their train ride ended. Unfortunately, their closeness ended abruptly too. Cal didn't exactly shove her away, but he kept a good distance between them as they made their way out of the station.

Back in the suite, he barely looked at her, suddenly seeming distant despite all the fun and laughter they'd shared during the day and the triumph with Dane Harrington. "I'm going to shower and wash off all this paint." Then he turned at his door. "I enjoyed myself today, Lyssa. More than I thought I would."

She saw something in his eyes then. A momentary lapse of his steely self-control, maybe? But he quickly regained it. "I've got a mountain of emails to get through and some phone calls to make tonight. I'm sure I'll need to work through dinner, and then I have several meetings for my other businesses tomorrow morning, so I'll meet you in the lobby tomorrow ninety minutes before our flight."

Just like that, Cal was gone, his door closed behind him.

* * *

Cal stood beneath the rush of water, the hot spray sluicing away the paint. His thoughts spiraled down the drain right along with it.

He could still feel Lyssa's body against his, still feel the heat of her palm on his chest, still feel every jostle and jerk of the Underground as it threw her against him. He could smell her sweet scent, feel her heat. And he remembered the look in her eyes that seemed to say he wasn't the only one feeling the attraction between them.

If he'd dipped his head, their lips would have touched. He could almost taste her right now, simply from the force of his imagination.

No, damn it!

She was the Mavericks' little sister. She was his employee. He was too old for her. She was completely off-limits.

He let those reminders run over and over in his head.

But it didn't stop the desire.

★ ★ ★

More than anything Cal had wanted in a very long time, he'd wanted to have a bottle of champagne sent up to their suite last night and to dance with Lyssa again. But doing that would have decimated what was left of his waning self-control. So he'd used the excuse of going through emails and worked in his room, not even emerging to order room service.

But that night she'd consumed his dreams anyway.

The next morning, he left early for a couple of meetings. Even as he was talking business, he was thinking about Lyssa. He'd never let a woman crowd into his thoughts while he was working. But somehow he couldn't seem to push Lyssa away.

When he returned to the hotel, she was waiting in the lobby, looking beautiful in a slim-fitting skirt that hugged every curve. Unbidden, he found himself fantasizing about stripping her out of it, covering her in spray paint, and taking her up against the wall.

Instead, as they got in a taxi, they made small talk about what they'd both accomplished since they'd last seen each other the night before. He wasn't sure if he was the only one who felt their conversation was stilted, no longer as easy as it had always been.

Once on the plane, they waited for Delilah to show up. He was surprised when a text came in fifteen minutes after their scheduled flight time.

Im so so sorry mr danniger but I met the most fabulous englishman here and hes asked me to stay so Im going to

There was no punctuation and no capitalization. At least she hadn't used heart emojis.

"I'm afraid Delilah won't be making the return trip." So much for having a chaperone to help him remember all the reasons why he needed to keep his distance from Lyssa. "I'll have to call for someone else."

"Actually," Lyssa said, "we don't need to wait around for someone else when I can use a coffee machine."

How long would it take to find a replacement for Delilah? They could be delayed for hours. But if he didn't find *someone*, that meant he and Lyssa would be alone on the plane for hours...and he didn't know if his self-control could withstand it.

Silently, he cursed. He'd never been led around by his body parts. He wasn't about to start now. He could do this, damn it.

"Are you sure?" he asked.

She looked at him like he was missing a screw. "Of course I'm sure."

"All right, then." Telling himself to stop acting weird, or she was surely going to figure out that something was up with him, he picked up the phone. "Captain Greer, we're ready to go without a crew member."

When they were both buckled in, Lyssa asked, "Are you going to tell me why she's not coming?"

"She met an Englishman who asked her to stay here with him. It sounds like it all happened pretty quickly."

Lyssa raised an eyebrow. "An Englishman, huh?" Then she grinned. "Good for her."

Her smile short-circuited the already badly firing synapses in his brain. Fumbling for something— anything—to say that would force them to focus on work, and nothing but work, he said, "Let's brainstorm ways we think Dane's participation could help the foundation, in addition to reaching out to his contacts to find new donors."

She nodded. "Good plan."

As they tossed ideas back and forth, he knew it would be nuts to throw away their incredible synergy as business partners for a roll in the hay. Even though a little voice whispered that being with Lyssa would be so much more than that.

An hour later, she said, "I need coffee. Can I bring you a cup too?" She was already rising from her seat.

He tried not to notice the way her pencil skirt molded to her hips. He failed. "You don't have to serve me."

She laughed, a light sound that reached straight inside his chest. Then she put her hands together and said in a breathy voice, "Oh, Mr. Danniger, please let me know how I can serve you. Absolutely *anything*."

Her imitation of Delilah was spot-on, and she was laughing as she headed back to the galley. He swiveled his seat, stretched out his legs, and scraped a hand down his face.

Her lingering scent filled his head. He told himself he'd feel more in control when they were back in San Francisco. Mary, their admin, would be there. Lyssa had her own office, he had his. Things could get back to normal. He would stop thinking about her once they were back in California. He *had* to stop thinking about her this way.

A few minutes later, the scent of coffee overtook the sweet perfume of her hair and skin as she returned with steaming mugs and sugar and cream, pushing his pad out of the way and setting the tray on the table.

Then she went on playing her part to perfection as she hovered over him. "Mr. Danniger, how do you want me to fix your coffee? As I said earlier, I could make it *any way* you like, sir."

He couldn't help but laugh, although he felt he should say, "You're exaggerating."

"Exaggerating? If anything, I'm *underplaying* it. Delilah was falling all over you. If I hadn't been here," she said with a cheeky smile, "she'd have been right in your lap, wrapping herself around you like a boa constrictor."

She was standing so close, and she was so beautiful, and he was so hungry for her that his brain malfunctioned, and his body took over before he could stop it.

He recognized the moment the same thing happened to her. The laughter died on her lips. And a hot flame grew in her eyes. Her pupils widened, and he could see his reflection, the need etching his features.

Resistance was futile.

At the same time that she moved to wrap her arms around him, he yanked her into his lap, shoved his fingers through her hair, and pulled her mouth down to his.

Chapter Seven

Cal's lips were hot and demanding. And *perfect*.

With his hand on her neck anchoring her to him, his other arm snaked around her waist, pulling her tight. She could feel in every hard, rippling muscle how badly he wanted her. When he groaned, it vibrated through her body. And she kissed him with all the need that had been screaming to get out.

She couldn't lie to herself about this, not even a little bit. Despite all the arguments to the contrary, she'd wanted this for months. Wanted *him* for months.

Right now, she didn't care about her job. She didn't care about her brothers or what they would say when they found out. She didn't care about their age difference.

All she cared about was kissing Cal.

Then suddenly he was lifting her to her feet and he was standing too. "This is wrong."

His breath was coming too fast, and so was hers. "I don't care."

"It's not right. We can't do this."

"We can."

He tried to fight it. For one second. Then two.

Then on three, he possessed her with his mouth once more. His arms went around her, lifting her against him, and she felt him turn, his lips never leaving hers.

She'd think about the consequences later. Right now, she wanted him so badly she ached.

In the bedroom, he let her slide down his body until her feet touched the floor. "I haven't stopped thinking about you since the night we danced." His eyes held fire as he ate her up with his gaze.

"I dream about you at night," she admitted in a whisper. She didn't tell him how long she'd been dreaming of him—for months, since Matt and Ari's wedding.

"I should be able to control myself around you." His voice was a low rumble. "But I can't."

"I don't want you to control yourself."

He fumbled with the buttons of her blouse. "Tell me to stop."

"Don't stop." She put her fingers to his, helping him undo all the buttons, pulling her blouse from her skirt.

He stroked her breasts through the lacy bra, moving his thumbs over the peaks, making her heart pound even faster. When he pulled the lace aside, Lyssa moaned softly as his fingers skimmed her bare skin. He shoved the blouse off her shoulders, then pushed the straps down. She reached in front, unhooking the clasp. Her blouse and bra fluttered to the floor.

"Lyssa." Her name sounded like a prayer on his lips. "You're so beautiful."

He toyed with her, each palm cupping a breast, until she begged, "Taste me."

He bent to her, taking a peak in his mouth, sucking sweetly, licking over her heated skin, making her knees weak.

He inched her skirt up until it rested high on her hips at the same time that she pushed his suit jacket off his shoulders, slipped his tie loose, then tugged on the buttons of his shirt. One tore as it popped free, flying across the room. She shoved her fingers beneath the material, ran them up his abdomen.

He groaned as if her touch was an exquisite pleasure. "You can't possibly know what you do to me," he said, his eyes closed.

"I do. Because it's the same thing you do to me."

Cal pulled back, his eyes so hot they burned into hers. "Are you sure you won't regret it?"

She placed a hand over his heart. "I'll never regret this."

Heat flashed again in his eyes as he slid his hand down her body once more. "You can change your mind anytime. You can stop me at any moment. All you have to do is tell me."

Didn't he know? There was no going back to the way things had been between them. Not now. Not ever. "I'm not changing my mind. And I'm not going to stop you."

The words were barely out of her mouth when he slid his fingers beneath her panties...and over the center of her arousal. She anchored her fingers on his shoulders, leaving marks on his skin as she held on, riding his touch.

"*Oh God.*" The pleasure was exquisite, intense, making her legs shake. "I'll never change my mind," she said on a gasp.

The next thing she knew, he was sliding off her panties. It was her cue to go for his belt. Unbuckled, unbuttoned, and unzipped, his pants slipped away, and he kicked his shoes aside.

She sucked in her breath at the length of him beneath the boxer briefs. She reached out for him and felt him shudder, heard his sharp indrawn breath.

"You make me crazy," he growled. "That's what I should've painted on the wall. *Crazy.*"

"You make me crazy too," she said. "The best kind of crazy I've ever felt."

She pulled his boxers down, then moved to kneel in front of him. Her mouth watered for a taste, and she gave him one long swipe of her tongue.

But that was clearly too much for him, because he hauled her to her feet, turned her around to yank down the zip of the skirt still up around her waist, and shoved it to the floor to land on the pile of their discarded clothes.

He trailed his fingers down the line of her spine. Then, with his front pressed to her back, he pulled her hair aside, kissed her neck, her earlobe. The bed was right there in front of her, and it was pure instinct to crawl onto it, on her hands and knees in front of him.

He let out a long, slow groan. "I tried not to want this. I tried not to want you." Each sentence was an admission she sensed he'd never wanted to make to her. Then he made an even bigger admission. "But I've wanted you *forever.*"

"I've wanted you too," she told him. Every step he took toward the deep end, she took with him.

The bed dipped as he knelt beside her, his fingers tracing down between her legs as Lyssa spread herself for him. She felt wanton and crazy with desire.

"You're so hot. So ready for me." He stroked her, stoking the fire building deep inside her.

"*Cal.*" She closed her eyes and reveled in the pleasure he gave her, moaning his name over and over. Then she turned her head and found his mouth. Kissing him with all the desperate desire he made her feel, she rolled to her back, pulling him down on top of her.

At last, she tore her mouth from his. "I need you inside me."

"I don't have a condom." His eyes were iron gray with regret.

"It's okay. I'm on the pill." Reaching down, she wrapped her hand around him, stroked, felt his heat and steel in her palm. "I need you *now*."

"Are you sure?"

"One hundred percent sure. One *million* percent! Nothing bad is going to happen, I promise." She kissed him again. "Please, Cal, take me. Love me."

His eyes blazed with heat as he flexed his hips, one long, glorious thrust, so that she felt him deep inside her. Her head fell back as she lifted her hips to take him even deeper.

His strokes were slow and measured as he braced himself on his arms, yet he shook with the effort to take his time, to push her higher, make her crazier.

"You." He sucked in a breath. "Feel." Let it out in an exhale that shook through him. "So damned good."

Then he closed his eyes, and the slow steady rock of his body was unbearable, the pleasure overwhelming. She clamped around him as all the tension stole down to her center, her very core. And broke inside her.

The world exploded. She called out his name. And that was when Cal slammed his hips into her, turning the climax cataclysmic.

★ ★ ★

Cal woke alone in the airplane bed to the sound of water running. He had never felt so languid, so sated. He stretched, breathed deeply, let it out. He hadn't looked at the clock, didn't know how long he and Lyssa had slept.

He was angry with himself for giving in to his need for her. For letting his insane hunger override all rational thought. But the sound of that water, and the knowledge that she was naked in the shower, made his desire rise higher than any self-recriminations could.

It was a siren's call he had to answer.

Sliding naked from the bed, he headed to the bathroom door, thinking he'd find her in the shower. Instead, he found her buried in bubbles up to the neck.

She shut off the water when she saw him, naked before her and boldly ready to do everything all over again. To experience the wonder of her against his body, the tight, wet heat of her around him.

She reached out a hand slippery with bubbles. "Come join me."

He knew he shouldn't. Hell, he shouldn't have let himself notice she was a beautiful woman, shouldn't have let himself touch her, shouldn't have given in to the powerful urge to kiss her. But of course, since he couldn't think straight around her, he climbed right into the tub, standing over her long enough for her to wrap her hand around his erection.

He had never seen such a wicked smile on a woman's face. She was magnificent, her breasts playing peekaboo with the bubbles.

She stroked him, and he did the unthinkable, curling his hand around hers and helping her. It was crazy good, the sight of their hands. He slid down into the water with her and kissed her.

"I love the way you taste," he said between kisses. "I love the way you feel." He reached beneath the water and played with the aroused flesh between her thighs, sending her to the edge of bliss in under a minute.

"Wait, not yet." She opened her eyes, her gaze stroking him. "I want to wash you. Then you can wash me."

She found a fruity body soap, squirted a dollop on her hand, and stood.

"I'd rather watch you do it yourself," he said.

Her smile was hot enough to make the water boil. And she soaped up, washed her breasts, slowly, lingering where he wanted his hands and mouth. Then her arms, but when she headed south, he stood, took the body wash, and lathered up. With his eyes on hers, he soaped away the residue of their lovemaking, washed every inch, all her sexy nooks and crannies as her gaze turned even more needy.

Then she started on him, making him want to beg. Yet he needed the slow, easy nature of it, the rising tension as he relished her touch.

When there wasn't another inch to be washed, they sank into the water. He rolled, bringing her on top, lodging himself between her legs before telling her, "I want to taste all of you." Hands under her hips, he raised her until she was a feast begging for his mouth. He lapped gently, savoring her before delving deep, finding the pearl between her legs. He gave her everything, holding her tight against him, licking, sucking, swirling until her legs started to shake.

He felt the clench of her body, knew she was close, and with his tongue still on her, he filled her with two fingers.

She put her head back, cried out, riding the long wave of pleasure, and finally she collapsed against him. Rising, he lifted her out of the water, stood her on the bath mat, and toweled them both dry.

Then, lifting her until she straddled him, he carried her back to the bed. Her arms were around his neck, her legs around his waist as he plunged deep, filling her up, filling himself up, and taking her to the pinnacle once more.

And when she fell, he fell with her.

Never, ever wanting to let her go.

Chapter Eight

Cal woke the second time to find Lyssa tangled around him, still asleep. She smelled like warm woman and hot sex.

He glanced at the clock. They'd be landing in less than an hour.

Not wanting to wake her, he slowly disentangled himself from her and stood beside the bed.

She was so beautiful. So sweet. And so damned sexy.

He didn't want to regret what they'd done. Didn't want to have to face it either. Not yet. So he let her sleep a few more minutes.

Normally, he would have taken a shower before he got dressed, but he didn't want to wash away anything they'd done. He wanted to keep the memories with him just a little longer, of her hands and mouth on him and his on her.

After dressing, he brewed a pot of coffee, then turned on his Bluetooth to check voicemails and email. Standing by the table in the main cabin, his mind and body were consumed with the feel of her, the taste of her. The last thing he wanted was to stand out here while she was in his bed. Wickedly, his brain—and body—told him that he had time, just enough time if he got back in there with her right now, to touch and kiss her all over again.

His phone rang just as he was about to give in to the irresistible urge to stride back to the onboard bedroom. Daniel Spencer's name flashed on the screen.

Lyssa's overprotective older brother was calling.

Cal's stomach twisted into a million tiny knots.

Jesus. The thoughts he'd had about this man's sister. The things he'd done to her in his bed. The things he had been about to do with her again before landing.

Every second with Lyssa had been glorious. *Beyond* glorious.

And yet Cal knew it was all so wrong, the two of them together. So damned wrong.

What the hell had he been thinking?

That was the problem. He hadn't been thinking at all. He'd acted on every impulse. He'd launched himself out of control.

He still felt completely out of control. Every time he thought about her. Just knowing she was still in his bed, naked and warm.

And still, the phone rang.

No matter how badly he wanted to let it go to voicemail, that wasn't the answer. He couldn't avoid

Daniel forever. Barely twenty-four hours, actually, given how many ventures they worked on together.

Cal swiped his finger across the screen. "Daniel, what's up?" Did his voice sound strangled? It did, but he hoped his friend and business partner wouldn't guess why.

"I was just talking to Gideon about the new donor." Lyssa and Cal had debriefed Gideon yesterday after talking to Dane Harrington. "Pretty damned cool he was also the guy who bought the painting."

Cal could barely find his voice. He'd had breathless, sweaty, mind-blowing sex with this man's sister. He'd slept with his employee. He'd crossed two decades of age boundaries.

He'd done the unthinkable, the irretrievable, the unacceptable.

The *unforgettable*.

He felt disgusted with himself. Turned out he was a chip off the old block, just like his good old dad, after all.

"Hey, are you okay?" Daniel asked.

Cal had to say something. "Yeah, it was pretty amazing."

Amazing, that's what Lyssa was. And he never should have touched her. No matter how irresistible she was.

"You must've done your damnedest to get the guy to cough up more money after already forking over sixty million." Daniel chuckled. "You the man, just like I always knew you were."

Cal couldn't take credit. "It was Lyssa. She reached Harrington right away and brought tears to the man's eyes, telling him Gideon's story. Every word was from her heart, and Harrington knew it. She's why he signed on."

Then Cal had pulled her into his lap, and kissed her, and—

With the sound of Daniel's voice in his ear, he felt physically sick. If her brother ever found out what Cal had done, he'd surely be ready to commit murder.

Cal closed his eyes and ran his hand over them. If only Daniel had called earlier, back in London, then maybe Cal could have stopped himself—

"She's a pretty amazing kid." Daniel said.

"She's not a kid." The words almost exploded out of Cal. And it wasn't just about the ways he'd touched her or the things she made him feel. It was how smart and funny and brilliant she was. "She's a damned fine accountant, and the foundation is lucky to have her."

"Wow. She really impressed you, didn't she?"

Cal felt a sudden, undeniable urge to stand up for Lyssa, and it wasn't because they'd slept together. "She impresses everyone who meets her."

"Of course she does," Daniel said. "She's always impressed me. But she's my little sister, and of course I'll always see her that way."

Cal almost told Daniel he needed to show Lyssa more often how impressed he was with her. But Cal clamped down, knowing Lyssa wouldn't appreciate him sticking his nose into their family business. Plus, he was worried he'd sound like a besotted fool.

Which he was. *Completely.*

"Where are you guys?" Daniel asked.

"We'll be landing in San Francisco in half an hour."

"Hey, let me talk to Lyssa, would you?"

Cal's heart dropped like a stone, falling thirty thousand feet to splat on the ground. He couldn't tell Daniel, *No can do, she's still sleeping after we spent the entire flight home in my bed.*

Instead, he opted for, "She's in the powder room. I'll have her call you."

"No need, I can talk to her later. I just wanted to say hi if she was around."

Once they hung up, Cal turned his phone off, threw it on the table, and turned to find Lyssa standing by the galley door. She'd put on her clothes, and he didn't think she'd taken the time to shower any more than he had.

"Thank you."

He felt sick. "For what?"

"For telling Daniel how well I did with Dane Harrington. I appreciate that."

Did she appreciate more than just what he'd said to her brother? Was she glad that he'd appreciated every inch of her beautiful body with his hands and mouth and—

He clamped down on the rest of his wayward thoughts, even as he had to face the truth that he'd do it all over again if there was the smallest chance he could.

He was out of control. *Completely* out of control.

The only way to fix it was to remove himself from temptation.

* * *

Tingles coursed through Lyssa's body. It wasn't just the things they'd done together in the bed and bathtub. It was what he'd said to her brother, praising her, every word ringing with sincerity.

Cal believed in her. And that meant the world to her.

He shrugged off her thanks. "It's the truth. You're a major asset to the foundation."

As he spoke, color crept up his neck as if he were embarrassed she'd overheard his conversation. In fact, he was having trouble making eye contact with her.

Oh no. Was he embarrassed about what they'd done? Did he regret it? Did he wish it had never happened?

"I made coffee, if you'd like any." He waved a hand at the galley, still not looking at her. Even his voice sounded off, each word too precise, his movements a little robotic.

He was acting as if he hadn't touched her, kissed her, taken her again and again. As if they were strangers. As if he'd become her boss again...and nothing but her boss.

Even though it felt like her insides were shattering into a million pieces, she tried to reply in a perfectly normal tone. "I'd love some, thanks. You want me to pour one for you?"

He shook his head, still staring out the window at the clouds they were descending through. "I'll get my own in a minute."

"It's okay. I can pour two."

A few moments later, he took the coffee from her, making a point not to brush his fingers against hers as he did so. "Thank you."

He was so damned polite that her teeth clenched in frustration, and her mood took a nosedive.

Everything felt awkward. *Horribly* awkward.

Okay, so she hadn't thought through exactly how the aftermath of an affair with her secret crush/boss/brothers' best friend would turn out. But she'd never wanted it to be like *this*.

She didn't expect him to declare his undying love for her or anything, but she'd thought they'd at least manage to be adults about it. She'd hoped they could keep the pleasure they'd shared in each other's arms from conflicting with their jobs.

Was it because her brother had called? Was that why Cal had gone all twitchy? Was he worried that Daniel would kill him if he found out? Was he worried that she was going to dash off the plane and tell everyone in her family what they'd done?

The pilot told them over the intercom to buckle up for landing, which meant they were now stuck in the same room for the next ten minutes. In that case, there was no time like the present to lay it all out in the open before things got any weirder.

"Cal, you don't have to worry. I'm not going to tell Daniel—or any of my brothers—about what just happened."

"About that…" Frown lines appeared on his forehead. "Today was great."

She nodded, doing everything she could to reply in an easy tone despite her twisting stomach. "It was."

"You're an amazing woman." He breathed in deeply, let it out.

She was about to say something to diffuse the fraught situation, but changed her mind, deciding to see where he went with it.

"But, uh, I'm your boss." His gaze focused somewhere over her left shoulder. "So—"

She couldn't stay quiet a moment more. She had to jump in. "So you're regretting what happened?"

At last, he met her gaze. "It can't happen again," he replied, not answering her question. "We work together. Your family trusts me with you. I'm much older than you. None of this is—" He searched for a word, his Adam's apple sliding. "Appropriate."

A devil on her shoulder urged her to show him just how much better their time in his bed had been than the teeny-tiny amount of pleasure they'd get from being *appropriate*.

But the truth was that she hadn't slept with Cal expecting a commitment—she'd simply found him irresistible. She'd acted first and decided to deal with the fallout later. What's more, her job was extremely important to her. She wanted to prove herself at the foundation, wanted to keep learning so she could be the best she possibly could.

So if being awkwardly brushed aside by Cal bruised her insides, she firmly reminded herself there was no point in being upset because he hadn't tossed a bunch of pretty words her way. Because he hadn't told her she was special. Because he hadn't said he couldn't imagine being without her. Because he hadn't begged to be with her again. Because he hadn't laid his heart at her feet. Because he'd put up a huge, thick wall in front of the idea of ever sleeping with her again.

"You took the words out of my mouth," she said without inflection as she tucked any and all secret feelings for Cal back inside and shoved them down deep where they would never again see the light of day. "We had fun. And neither of us needs to feel weird or uncomfortable about what happened." She forced a smile. "Especially when we both agree that nothing like that will ever happen again."

No matter what.

Just like that, it was as if the hours she'd shared with Cal had never happened. As the pilot brought them down for a landing, they discussed a couple of questions Dane had emailed after their meeting. Then they landed and prepared to say good-bye, given that it was already late afternoon.

"I've been meaning to tell you," Cal said as she got into a taxi. "I'm heading to Miami for a new project I've got going and then up the East Coast for some Maverick ventures. While I'm on the road, I'll put in some face-to-face time with potential donors from Dane's list, and you can stay in San Francisco and deal with the administration and accounting work and any overflow."

She stared at him, speechless for a moment. Until finally she managed to say, "But you told Daniel I was great with Dane Harrington. That I can handle the donor stuff."

He nodded, though she couldn't help but think he looked distinctly uncomfortable and unable to meet her eyes. "You were great with Dane. And if there are potential donors in the Bay Area, you should definitely meet with them. But we don't need to be in each other's pockets at the foundation. I trust you to take care of anything that comes your way. And I'll be just a phone call away if you do need anything."

Hadn't he believed her when she'd agreed they should keep their relationship all business?

Or maybe she was blowing his comments out of proportion, unable to think straight after everything they'd done on the plane, and attributing meaning to his words that simply wasn't there.

"Okay," she said, "you take care of business and bring in a ton of donors, and I'll call if I run into any problems on my end."

His gaze connected with hers again for one brief moment, and she swore she saw a flash of heat before regret came smashing down. Then he closed the door, and the taxi took her away.

Away from Cal.

Chapter Nine

Three weeks later…

Lyssa and Cal spoke on the phone, texted, emailed. It was all business. She went out of her way to act as if they hadn't danced in a private capsule on the London Eye. As if they hadn't painted each other. As if they'd never touched or kissed or climbed into his bed together. In fact, she'd never been so businesslike in all her life.

When she was by herself, however, it was a different story. No matter how much she tried to tell herself she didn't miss him, the truth was that she did. A lot. Missed brainstorming with him in the office. Missed sharing a burrito at lunch. Missed staying late poring over spreadsheets and secretly being glad that he was with her instead of on one of his many dates.

It was even worse at night, when she was alone in her bed and couldn't stop remembering how it felt to be in his arms. How it felt as though all her romantic dreams had come true.

Even though they most definitely had *not*.

Just then, the outer door to their office opened, and with a glance at the clock, she realized Dane Harrington had arrived for their meeting. Mary, their receptionist, lost the power of speech when she looked at him. With his dark hair and devilishly blue eyes, Dane was a seriously handsome man. Other women must fall at his feet, literally go weak in the knees and need to put out a hand to remain standing. But there was only one man who had ever made Lyssa's heart race and turned her knees weak.

She put a stop to her train of thought. Lyssa was done mooning over men she worked with. She'd never make that mistake again. Besides, although there was no question that Dane was a great-looking billionaire, there was no spark between them.

No, Cal had taken all her sparks with him when he'd left.

Rising from her desk to greet Dane, she held out her hand. "It's so good to see you again. I hope everything went well with your resort opening."

"We had our fair share of glitches, but it all worked out in the end." He grinned. "And I was very happy to hear in my recent chat with Cal that things are going well on your end too."

"They really are," she said with a smile, although it felt a tad stiff. Almost as though her lips weren't used to curving up anymore. "Cal's doing a great job of wining and dining new donors on the East Coast. Most of them are from your list, thank you very much."

Dane looked pleased that his contacts were stepping up to the donation plate. "Has he told you that I've lined up a few additional prospects, particularly a man in the Caribbean named Westerbourne?"

"Yes, Cal told me you two would be heading to his private island after Thanksgiving. We can't thank you enough for all your help with the foundation."

"It's my pleasure," he said, waving away her thanks. "Although I'm confused about why he's doing all the donor recruiting by himself when you did a fantastic job talking me into donating. Seems to me you should be out meeting with everyone too." His gaze sharpened. "Is something not right between you and Cal?"

"Me and Cal?" Her voice was too high. "Of course not." Now she sounded strident, darn it. "He handles donors. I handle the accounting. We have complementary strengths."

"Sorry," Dane said with a shake of his head. "I must have gotten the wrong impression. I know it's none of my business, but I assumed you were a couple."

Really? He thought she and Cal looked like they were *together*?

She was astounded Dane would even think that, especially since she and Cal hadn't gotten together until the day after they'd met with him. Although, if she was being completely honest, there'd already been a few sparks.

Warmth moved through her at the thought of being in a real relationship with Cal—rather than on the weird back end of a one-night stand—before she ruthlessly tamped it down. Giving Dane as carefree a smile as she could manage, she forced herself to brush off his words. "We're just really comfortable with each other. He works with my brothers, and I've known him a long time." She shrugged. "It's years of family barbecues and weddings and holidays. He's almost like another brother to me."

Ugh. She was overexplaining, practically about to declare that there was no way, no how, not a single teeny-tiny chance that she and Cal had ever looked at each other as anything more than business associates and friends.

She quickly changed the subject.

"I've been reviewing the IRS requirements for maintaining nonprofit status. One of the main things we need is public funding." Then she threw the ball into his court. "I was thinking we should hold some fundraisers, if you think that's a good idea."

"As a matter of fact, I've hosted many fundraisers at my resorts. We could put together a hell of a charity gala. I can donate the use of the resort facilities at no charge to the foundation."

"Wow, that's great! If you have a few minutes,

maybe we could start to put together an action list for
me to get going on."

Dane pulled out the chair opposite her desk. They
talked for an hour about all the possibilities. He finally
stood and was heading for the door when he turned
back. "For what it's worth, I still think you should
come to the Caribbean with us to speak with Westerbourne. Think about it, would you?"

★ ★ ★

Cal hadn't seen Lyssa in three weeks. Three long,
arduous, frustrating weeks.

God help him, he'd wanted to call her up late at
night, every single night, just to talk to her while she
lay in bed. To hear her voice. And to know if she
missed him as much as he missed her.

Of course, right while he was thinking about her—
who was he kidding, he was *always* thinking about
her—Cal got a call from the Mavericks. All of them. On
speakerphone.

"Hey, Cal." It was Will. "What are you doing on
Saturday?"

"Why do you ask?" He felt as though a neon sign
over his head flashed GUILTY, GUILTY, GUILTY.

"We're down to the wire on Mom and Dad's
house, and we need your help." That was Evan.

"So strap on your tool belt," added Daniel.

"Saturday, eight a.m. sharp," Sebastian said.

"We're not taking no for an answer," Matt put in.

Since Cal couldn't tell them it was dangerous for him to be in the same state as Lyssa, having no control whatsoever around their sister, he had no choice but to agree. "I'll be there."

He flew into San Francisco late Friday night so he wouldn't have to test his self-control by dropping in at the office to see Lyssa. He just hoped she wouldn't end up pitching in with the guys on the house renovations. He'd heard something about a pool party Ari was throwing, so hopefully Lyssa would be there all day, rather than anywhere near him.

The guys were in the backyard when he arrived the next morning. "We're planning to lay down the redwood deck today," Will said. "All along the back of the house and down to the pool patio."

The house was a five-bedroom, five-bath bungalow with a great room that included a dining area, plus a breakfast nook and large kitchen. There was still work to be done both inside and out, but Cal was impressed by what the guys had already accomplished. The pool and hot tub were in-ground, surrounded by a new concrete pool deck. They'd laid sod in the big backyard and planted flowers and shrubs all around the fence they'd erected. Outside the fence was another treed acre that would grow wild. This inner sanctuary was where Susan could grow her roses and the flowering shrubs she adored. She'd be in heaven not having to work around a Chicago winter for the first time in her life.

"You guys have done a great job," Cal noted.

"You think Mom will be pleased?" Matt was a big, muscular man, though Cal had heard tales that he'd been scrawny as a kid.

"Susan is going to feel like you've created heaven on earth for her."

The Mavericks all grinned like little kids who were about to get a gold star from the teacher.

Gideon sidled up to Cal. "You and Lyssa are doing a very impressive job with Lean on Us. I can't thank you enough."

He told Gideon the absolute truth. "It's all Lyssa. She works tirelessly for your foundation and loves every second of it."

"I feel lucky to have her on board. Both of you." He slapped Cal on the back, then said, "She gave me the details on that gala she and Dane are planning. Sounds like it's going to be quite the shindig."

Dane. That was all he'd heard out of Lyssa's mouth recently. *Dane said this. Dane said that.*

Was Dane going to ask her out? Or had he already done so?

Cal's blood pressure rose as jealousy ate him up. *No.* He couldn't go there. Couldn't let himself think that he had any hold on her. Just because he couldn't have her didn't mean she was off-limits to anyone else.

Especially a handsome billionaire like Dane Harrington.

"Lyssa always has brilliant ideas," he told Gideon.

"You're right, she does. But I'm wondering if you're working her too hard. She couldn't make the pool party today because she had to go into the office."

Cal held up his hands. "She never listens to me when I tell her to take time off."

Gideon shook his head. "Figured as much. She's a Maverick, after all." Gideon was a big, strapping guy who looked like he'd only just come out of the military, rather than having left ten years ago.

Jorge, Rosie's son, was running laps with Noah around the pool, his arms out as he pretended to be an airplane. Gideon had fallen head over heels for Jorge as well as his mom. Jorge was the same age as Noah, Matt's son, and the two boys were best friends.

"Careful," Matt called as his son skidded close to the pool's edge. "You're getting close to falling in."

"I know how to swim, Daddy. So does Jorge."

"That doesn't mean I can't watch out for you." Matt tickled both boys in the ribs, and they giggled like two very happy six-year-olds.

Cal felt an ache around his heart. Once upon a time, he'd dreamed of this—having a family, a loving wife, the white picket fence, laughter. But when he was seventeen, everything in his family had gone sideways, and after that, it had been easier to focus on school, then jobs, then building his business. So much easier than facing his past, or delving into his emotions and the darkness he'd shoved way down deep inside. He'd never met a woman who made him want to dig deep enough to make things last, because he couldn't live without her, because he couldn't stop thinking about her.

Not until Lyssa.

She was the only woman he'd never been able to get out of his head.

Lyssa, the Mavericks' younger sister.

Lyssa, the woman he'd taken again and again on a transatlantic flight.

Lyssa, the woman he couldn't stop fantasizing about. Even when he was surrounded by her brothers, all of whom would tear him apart with their bare hands if they knew what he'd done. The way he'd made her gasp and cry out with pleasure. The way she'd—

"Hey, you guys, get your asses down here," Sebastian yelled, breaking through his wicked thoughts. Thoughts that should have damned him to hell already.

"Did you hear?" Gideon asked as they walked over to the others. "They want to finish the deck today. The whole thing, start to finish."

Cal nodded. "Normally, I'd say it's an impossible task. But with seven of us—and the Maverick energy flowing strong—I'm thinking it won't be a problem." If he didn't explode from guilt, leaving them with only six.

"We put in the concrete piers last week, along with the posts," Sebastian said as they approached. Tallest of the guys, he had dirt on his hands and holes in his jeans, as if he wasn't worth several fortunes.

"Today we'll set down the support beams and lay out the decking," Evan added.

The Mavericks were like one being. They finished each other's sentences. They knew one another backward and forward, all the family secrets.

Except Cal's big, humongous, they-would-kill-him-a-hundred-times-over-if-they-knew secret.

God, it was going to be a long day.

Cal pulled out his hammer. "Tell me where to start."

"Over here," Daniel said.

Faced with Lyssa's big brother, Cal felt yet another wave of guilt. Would it never stop?

It wasn't as if the Mavericks didn't have their demons. Each of them had a shadowy past they rarely talked about. Fortunately, they'd all found amazing women who'd helped them move forward and forgive, even if they couldn't forget.

Lyssa was an amazing woman too. More amazing than any woman Cal had ever met.

Out of the blue, the thought occurred to him that if

he'd dealt with his own demons the way each of the Mavericks had, rather than forever shoving them deeper into the shadows, then maybe he and Lyssa could—

Damn it! He was doing it again. Getting lost in fantasies. Even if they could somehow circumvent her brothers, the truth was that she could do so much better than her boss, who was twenty years her senior.

She had her whole life ahead of her. Cal couldn't stand the thought of holding her back in any way. And given his track record with relationships, it wasn't lost on him that the women he dated usually had the same complaint, that he held something back, or worse, retreated altogether if things started to get even the slightest bit serious. Lyssa could do a hell of a lot better. *Dane Harrington* kind of better, in fact.

Furious with himself for continuing to want her even when he knew he could never have anything beyond their one-night stand, he hefted a beam with Evan and worked for the next hour without so much as a water break. His muscles heated, and sweat poured from him, but he was intensely glad for the hard physical work. Anything that would keep his thoughts from straying to Lyssa.

It didn't help that the guys kept talking about her. "Tell us more about this gala Lyssa and Dane Harrington are planning," Daniel said.

"I don't know much," he had to admit. "They've

been running with it while I've been out of town."

Thinking about how much time Lyssa was spending with Dane made him unnaturally clumsy. He lost his grip on the beam, scraping his finger and drawing a little blood.

"What's got you so jumpy?" Matt tossed him a pair of work gloves.

He wasn't jumpy. Except when he thought about how he'd slept with their sister.

"Too much caffeine," he lied.

Too much dreaming about Lyssa Spencer.

"Wait a second," Daniel said. "Is there something you're not telling us?"

Oh shit. How could they possibly know? "Like what?"

"Is Dane hitting on my sister?" Daniel asked, his chest puffing out like he was ready to avenge her right that second.

"He'd better not be," Cal said before he could stop jealousy from surging through him again.

"You're right about that," Will said. "Because we would tear him limb from limb if he so much as touched a hair on her head."

Sebastian nodded. "I don't care how much money the guy has, or how much he's helping with Gideon's foundation, she's got no business being with a guy that old, or that experienced."

Gideon and all the rest of them nodded. While Cal

stood there and tried to act like he hadn't done a damn thing with Lyssa beyond hiring her and complimenting her accounting skills.

"Speaking of experience," Matt said, "how are things going with you and the ladies lately?"

Cal hammered a beam in place as another wave of guilt hammered his gut. He was almost getting used to the queasiness. Almost.

Until he stood among the Mavericks.

They would smash him into pulp if they knew what he'd done. And he would deserve every last bit of punishment meted out to him.

"Sorry, guys, I got nothing." He tried to distance himself from the conversation by focusing on repositioning a beam that was slightly out of line with the others. "I've been really busy with work."

Now that the Mavericks had each found their soul mate, they couldn't resist ribbing him since they could no longer rib each other. Which was why Daniel elbowed Sebastian and said, "That means he's got a hot one on the hook."

Sebastian laughed. "If he doesn't want to talk about her, she's got to be pretty special."

If they only knew, they wouldn't be laughing. They'd be going for his throat.

* * *

When they were done for the day and packing up,

Evan approached him. "Hey, I think your email address was accidentally left off the invite."

"What invite?"

"Catalina. Paige and I want to have Thanksgiving on Catalina Island with everyone. It's her birthday a couple of days after that, and we thought it would be a great way to celebrate with the whole gang."

Lyssa would be there. What the hell was he going to do when he saw her? How was he supposed to get through twenty-four hours on an island with Lyssa?

"I'll do my best," he said as he tried to think of an excuse his friend would buy, "but I've got meetings back East and I have to fly out again right away after today."

Evan narrowed his eyes. "No one meets on Thanksgiving. That and Christmas are the only two days of the year when the business world shuts down. Besides, I know you wouldn't want to disappoint Paige, would you? She's pregnant and might burst into tears if she hears you're not coming. Don't do that to me."

Cal couldn't help but laugh. "Boy, are you ever laying on the guilt trip." Didn't Evan know that Cal already had a guilt trip crushing him?

"Fly from wherever you are directly into LAX and meet us at the ferry," Evan insisted. "You're family. It wouldn't be the same without you."

It was an honor to be considered part of a family

like the Mavericks. Strong. Steady. Always there for each other. Only Cal and Lyssa knew the truth—that he was scum who'd indulged in a sexy afternoon with the Mavericks' younger sister, then run as fast and far as he could because he couldn't stop wanting her...and didn't trust himself to have the strength to keep his hands off her.

All his life, Cal had thought he was a better man than his father. Now he knew how wrong he was. Their situations might be different—Cal hadn't cheated on anyone the way his father had cheated on his mother—but in many ways, Cal wondered if his situation was even worse.

He'd broken the trust of *all* the Mavericks. He'd broken Susan's and Bob's trust. He'd broken his own trusted rules about never mixing business with pleasure. And worst of all, he was afraid he'd broken Lyssa's trust in him. Because he was no longer the good guy she could count on to be there for her as a business partner...and as a friend.

Chapter Ten

The moment she received Paige and Evan's invitation, Lyssa knew Cal would finally be forced to face her. Paige had said the guest list was just family since it was Thanksgiving and Paige's birthday.

And Cal was family.

Lyssa felt totally fine about everything now. No one knew what they'd done, and no one ever would. She could maintain her equilibrium. She wasn't angry. She wasn't even hurt anymore.

Instead, she was wholly focused on moving forward. And right now, the entirety of her life was her job. She didn't want to leave the foundation, so that meant she and Cal had to efficiently and unemotionally clear up any garbage left in the aftermath of their very short affair. It was her one big goal for the weekend—to tidy up loose ends with Cal, put the past in the past, and move on.

Then Cal could stop running away and get back to San Francisco where he belonged. There was so much to do at the foundation, so much she still had to learn.

And if, in the middle of the night, her heart sometimes felt a little weak, and her body sometimes felt a little needy, and all she could think about were his kisses and his touch and his mouth on her…well, she'd forgive herself those tiny lapses and trust she would soon forget. One day, she vowed, their hours on the plane together would be nothing but a distant memory.

But as she stepped out of the limo Daniel had rented for them at LAX and saw Cal on the Catalina Island ferry dock, despite her vows to be strong and relaxed and determinedly positive, an ache closed around her heart.

Daniel and Evan had flown everyone down from San Francisco—her parents, who'd come in from Chicago, the brothers, their ladies, plus the immediate family. Of course, Tasha was with Daniel. But Lyssa noted the absence of Tasha's brother Drew. She wondered if he'd been invited. He was a bit of a black sheep, but he'd been a tremendous help to her with the foundation.

Charlie's mother, Francine, had decorated her walker with cardboard cutouts of turkeys, pumpkins, squash, and horns of plenty. She was a doll. In her eighties and suffering from debilitating arthritis that never got her down, she walked a mile every day. She was an inspiration.

Paige was very pregnant now. She didn't have just

a baby bump but a watermelon, and she also looked super happy, especially since Evan's mother had come too, along with the twins. Tony and Kelsey were Lyssa's age, which was ten years younger than Evan. His mom, brother, and sister had come back into Evan's life only a year ago. Having been separated from his mother when he was a kid, he hadn't even known about the twins. But it was all good now.

Gideon had Rosie and the adorable little Jorge with him. Chi had come too. Rosie, Ari, and Chi were best friends dating all the way back to their time in foster care together.

Jorge and Noah, and Harper's brother, Jeremy, too, were bouncing around Lyssa's parents, happy to see Grandpa and Grandma. Jeremy was a wonderful big kid, and Jorge and Noah adored him.

And then there was Cal.

He was gorgeous. The well-built body, his beautiful face, that kissable mouth.

Get yourself under control, she thought, her teeth gritted as she worked to regain her equanimity before she came face to face with him.

Kelsey, her sun-streaked chestnut hair pulled back in a ponytail, found her in the crowd of Mavericks. "It's been ages since I've seen you." She gave Lyssa the biggest, warmest hug.

"I've been really busy at the foundation. But it's amazing work, and I love it." And, if Lyssa was being completely honest, she would have to admit she'd been working extra hard to prove to herself that she was totally over her afternoon with Cal on the plane. As if to say, *See, I'm not heartbroken. I feel totally fine!*

Then Chi, Rosie, and Ari were rushing to hug her too. Of course, Noah and Jorge couldn't be left out.

Lyssa tried to swing Noah into her arms the way she usually did. "Wow, you're getting so big, I can barely pick you up anymore."

At six and three-quarters—because Noah wanted to make sure he got credit for every quarter year of age— he was growing like a weed.

Giving Jorge a big hug, she smiled at Rosie and Ari. "They grow so fast."

"And they eat like elephants," Rosie said, her hair the same dark, curly silk of Jorge's.

The boys made trumpeting noises and whooped around. Those two never slowed down.

"How's prep for the gallery show going?" All of them were so excited that Rosie had a show at the end of January at a huge San Francisco art gallery. No one could have been more thrilled than Gideon, who absolutely adored everything about Rosie.

She'd worked as an accountant, but she was an amazing artist, her paintings beautifully detailed. Having quit her job at the end of September, Rosie was now painting full time, which was why she and Gideon hadn't yet set a wedding date.

"I've got the whole first floor of the gallery to fill." Rosie's eyes were wide, as if she thought the feat was impossible. But she would do it. "I want to show a bunch of new paintings as well as works from over the years."

Lyssa hugged her tight. "I'm so happy for you."

A few moments later, the ferry began boarding. Lyssa couldn't tell whether it was on purpose or by accident, but no matter where she was, Cal seemed to be on the exact opposite side of the group.

Evan had rented a room for all of them on the ferry's top deck. Though it was chilly outside with the wind off the ocean, the big room was warm, with all-around windows for a great view. They snacked on finger food, champagne, and hot chocolate. Making her way to her mom and dad, she gave them big hugs.

"I haven't seen you for so long, honey. It feels like years."

Susan and Bob were both in their late fifties. Lyssa had always considered her mom beautiful—tall and slim, her hair a lovely silver she'd never dyed. And her father looked hearty and healthy, his smile wide. The back operation her brothers had paid for a few years ago had given him a new lease on life.

"I've only been gone a few months, Mom." But she knew how her mother felt. In Chicago, they had seen each other all the time.

"I know. But I miss my little girl." She cupped Lyssa's cheeks. "I can hardly wait until we move to California. The house will be ready for us in only a few weeks, or so I'm told."

Her dad threw his arm about Lyssa. "Your mom's been going through everything around the house. I can't believe all the stuff she's throwing out. You'd think we were pack rats."

Mom laughed. "Every time I put something in the giveaway box, your father takes it out and tells me he needs it, and we can't possibly throw it out."

They'd lived in Chicago all their lives. When they were first married, they could afford only a cramped walk-up in a not-so-nice neighborhood. And that was putting it politely. But they'd raised her and Daniel there, done their best, and when Daniel had been eleven, they began bringing in the Mavericks, boys with not-so-happy pasts—and that was putting it mildly too. Her parents always had more than enough love to go around. Matt, Evan, Sebastian, and Will had been Daniel's friends at school, and they'd all come to feel that Susan and Bob Spencer were more like real parents than their own. When her brothers—she never thought of them as foster brothers—had started making money in their various endeavors, the first thing they'd done was move Mom and Dad to a big house in a good suburb. Until recently, her parents had wanted to stay right there. But now that Lyssa had moved away, and with no more family ties in Chicago, her parents had decided to leave too.

"I'm so excited to see the new house for the first time."

"Your brothers won't let me come out and help," her dad groused, rubbing his almost-bald head. He'd taught them everything they knew about home improvement. Daniel always credited their father for inspiring him to start Top Notch.

"You know they want to surprise both of us with the finished product, honey," Susan reminded him. "They're out there every weekend. Cal was there this past Saturday, as well. I heard he helped them build the deck."

Lyssa worked to keep her expression neutral. So. Cal had flown into the area for the weekend, but hadn't stopped by the office, or even let her know he was in town. Clearly, they needed to have their face-to-face sooner rather than later. Before things got any weirder, it was time to nip his awkwardness around her in the bud.

But while Cal might be able to avoid Lyssa, at least for these past few weeks, he couldn't avoid her mother. Susan beckoned, and of course Cal immediately came over, making his way through the crowd of Mavericks. He gave Susan a big hug and clapped Bob on the back. All Lyssa got from him was a faint approximation of a smile.

Fortunately, her mother didn't seem to feel any of

the tension. "The boys tell me you've been working on the house too." She clasped both his hands in hers. "Thank you so much. We can hardly wait to move in."

"It was my pleasure," Cal said politely. "Good to see you both." Then he glanced over Bob's shoulder. "I see Gideon gesturing at me. I'd love to catch up with both of you later, if you'll excuse me."

Then he took off, clearly desperate to put distance between himself and Lyssa.

As she watched him go, there was that ache around her heart again, squeezing the breath out of her.

She shoved it away, put a smile on her face, and proceeded to tell her parents all about the gala she was planning with Dane Harrington.

Chapter Eleven

This twenty-four-hour Catalina Island celebration would be the death of him.

Cal surreptitiously surveyed the name tags on the dining table's place settings and was simultaneously thankful that Paige had put Lyssa between Kelsey and Chi, rather than next to him—while also suffering from the emptiness of all these weeks without her smile, her beautiful face, her laugh, her scent.

The ferry ride over to Catalina had been the first hurdle. He looked at each of the day's events as additional hurdles he would have to jump before he could hurry back on the ferry and get the hell away from her again.

Not that he didn't love the Mavericks and their parties, but standing among them, knowing what he'd done, felt worse than sticking his hand in a basket of rattlesnakes. Talking with Lyssa and her parents, he was sure he'd felt the fangs sinking into his flesh—and he deserved every poisonous bite.

The Mavericks had taken over the entire hotel. The

banquet hall was decked out festively for Thanksgiving, the tables set in a big U and decorated with dried gourds, small pumpkins, and squashes along the inside edge. A parquet dance floor took up the other half of the hall, while a buffet table rested along one wall, ready for the turkeys to be carved and warming plates to receive the yams and mashed potatoes and stuffing and vegetables. Along the other wall was a full bar, including champagne, plus juice and sparkling cider for the kids.

After the ferry dropped them off, they'd checked into their rooms, and now everyone was dressed in their finery. The Mavericks wore dark suits and ties, while the women were all beautifully dressed in a variety of colors. They were each different and stunning in their own way. Charlie was the only redhead. Harper was blond, yet somehow more serious than the others. Tasha had long, midnight-black hair. Ari, the youngest, looked like a blond girl next door.

But all Cal truly saw was Lyssa. Her silky teal dress hugged her curves and flowed around her calves. She wore a pair of heels that made her legs look endless.

He thought of the teal paint splotch she'd sprayed on his shirt in London and how she'd pressed tight against him as they'd fought for the can. Which made him remember the taste of her, the softness of her skin, the sweetness of her lips.

He lived in fear of accidentally doing or saying

something that would reveal to the Mavericks what he'd done. Surely it must be written in his gaze whenever he looked at Lyssa, or even stood in the same room, despite trying his hardest *not* to look.

"Where's Evan?" Daniel said by his ear, and Cal damn near jumped out of his shoes.

"I haven't seen him. Paige would know."

He could only hope Daniel hadn't seen him staring at Lyssa with all the lust in his heart. He loved this family. He loved these guys. And he'd screwed up everything by giving in to his craving for someone he should never have been with...and couldn't stop thinking about.

At that moment, Evan entered the banquet room, dressed to the nines in an impeccable tuxedo. He strode straight to the arbor that had been set up by the dance floor, flowers threaded through it like a trellis.

Cal had thought it was a backdrop for photos. But now it dawned on him what the arbor was *really* for.

Susan gasped, clearly having realized the same thing, and took Theresa Collins's hand in hers. Evan's mother had come back into his life only a year ago, after disappearing when he was a kid. And she'd returned with the twins. More aptly, the twins had brought her back.

No question, Paige and Evan had been through the wringer. First, there'd been Evan's horrible ex-wife, Whitney, then the amazing love story with Paige, who was Whitney's sister, all while Evan had to deal with the return of a family he hadn't even known he had. It had been a long year for all of them. Yet Evan, standing before them, seemed bathed in the glow of love.

Cal couldn't help but think of his own family. Not one of them had ended up basking in the glow of love. Not even close.

When everyone was silent, Evan announced, "Paige and I got you here under false pretenses. While, of course, we want to celebrate Thanksgiving and Paige's birthday, we have something extra special planned for you."

With a flourish of his hand toward the door, the "Wedding March" began to play.

Paige stood in the doorway, her hand looped through the arm of Evan's brother, Tony. She held a bouquet of brightly colored peonies. Her auburn hair was pulled up, her dress a cream-colored silk with a beaded bodice, the skirt flowing over her baby bump. Her pretty brown eyes glittered with joy. She was a truly beautiful bride.

It was on Cal before he knew it, an ache squeezing his heart. Evan and the rest of the Mavericks were ten years younger than he. Yet each of them had found the perfect love. Paige would have her baby in the new year, and Cal would watch them all start their families.

Looking back at the past twenty years of his life, what did he have to show for them beyond piles of money, a plane, and a bunch of expensive properties around the world? Though those things were all great, they couldn't give comfort in the middle of the night when he was feeling low, and they sure couldn't make him laugh unexpectedly when they nailed him with spray paint, or danced with him far above London with the city skyline as a backdrop.

Instinctively, his gaze was drawn to Lyssa. She was gorgeous, her features glowing, her eyes glistening with happy tears as she watched Paige walk to the love of her life.

The Mavericks had it all—love, family, happiness.

Whereas when Cal had finally found the first and only woman who had ever made him think about *forever*, she was the woman he could never have.

He had good friends, a great career, and the money to have whatever he wanted. Except the one thing he now realized that he truly needed—a family. Bitterness welled up in him, and he hated it. He didn't want to envy the Mavericks. He was happy for Evan and Paige, happy for all of them.

He dragged his gaze away from Lyssa. It was too painful even to look at her.

Paige finally reached Evan, and Tony kissed her and stepped back as she took her place at her bridegroom's side.

"She's so lovely." Susan dabbed her eyes with a tissue, still holding hands with Theresa Collins, whose eyes were shiny with tears too. While she was probably Susan's age, she looked older, her difficult years having taken a bigger toll.

The middle-aged minister, in a dark coat, a sliver of white at his collar, joined Paige and Evan beneath the arbor.

Standing together, their hands clasped, Evan said, "We wanted something small and informal, with the people most special to us in all the world."

Everyone's cameras and phones were exploding with the pictures they were taking as Evan raised Paige's hand to his lips.

Their love was an aura surrounding them. Paige was the woman Evan should have married all those years ago, not her sister. Finally, the two of them had everything they wanted.

Cal rejoiced for their love and their union and the new baby to come. And worked like hell to squash every dark speck of bitterness inside him.

Paige and Evan turned to each other, and the minister began to speak, his voice resonating in the hall. "I don't believe I've ever had a greater pleasure than bringing this couple together, a couple who are so in love and who give each other such unconditional support." He smiled at them both. "I believe you've written your own vows."

Paige smiled and held Evan's hands in hers as she spoke the heartfelt words. "We were friends first. I admired you for your intelligence, your hard work, your kindness. You had a purpose, and you never let anything sway you. I fell in love with the good man you are. It was never about how handsome you were or the millions you were going to make. It was always about the beauty of your spirit." She put her hand to her belly. "It's about the wonderful father I know you're going to be. I have always loved you, Evan, and I always will."

Evan reached out, tenderly wiping a tear that trickled down Paige's cheek. "I love you with every fiber of my being. I was never as smart as you about how to be happy, how I should live, and the best choices I could make. I made some horrendous mistakes. But in the end, all those mistakes led me to you. To this moment. To the life we're building together." He gently laid his hand over her curved belly. "And to the new life we've made. I will always strive to be the man you need. To be the kind of father our children need. I will always be here for you. And I will always love you with everything in me."

There wasn't a dry eye in the house. Even Cal felt an ache behind his eyes.

He looked at Lyssa. At the same moment, she turned to him. And gave him a misty smile.

And he was lost.

* * *

As if she didn't have a will of her own, Lyssa's gaze was drawn to Cal during the vows. Despite how shaky things had been between them since their plane ride home from London, she couldn't help but smile as she looked at him.

She smiled for the beauty of the moment. For the sweetness of the love between Paige and Evan. Even for the pureness of the emotions she felt for Cal as her guard fell away in this moment, emotions that were stronger than anything she'd ever known.

Cal didn't smile back. But he didn't turn away either. She had no clue what was in his mind, if he still thought about holding her, kissing her, the ways they'd touched each other, the things he'd said when he was bringing her to the peak of ecstasy. All the things she'd been working so hard to forget.

Then the minister was saying, "I now pronounce you husband and wife. You may kiss the bride."

Evan cupped Paige's face, and he kissed her so softly, so gently, so sweet and long and lasting—just the way Lyssa knew their marriage would be.

Everyone agreed that Evan should never have married Whitney all those years ago. It should have been Paige right from the beginning. Lyssa wanted to be absolutely, positively sure that the first time she got married would be the *only* time.

She refused to let her eyes drift back to Cal and give in to the urge to drink him in. Clearly, their hours together on his plane had been a mistake, but hopefully not big enough to cause permanent damage to their careers, their friendship, or their hearts. Anything more between them, however, would surely turn their mistake into a catastrophe. There was no way she could allow that. As soon as she said her congratulations to the happy couple, and there was a chance to sneak away from the festivities without anyone noticing, she would pull Cal aside and put everything to rest. They could then move forward without any of this lingering weirdness.

The minister announced, "I give you Mr. and Mrs. Collins!"

As everyone cheered, Paige and Evan kissed again. Then Paige turned to the room and her whole family. "We have one more announcement. It's been terribly hard to keep this secret, but we wanted it to be a huge surprise for everyone."

A smile lit up Evan's face like fireworks at the seventy-fifth anniversary of the Golden Gate Bridge. And he took over the announcement. "We're having *twins!*"

The Mavericks all rushed forward, surrounding Paige and Evan, the brothers clapping him on the back and kissing her on the cheek. Lyssa's mother hugged Paige. "I'm so happy."

Theresa Collins came next. "You did such a great job of keeping it all so secret—the wedding, the twins."

The brothers stepped back for their mom to throw

her arms around Evan. She whispered something that made his hug even tighter. Then his mother, Theresa, hugged him tearfully.

When it was Lyssa's turn, she told Paige, "I'm so glad you're my sister now. Thank you for making Evan so happy."

"You're the best sister I could ever wish for."

When she hugged Evan, she teased, "I'm glad you finally got it right."

"I sure did," he said, looking happier than she'd ever seen him.

When she stepped away to let the others say their congratulations, Kelsey grinned at Lyssa. "Now we're truly sisters."

"We've been sisters of the heart all along," Lyssa said. "But I'm so glad it's official."

The waitstaff moved through the party, handing out champagne. And when everyone had a glass, Lyssa's dad raised his. "To the happy couple. May your love last for all eternity and your joy in each other be boundless."

They all shouted "huzzah" to the toast and drank.

"To forever and a day," came from Gideon, surprising since he was such a quiet guy. But he had eyes only for Rosie as he made the toast. Same with her brothers and their beautiful ladies. After that, everyone mingled, telling one another how surprised they were, how heartfelt the vows had been, how beautiful Paige was, how excited they were to welcome twins into the family.

"He's your brother," Lyssa said to Kelsey. "Did you really not have a single clue about any of this?"

Kelsey shook her head. "The only one he told about the wedding was Tony, and that was half an hour before it all went down."

"Frankly, I'm amazed they were able to keep it on the down low." Rosie smiled, tucking an errant dark curl behind her ear. "I would have been blurting it out to everyone!"

Jorge and Noah raced around the room with Gideon chasing after them, making sure they didn't knock too many things over.

"She was the most beautiful bride ever," Ari said.

Lyssa grinned at her friend. "I know another beautiful bride."

"Yes, but I didn't have the baby bump," Ari said. "That made all the difference."

Every one of them—Lyssa, Rosie, Chi, and Kelsey—stared at Ari. Until Lyssa asked, "Are you?"

"We're certainly trying." Ari beamed.

Lyssa's friend adored Noah. Though he was her stepson, she loved him as though he were her own flesh and blood. She wanted a huge brood, though. She was even a kindergarten teacher—that's how much she loved kids.

"I hope it happens soon," Kelsey said. "So, Lyssa,

fill us in on the new job at the foundation. Especially about Dane Harrington. I've never met him, of course, but I heard he's gorgeous and that you've been spending a lot of time with him putting together a big gala."

"Dane bought the painting," she said with a smile, "and he wants to help the foundation in any way he can. He's been spearheading the whole gala and is hosting it at his resort in the wine country."

"Any sparks between you that you care to mention?" Ari said, giving an eyebrow waggle that made them all laugh.

Lyssa shook her head. "It's nothing like that. He's just a business associate who has also become a friend during the time we've worked together."

"Is that too much denial?" Chi asked, winking. She wore her straight black hair in a delicate chignon.

"I'd tell you if there was something going on between us," Lyssa promised, though there were plenty of things she *hadn't* told them when it came to another handsome, wealthy man she worked with. "But I swear there isn't."

Kelsey nudged her, keeping her voice low. "Okay then, what's it like working for Mr. Danniger?"

Chi's expression held a wicked glint. "At the last Maverick wedding, I believe you said something about wanting to write your name all over him in lipstick?"

Of course, Cal chose that moment to glance at the posse of girls, who were looking at him. Lyssa prayed he wouldn't think she'd told her friends about their one-flight stand. She wanted to close her eyes and groan. But that would only add fuel to the kindling.

Instead, in the calmest of voices, she said, "He's my boss. I don't even wear lipstick around him. Besides," she said with an airy wave of her hand, "I only said that to get Daniel's goat. You know how he's always been so overprotective."

"He's a Maverick," Ari said with a knowing smile. "They're like a pack guarding their den."

Ari was married to a big, overprotective Maverick, especially where Noah and she were concerned. But Lyssa was the one who'd been told in no uncertain terms that a certain man was off-limits.

Kelsey wasn't letting up. "What if he wasn't your boss?"

"Well, since I hope to continue working at the foundation for a very long time, it's not something I've ever really thought about."

She couldn't stand lying to her friends—it felt like chewing on nails—but she could never come clean with them about London, or the trip home. She had no choice but to get through their line of questioning and hope they didn't ask about Cal ever again.

★ ★ ★

Cal had to get on the first available ferry off the island after the Thanksgiving dinner. There was no way he could keep his head straight around Lyssa for even one minute past the pumpkin pie.

She had looked at him, and he was a goner.

One glance at her lips, and he remembered how good she tasted.

One whiff of her perfume, and he remembered how sweet she smelled.

And if he kept gazing at her as if he wanted to devour her, there was no way the guys would miss it.

Luckily, he was seated far enough from Lyssa that he couldn't see her, couldn't drool over her. Next to him, Theresa Collins was ecstatic about the wedding and the twins. She chattered away happily without expecting a reply. The turkey and all the trimmings were surely delicious, but could have been straw in his mouth for all he enjoyed them.

Bob Spencer rose, clinking his fork against his glass. "Although I didn't have time to prepare a toast, I'd still like to say a few words to the happy couple." He raised his glass. "Paige, you know Susan and I love you like our own daughter. We couldn't be happier that you've joined the family and that you're bringing us not only one grandchild, but two. It's all the more important that we move out to California ASAP, because we want to be here for the twins' arrival." He laughed. "We're going to be spending so much time with your kids—" He looked at the parents in the group. "With *all* of your kids, that you're bound to get sick of us and want to send us back to Chicago."

Paige—and everyone else—called out, "Never!"

He raised his glass. "Evan, you done good, son. Real good."

Then Will rose. "You caught us by surprise, bro. The best possible surprise. So, like Dad, I'll be short and sweet. All I'll say is that after it took you ten long years to get your head out of your butt and marry Paige—" Everyone laughed and cheered. "—I'm glad you can finally see the sun shining again."

There were guffaws and more *huzzahs*, and everyone toasted with glee because Evan had finally picked the right sister.

But Cal didn't touch a drop. Champagne reminded him of the London Eye and holding Lyssa in his arms as they danced the unforgettable night away.

He had to be on the next ferry. He wasn't going to be able to keep his distance for much longer. And if he touched her again?

On a silent curse, he picked up his glass and downed it in one gulp, consumed by the seriously hot sparks that would fly if he gave in to his desperate need to pull Lyssa into his arms and kiss her breathless.

Sparks that would surely burn to ashes any friendship or business relationship left between them.

Chapter Twelve

With the fabulous meal over, the staff cleared away the plates. A waiter rolled in a trolley with a one-tier wedding cake covered in fondant icing and beautifully made sugar flowers.

In all the hubbub, Lyssa saw Cal slip out. Knowing this was the chance she'd been looking for, she followed him as he made a beeline for the rear exit. By the time she reached the French doors, he'd already wended his way through the tables on the patio and was heading along the path to the cliff.

She couldn't run in her heels, so she slipped them off, lifted her dress, and jogged after him. Fortunately, the patio was empty, and no one would see her making a fool of herself.

She was breathless by the time she caught up to him. "Cal," she called.

Cal finally turned.

The look he gave her made her whole body tremble. He didn't look angry or annoyed. His gaze simply ate her up, his eyes hot, blazing, taking in her heaving chest, sliding down her body to her shoes in her hand and her bare feet. Then he licked his lips as if his mouth had dried up.

She couldn't catch her breath, and it wasn't just the running. It was that look.

That *hunger*. For *her*.

Working to think clearly, she said, "I wanted to talk to you face to face. Clear the air."

"What things do we need to talk through?" His voice was rough-edged.

She'd planned on being calm, cool, and collected. But his question—one that was so full of denial it might as well be a river in Egypt—made her see red.

"Are you kidding me?"

He'd flown up and down the East Coast for over a month just so he didn't have to be near her. He'd run from her parents on the ferry because she'd been with them. And now he intended to skulk in the garden to avoid her?

Without stopping to think whether it was a good idea or not, she grabbed his arm and pulled him into a secluded glade off the main path. Surrounded by tall hedges, a fountain babbled prettily, a bench beside it. It was the perfect place to yell at him without anyone seeing.

She deepened her voice, doing her best imitation of him. "I have to fly off to Miami. I don't have time to talk. I've got to run here, there, and everywhere to make sure I'm not in the same city as you." Her entire body was vibrating with emotion. "Okay, so we had sex. But it's no big deal." She defiantly ignored the fact that the words didn't ring the slightest bit true. "We're both adults. We can handle this. You don't have to avoid me like I carry the plague. I don't know why you've turned the whole thing on the plane into a federal offense."

"It shouldn't have happened." His voice was low, his tone raw.

She gave a painful snort of laughter. "So that means we can't even talk anymore?"

"We talk," he insisted. "I answer every question you have about the foundation, don't I?"

"Okay, so you talk to me over email or the phone. But you haven't been to the office since London. You didn't even let me know you were in town when you worked on Mom and Dad's deck on Saturday." She rolled her eyes. "What's going on with you, Cal?" She flashed back to the heat she imagined she'd seen in his eyes a few moments earlier, and the devil climbed up on her shoulder. "Are you afraid you can't resist me or something?"

"Yes, that's exactly it." It was the very last thing she'd expected him to say. "I can't resist you. No matter how hard I try."

Oh. My. God.

Her knees went weak, and her heart pounded. So

hard that she thought it might actually leap out of her chest. She *hadn't* invented anything in her head. She *hadn't* made up the heat or the hunger. Which meant she *wasn't* the only one who had been left struggling with unquenchable desire for the past several weeks.

"You should never have come out here to find me." His voice was deep and harsh. "I should never have agreed to come to the island at all."

But even as he was listing all the things they shouldn't do, his hand slid beneath the fall of her hair and wrapped around her nape. His skin was warm, and his eyes were hot as he hungrily drank in the sight of her. Then he devoured her, tasting her, consuming her as if he'd been starving.

For *her.*

She forgot all about clearing the air. Forgot about burying the past. Forgot every vow to be nothing more than friendly and professional. Forgot how difficult the past weeks had been, how awkward, how weird. Forgot about needing to move forward with a clean slate. Forgot how much she wanted her job and how determined she was not to make another mistake.

All she could think about, all she could feel was Cal. How much she loved his kisses, his touch. How much she longed to be with him again. And how sure she was that this time, things would be different.

They could both see now that there was no point in trying to stay away from each other. They both knew what they shared was too special, too wonderful to ignore.

They would have to find a way to make everything work—from her brothers to the foundation to their age difference.

None of those things mattered anymore. Only this.

Only Cal.

She dropped her shoes, wrapped her arms around his neck, and held on for the wild ride. His hands were all over her, caressing her breasts, slipping down her sides, cupping her bottom, and bringing her tight against him. She could feel every hard inch of why he'd been avoiding her. She pushed her hands beneath his suit jacket, shoved her fingers down the back of his slacks.

Cool air bathed her thighs and bottom as he lifted her skirt. He slid his hands inside her panties, knowing exactly how to touch her. Knowing exactly what she wanted. What she needed.

What she'd been craving every single second since he'd been gone.

She tugged at his belt, his zipper, and somehow they were on the bench, and she was straddling him, her panties gone.

"Yes yes yes yes," she whispered. He was in her hand, hot and hard, like steel.

He held her face in his palms as she stroked him, his eyes closed. "You don't know how many times I've thought about you, needed you, made myself crazy thinking about you. Remembering every glorious moment we were together." When he opened his eyes, his gaze burned through her, deep and dark and bleak all at the same time.

"I want you, Cal. Please. *Now*." She'd never begged before in her life. But she wouldn't stop begging him until he gave her what she wanted. *Everything* she wanted.

She rose, sliding down on him until he was so deep she swore she felt him in the center of her soul. And finally—*finally*—she felt whole again.

"You feel good. Too good. *So* good." Then he kissed her, ravenously, with everything he had.

Their lovemaking was crazy and wild and frenzied, his mouth and his body consuming her at the same time she consumed him. She'd never been so out of control. Never needed anyone like she needed Cal.

Sensation shot down to her center, their bodies joined as one. When she felt him pulse inside her, it was her undoing. His name was on her lips, and he took the sound into his mouth.

Bliss was all there was. All there ever needed to be.

As long as she was with Cal, she'd never need anything more.

★ ★ ★

He had lost himself in her. It didn't matter how wrong

it was. Lyssa was all he'd thought about—obsessed about—for more than a month. And now that she was in his arms again, he didn't know how he'd ever convince himself to let her go.

But in the back recesses of his mind, he couldn't forget that she deserved so much more—he could give her jewels, but he couldn't give her a whole, undamaged heart.

At last, the music drifting down from the hotel seeped back into his senses. And he belatedly remembered where they were and what they were doing. The place was swarming with Mavericks. Her brothers or parents could stumble upon them at any moment.

Something broke in him when he forced himself to lift her away.

She swept her thumb across his mouth. "My lipstick," she whispered. "It's all over you."

There wasn't even a smudge left on her luscious mouth. It was all over his lips, a beautiful, heartrending symbol of what they'd done.

With one last caress, she said, "There, all better."

He was dazzled, he was dazed, but he wasn't even the slightest bit sated. He needed so much more of her. More he couldn't have.

He smoothed her dress down her thighs, then bent to retrieve her shoes and hand them to her. She was slipping into them as he did up his belt buckle.

Which was when he heard footsteps on the path.

He found himself at the opposite end of the bench without even knowing how his feet moved. A good, safe distance.

Until he saw her panties on the ground just under the bench. His heart pounded, his gut twisted, and he'd only just scooped them up and shoved them in his pocket when Daniel Spencer stepped through the break in the hedge.

"Hey, I wondered where you'd got to," Daniel said.

Cal now knew exactly what *my blood ran cold* meant.

Daniel was looking at Lyssa. Did he notice her lips were bare of lipstick? Had she gotten every smudge off Cal's face?

Being with Lyssa had been fast and cataclysmic, unbearably divine, and insanely stupid. If Daniel had arrived thirty seconds earlier, he'd have caught Cal buried gloriously deep inside his sister.

Cal knew he was all kinds of an idiot, but his fingers caressed her silky panties in his pocket.

"I needed a few minutes to talk to Cal about the gala," Lyssa lied smoothly. "He hasn't been around the office much lately."

"The gala?" Daniel asked, a little dumbfounded.

"Yeah," she said. "The fundraiser for the foundation. The one Dane Harrington is spearheading out of the goodness of his heart."

She sounded so normal, so in control, as if they

hadn't just screwed the hell out of each other five minutes ago.

Screwed. It was the wrong word. Hot and crazy and amazing, what they'd done couldn't possibly be called *screwing.* It was something more. So much more. Something he was terrified to put words to.

He'd never felt wild like this, not until Lyssa. But when he was with her, such warmth blossomed deep in his chest. A warmth that would spread through him, if only he could pull her into his arms again and never let her go.

But even then…he could feel the brokenness inside him. He could never give her everything she truly deserved.

"I thought Gideon told you." She prodded Daniel. "We'll all be dressed to the nines again and heading to Dane's resort in the wine country to inspire as many Silicon Valley moguls as possible to give freely to the foundation."

Whatever her brother might have been on the verge of suspecting, she was quickly making him forget. She was beautiful, magnificent. Even regal as she handled her older brother.

"Oh, yeah," Daniel said, clearly having forgotten all about it.

"And wasn't the surprise wedding absolutely fabulous? Evan looked so happy, don't you think?"

"Yeah, sure. It was great." He looked a little dazed

by his sister's fast talk.

As dazed as Cal felt.

"I hear music. Has the dancing started?"

Daniel cocked his ear toward the ballroom. "I guess so."

"What are we waiting for?" She linked her arm through her brother's. "I've got my dancing shoes on."

Daniel looked down at her heels. "You'll break your neck in those things."

She laughed, and Cal felt it wrap around his heart and squeeze.

She led Daniel out of the glade.

The moment before she disappeared, she looked over her shoulder at Cal.

And winked. Only Lyssa would go commando to a wedding dance.

★ ★ ★

Lyssa wondered if Cal would dance with her. Probably not. He wouldn't want to give her brothers any food for thought. Especially if they realized just how much heat was radiating off the two of them.

Back in the banquet hall, she'd thrown herself onto the dance floor, partnering with Kelsey and Chi and Ari, Rosie and Noah and Jorge, her mom and dad, the newlyweds, all her brothers, their wives or fiancées. It was a dancing free-for-all.

She thought about making a quick trip to her room

for another pair of panties, but the loss of them was a sexy reminder of her encounter with Cal in the garden. And her skirt was long enough to hide bare skin, even when she was in full twirl.

Being with Cal with everyone so close had been risky, but the need that came over her had been irresistible. Now all her senses were on high alert as she waited with delicious anticipation for him to reappear.

Her feet were aching, and she skipped to a nearby table, slipping off her high heels and grabbing a glass of water. Maybe it was crazy to be with her boss—and one of her brothers' best friends. Okay, it was *definitely* crazy. But being with Cal was so good. So sexy. So right. She made herself shove away any misgivings about how crazy, and potentially destructive, their affair was. They were two intelligent people. Surely they'd figure out a way to make it work, wouldn't they?

Over the music, she heard Evan talking with Will on the sidelines. "Cal said he had to take off, some big emergency. He just chartered a helicopter to get off the island since the ferry doesn't arrive for another hour."

Between one heartbeat and the next, the sexy, giddy thrill inside her shriveled up and died.

She'd assumed Cal wasn't going to try to fight their connection any longer. That he'd recognized what they shared was something special, something unique, something that came along only once in a blue moon.

She'd been wrong.

★ ★ ★

Two hours later, Lyssa was amazed by how normal she was able to act. As if nothing special had happened in the garden. As if she hadn't let herself believe she and Cal had begun something real, rather than just a series of sexy flings between co-workers. As if she hadn't felt they were on the precipice of falling in love. As if her heart hadn't soared…then crashed headfirst into the rock-hard ground and splintered into a million pieces.

As if Cal hadn't chartered a helicopter to get away from her—and what they'd done wasn't a miracle that changed everything.

While she was dancing, she didn't have to think or talk to anyone. Eventually, she'd have to stop from pure exhaustion, but for now she downed water. In the state she was in, downing a glass of champagne and getting tipsy would make her maudlin. Especially since all her best memories of drinking champagne were with Cal.

And really, she tried desperately to convince herself, what difference did it make that Cal had left? She was young. She had the rest of her life to find someone who would make her forget him. Forget every kiss, every touch, every taste, every pleasure.

It was no use. She'd never forget him. No one would ever make her feel as good as he had. She would never feel as safe or as at home in anyone else's arms.

Which was funny, given that being with Cal had been the riskiest thing she'd ever done, both personally and emotionally. And now, he'd torn off little pieces of her heart and thrown them in the sea as he flew away from the island.

He couldn't even wait an hour for the ferry. He'd chartered a helicopter to get away from her as fast as he possibly could.

She was angry, she was hurt, she wanted to scream. But she wasn't stupid. She would continue to trust him on a professional level—he was a master at business, and she'd always have a deep respect for that part of him.

But she would never, ever again be foolish enough to trust him with the remaining pieces of her heart.

The aftermath of their sexy fling on the plane had been awkward, but she hadn't gone into it expecting anything more than a good time. This interlude, however?

This time she'd believed things would be different. That if they had a connection this powerful, this special, it meant they would figure out a path forward, no matter how difficult. She hadn't even braced herself for his disappearance. Had never imagined for a minute that he would leave her high and dry. Not this time. Not after how good, how wonderful, how special it had been.

It hurt to be so wrong.

She didn't hear her mother approach until she said, "Are you okay, sweetheart? You look a little peaked."

When Lyssa was young, she'd cried a few times on her mother's shoulder about boys, about school. But she absolutely could not talk about this.

She rubbed a hand across her brow and forced a smile. "I'm fine, just overheated from too much dancing."

Her mother, always caring, always noticing when something was wrong, put her hand on Lyssa's forehead. "You don't have a fever." She held Lyssa's chin in her hand. "You haven't started getting cramps again, have you?"

For years, her period had been bad enough to keep her out of school one day a month. Thankfully, as she'd gotten older, the pain had subsided. "I'm fine, Mom."

But her mother didn't let up. "If it's really bothering you, I can get you something." She rubbed Lyssa's arm. "I thought you'd grown out of those cramps and hormonal swings."

She couldn't tell her mom that her mood swing had nothing to do with her cycle and everything to do with Cal. "I swear, I don't have those bad periods anymore. They stopped a few years ago."

"Then what's wrong, honey? Are you coming down with something, do you think?"

Lyssa was trying to think of an answer that would satisfy her mom when it hit her, as though someone had boxed her ears so hard, they'd started ringing.

Oh no.

No no no no no no.

When *was* the last time she'd had her period? Her mind quickly ran the numbers as the horrible, terrible, debilitating realization sank deep into the pit of her belly.

It couldn't be true.

But, somehow, she already knew it was.

"Lyssa, honey? I think you need to lie down. The color just drained right out of you."

What was she supposed to say? *I'm freaking out because I think I'm pregnant with Cal Danniger's baby.*

Her mom was having the time of her life at Evan and Paige's surprise wedding. Even if she could have voiced her fears, Lyssa couldn't stand the thought of bringing her mother down today.

"You're right. I probably just need to lie down." Lyssa fanned her face. "I'm sure it's too much champagne and too much rich food."

"Shall I come with you?" Her mother was so sweet and compassionate, Lyssa nearly crumpled to the floor.

"I'll be fine, Mom. I'll take some aspirin and rest for a bit." She pressed a kiss to her mother's cheek. "You should go back to the wedding, and don't worry about me even for one second."

Though Susan looked uncertain, she finally nodded and left Lyssa, after extracting a promise to call immediately if she felt worse or needed anything.

Hell yes, she needed something. She needed to find a drugstore this very minute and get a pregnancy test.

They hadn't used condoms because she was on birth control. Had she forgotten to take a pill? No, she would have noticed.

When she got to her room, she fumbled with the card key. Finally, she got inside, grabbed a pair of panties out of her suitcase, and stepped into them. Before, she'd felt sexy and giddy and powerful, but now her semi-nude state felt sordid.

Everything was tainted now.

And she needed that test.

She tried to look nonchalant as she headed out to the drugstore. The concierge said it wasn't far, and she didn't care that she looked ridiculous, wearing tennis shoes with her fancy teal dress.

At the store, she walked the aisles, looking for what she wanted, her heart beating fast. Finally, she found several different pregnancy-test brands in the same aisle as the tampons.

"Don't tell me you're in the same pickle?" a familiar voice said.

Lyssa turned like a robot.

"My period came early," Rosie went on. "Maybe it was the dancing that shook things loose."

Rosie, Ari, Chi, and Kelsey were all grouped in the aisle, waiting for Lyssa to respond. The only thing she could do was grab a box of tampons she definitely didn't need. There was no way she could pick up a home pregnancy test now.

"It'll happen soon," Ari said to Rosie, putting her arm around her friend in empathy that her hopes had been dashed for another month. Ari surely felt a pinch around her heart too, since she and Matt were trying.

"Whenever it does," Rosie said, "Gideon and I are so ready."

Another thought struck Lyssa: If the test turned out to be positive, how on earth was she going to give the news of her accidental pregnancy to her friends without feeling like she'd stolen their dreams right out from under them?

Chapter Thirteen

It was the longest twenty-four hours of Lyssa's life. After flying everyone home on his private jet, Daniel wanted to drive Lyssa into the city. She told him she was perfectly happy taking BART out of SFO, since he and Tasha were heading down to Portola Valley to check on the new house now that their mom was so eager to get the move rolling.

Of course, instead of heading to her apartment, she dashed to the drugstore and bought five different pregnancy tests, practically running home to use them all without looking at any of the results until she was done.

She washed and dried her hands, then finally looked at the row of tests lined up on the countertop. All five said the same thing.

She was pregnant.

She didn't have any symptoms, because of course she'd looked that up. In fact, she felt sharp, energized. There could have been fatigue and tenderness and mood swings. But she felt better than normal. She put her hands on her stomach, where everything felt exactly the same as always, no fluttering or swelling.

Yet five pregnancy tests couldn't be wrong.

And now that she knew for sure? A slow unfurling of joy bubbled up from deep within her.

She hadn't planned for this baby. She hadn't even known she *wanted* this baby. But despite knowing her life had just changed forever, there was an undeniable and profound new light coming from deep within her soul.

The light of a love she knew would always be true, always be pure, always be solid and unconditional, no matter what.

Ever practical, however, she had so many questions—and concerns—about how things were going to play out.

First and foremost, she needed to understand *how* this had happened. Of course she understood the birds and the bees. But she'd been on the pill. She hadn't missed a day. She hadn't started the pack at the wrong time. She hadn't been sick and thrown up a dose. She wasn't on a medication that could interfere with it.

Her one-bedroom apartment was small, and it was only a few steps from the bathroom through the bedroom to the one main room with a kitchen and living area. Barefoot, she flopped down on the couch, crossed her legs, opened her laptop, and typed into the search bar: *How did I get pregnant on the pill when I did everything right?*

The simple answer? The pill, when used correctly, was only ninety-nine percent foolproof. Which meant she was one percent with a bull's-eye.

From that point forward, the questions came fast and furious.

How would she tell her parents?

How on earth could she tell her brothers without them losing it?

And what was Cal going to say when she told him? *Surprise! We're the one in a hundred odds, and I'm going to have a baby. Our baby.*

She felt sick for the first time, but it wasn't because of the baby inside her. It was because she was trying to imagine a good way to tell Cal and realizing there wasn't one. Especially when she'd assured him there would be no problem having sex without condoms because she couldn't possibly get pregnant on the pill.

Cal Danniger hadn't signed up for an insta-family. Heck, given how fast he'd fled the island after their second time together, he hadn't even wanted to sign up for a *date*. She was certain he loved his life exactly as it was. Footloose and fancy-free with no one to answer to.

Her chest clenched as it grew harder and harder to breathe. She wasn't a person who tended to live racked by fear and anxiety. Though she'd been a fun-loving, career-oriented girl in the city who went to shows and movies and bars and dance clubs, she was honestly okay if that phase of her life was over.

But she was still terrified that Cal might think she was trying to trap him into being with her—which she most definitely wasn't. And nearly as terrified that when her brothers found out who the father was, they would hate Cal. And worse, they'd tear him to pieces.

The shock of it all was a good excuse to hibernate for the weekend, to process what had happened on a subconscious level before she had to go out into the world and actually deal with it.

She watched movies, good ones and bad ones, but even the funny ones made her cry. She ate a carton of ice cream—comfort food, not because she had cravings. Her mom called, and she let it go to voicemail. Her friends called, and she didn't call back. Late Sunday afternoon, she was watching *Bridget Jones's Diary* for the second time—because the kiss at the end was the absolute best kiss ever, except for Cal's real kisses—when her phone pinged with a reminder.

She glanced down, read the message. And groaned.

She'd completely forgotten about the blind date she'd agreed to with the brother of her old college roommate. Lyssa had said yes only because she'd been so intent on trying to wash Cal right out of her hair, as the old song went.

She was about to call Gary to cancel. But then she stopped, her fingertips barely touching the phone. This was probably the last date she'd have for the next several years. The very last time she'd feel like a fun-loving girl in the city. And Polly had said her brother was super funny.

She met Gary at a place in the theater district called The Back Door. The alley was well lit and filled with restaurants that catered to the theater crowd. Gary had told her she'd recognize him by the rose boutonniere on his lapel.

Gary Roberts was handsome, tall, blond, and muscular, just the way Polly had described him. When Lyssa waved back, Gary sauntered over and held out his hand to shake.

"Polly said you were gorgeous, and she was right."

Though she knew it wasn't fair, it irritated her slightly that the first thing he remarked on was her looks. What if she'd been an absolute mess? Would he have run away? And did he care as much if she was also smart and funny?

"It's nice to meet you, Gary." She smiled, though it felt brittle.

He took her hand and pulled her through the crowd in the alley. "I've checked us in. There's a slight delay. Can I get you a drink while we wait?"

"Club soda with a twist of lemon would be great, thanks."

"What about a glass of wine?"

"No, thanks. I had too much at Thanksgiving. I

don't think I'll be able to look at a stiff drink for a while."

Now he probably thought she was an alcoholic. But that was better than thinking she was pregnant. But if he knew that, he would surely call off the rest of their date, and she could go home and curl up on her couch again with the TV remote.

Gary came back with the club soda. "I remember my big party binges at the frat house in college." He put his hand to his forehead in mock misery.

His name was called, and the hostess led them to the table. The restaurant was packed, and the high ceilings turned conversations into a roar. Their table was café size. Otherwise, they wouldn't have been able to hear each other.

Gary didn't open his menu, but leaned close to say, "One time at the frat house, someone brought in a donkey, and we were supposed to play pin the tail on the donkey. Until the donkey kicked one of the guys in the head." He laughed, then added quickly, "But he was fine."

She laughed politely. Under other circumstances, she might have found the story amusing. But she was pregnant, and her whole life was changing, and she still didn't know exactly how she was going to tell Cal. So she didn't care about frat parties from a decade ago or pinning tails on poor donkeys.

She picked up a menu, saying as nicely as possible,

"Maybe we should figure out what we want to eat." In this crowd, if they weren't ready when the waiter came back, it might be another half hour before their order was taken.

Gary waved expansively. "Pick whatever you want. Don't worry about the price."

She tried for more than a pinched smile. "Let's go Dutch."

"No way. Polly would give me the ribbing of my life."

She leaned forward and said conspiratorially, which was hard to do when she had to shout, "I won't tell if you won't."

He laughed. "My treat anyway, no matter what you say."

She chose cordon bleu, not nearly the most expensive thing on the menu, and Gary ordered a massive steak.

"That'll give me leftovers for a week."

His remark reminded her of the flight to London, when she'd planned to take home the leftover lobster and steak, except that she'd eaten it all.

Which made her think of Cal.

Which made her realize she hadn't stopped thinking about Cal since the day they'd started working together.

Which made her face the fact that she'd *never* stop thinking about Cal, no matter what happened from here on out. She'd never again make the mistake of trusting him with her heart. Only a fool would set herself up to have her heart smashed to smithereens a third time.

But convincing her heart to forget what it felt for him?

That would be like discovering all those pregnancy tests were wrong. Wasn't going to happen.

After the waiter left, Gary said, "Polly tells me you're an accountant." He winked. "I thought all accountants were boring."

"I try not to be." Once upon a time, she might have said something flirty back. But she was feeling a million miles from flirty. "I work for a nonprofit organization. And I love my job."

Loved it so much that she'd have sworn she'd never do anything to put it at risk. Only to end up committing the cardinal sin of sleeping with her boss. Not just once, but twice.

Of course, she knew Cal would never fire her. Not only was it illegal to let someone go because they were pregnant, but he'd made it abundantly clear that he thought she was doing a great job.

But that didn't mean staying at the foundation would be easy, especially if they couldn't figure out a way to make things work between them, or come up with an arrangement they could both agree on.

For a very brief amount of time—for the exact

amount of time she'd been in blissful ecstasy on Cal's lap on Catalina Island—she'd let herself fantasize they could have it all. Romance and a great working partnership. She'd wanted to believe they could smash through any walls in their way, leap over any hurdles.

Cal, clearly, didn't feel the same way. Both times they'd been together, he had immediately disappeared afterward. Yes, he'd said he couldn't stop thinking about her, but now she realized—too late—that he'd been talking about physical attraction, nothing more.

Instinctively, she pressed the flat of her hand to her stomach. The warm glow lit her up again as she reminded herself that no matter how Cal reacted, she was going to love this baby with everything in her.

Belatedly, she realized Gary was talking. "I'm a stockbroker. It's fast-paced. When the markets are up, you're riding high. When the markets are down, you're freaking out. But then there's always great deals on great stocks that are undervalued."

He told her stories about some of his craziest moments on the trading floor. Her meal came, along with another beer for Gary and club soda for her. She realized then why Gary always had leftovers—because he didn't stop talking long enough to eat. He could probably live happily on a diet of stock deals and leftovers from expensive dates. He could talk and not care that no one listened.

Whereas Cal made it a point to listen more than

talk, regardless of who he was with. And instead of spending all of his time working for himself, he chose to run Gideon's foundation without taking a salary and without spending a dime of the foundation's money on himself.

Poor Gary, stuck with her as a date tonight. He seemed very nice and was probably talking so much only because she wasn't talking at all. He could very well be perfect for any other single woman who wasn't pregnant with another man's child.

He stopped talking about himself long enough to ask, "Are you all right, Lyssa?"

"Actually," she said as gently as she could, "I'm really sorry about this, but I should probably go."

His face fell. "Was it something I said? Did I tell too many stockbroker jokes?"

"There could never be too many stockbroker jokes." She tried to smile and hoped he bought it. "It's just that I think you're a really great guy and I don't want to waste your time." She opened her purse. "And now that I've ruined our date, I insist on going Dutch."

He shook his head before she could get the money out. "It's another guy, isn't it?" Before she could answer, he added, "I thought as soon as I saw you that any guy lucky enough to have you would never be crazy enough to let you go."

She didn't know whether to laugh or cry at his comment. Because Cal *had* let her go. Twice.

"Thanks again for dinner, Gary," she said in lieu of answering his question. "I hope you find the woman of your dreams."

She went home to figure out how to tell the man of her dreams, who had made it abundantly clear that she *wasn't* the woman of his dreams, that she was having his baby.

* * *

It came to her as soon as she stepped into the office on Monday morning. She didn't want to tell Cal over text or email or the phone or on a video chat. News like this needed to be given face to face. And since he was never in San Francisco anymore, she would go to him.

Thankfully, she'd figured out exactly how to do it.

She called Dane. "Good morning. I hope I'm not disturbing you."

"Actually, I was just about to call you," he replied.

"You were?"

"Yes. I need you to go to the Caribbean in my place."

"Seriously? That's just what I was going to ask you about—if you're still on board with my attending the meeting with Mr. Westerbourne."

"Not only on board," he replied, "but grateful. There's been a bit of a staff mutiny in the kitchen at my just-opened British resort, and my chef is threatening to walk out. If Henri wasn't such a big part of the resort's draw, I'd find another chef, but I need to speak with him in person to find out what's happening with morale and fix it ASAP. Which means I need you in the Caribbean to tag-team Westerbourne with Cal."

"It will be my pleasure, Dane. And don't worry, I'll let Cal know about the change."

"That's great, Lyssa. I'll let Westerbourne know you'll be coming in my place. Before you go, however, you should know that he can be a hard case. He's seen it all over the years, and he's been cheated more than once, which has made him wary. Which means the story you told me isn't going to work with him. But I trust that between you and Cal, you'll pull it off."

"Tell me everything about him. I'll figure out what he needs to hear from us that will help him want to contribute to the foundation." She'd never lie or make up stories. But she believed she could find a way to touch Mr. Westerbourne's heart.

Then she'd face Cal with her news.

She had to get it done, and soon, even though she'd never be able to touch *his* heart.

Chapter Fourteen

The suite Dane had booked for Lyssa at his island resort in the Caribbean was sumptuous. The best part was the tub that overlooked an expanse of blue water. After the long flight, she soaked until her eyelids wouldn't stay open anymore, then fell into bed and slept like the dead. When she woke in the morning, she felt fresh and ready to go.

She'd told Dane one little white lie—that she would call Cal about the change of plans. She hadn't, deliberately, for one good reason: If Cal knew she was coming, he would surely find a reason to fly away before she could speak with him.

In the morning light, she appreciated just how stunning the resort truly was. Its immaculate grounds were landscaped with palm trees, lush flowering bushes, and bountiful native plants.

Dane sent a car for her, and she was glad to have someone else do the driving. The road to Wester-bourne's estate was narrow and winding, leading high up a mountain she guessed had once been a volcano.

The jungle was lush, often hanging over the road like an arbor.

With every mile, her heart beat faster, and she worked to slow it down. No matter how Cal reacted, everything would be okay.

That was her current mantra: *No matter how Cal reacts, everything will be okay.*

She'd said it to herself enough times that she almost believed it, she thought with a small smile.

Thank God she was still able to laugh at herself—and her predicament. Laughter, her mother had always told her, was a brilliant way to be strong in the face of adversity. Lyssa was seeing the truth of her mother's wisdom for herself.

Her driver took them through a massive wrought-iron gate that slid open as they approached, and knowing it would help quell her nerves, she asked to be dropped off at the base of the garden so that she could walk up to the house.

She instantly lost all track of time. How could she not when she was surrounded by a tropical landscape far more beautiful than anything she'd ever seen in a botanical garden's hothouse? For several minutes, she meandered down one path and then another, before she finally headed toward the driveway, which was lined with ferns in all shades of green. The house was colossal, even by Maverick standards, with marble steps flanked by stone lions. The butler opened the door before she even knocked.

In a cultured tone much like Dane's butler, Fernsby, in London, he said, "Welcome. It will be my pleasure to announce your arrival, Miss Spencer."

She took a deep breath and squared her shoulders, preparing herself to be at her very best. It was showtime. For the foundation…and her future.

★ ★ ★

"Your associate has arrived, Mr. Danniger," the butler announced from the doorway. "Mr. Westerbourne, may I present Miss Lyssa Spencer."

Cal, who had arrived only minutes earlier, was stunned speechless. He stood while Lyssa held out her hand to the wizened man in the wheelchair.

"You're late," was the decidedly gruff welcome.

"I'm so sorry. I'm afraid I couldn't resist the lure of your garden." Her eyes sparkled. "It's *magnificent*."

The age lines on the man's face softened slightly as he took in her words. "You should have left your hotel earlier, in that case, so that you could have some time in the garden and still be on time for our meeting." Then he relented a bit. "I chose all of the plants myself."

Her eyes widened. "Of course you did. Only someone who loves where they live could pick the perfect plants for the perfect garden."

"Now you're just trying to butter me up."

She laughed. "Believe me, you'd know if I was trying to butter you up. My mother always says she can see right through me." She held out her arms. "What you see is what you get."

At last—miraculously—Westerbourne cracked the hint of a smile. "Well, in that case, you might as well come in, since you're already here. But kick off your shoes first. You've got dirt on them."

Sliding out of her shoes, she approached their host. "It's so nice to meet you, Mr. Westerbourne."

"Believe me," he said in a crackly voice, "it's far nicer to have such a lovely young woman in my living room. Particularly when she appreciates the work I've done on my grounds."

"Dane sends his regrets. He had a crisis at his new resort and had to fly to England at the last second, so he asked me to come in his place." At last, she turned to Cal and said, "Hello, Cal."

Though he smiled and said, "Hello," in an easy voice, inside he was anything but *easy*.

No one had called him about the change, though he assumed Dane thought Lyssa had. But he couldn't be upset. Not when he could guess why she'd come without warning him.

Clearly, she wanted to have it out about the helicopter he'd chartered to get off Catalina Island mere minutes after they'd been together.

And though his heart was galloping, seeing her was

a breath of fresh air. Cal realized he hadn't truly been able to breathe since the moment he'd left the island on Thanksgiving Day. The sight of her wrapped around his heart, squeezed, and all he wanted to do was grab her up and hold her close.

"I'm not sure how much of the presentation the two of you have already gone through, but I hope you don't mind my joining you." Her smile pulled him closer.

"Your associate only beat you by a few minutes, so we haven't yet started. Would you like tea or coffee, my dear?" Despite his initial gruffness, Westerbourne was as dazzled by Lyssa as everyone else. And no wonder—she was the very definition of the word.

"I'd love coffee," she replied. "I haven't had my first cup. Although I should warn you, be prepared to watch me bounce off the walls as soon as I've had a few sips." She gave the other man a cheeky smile that lit up the room.

Cal was amazed to see that Westerbourne looked more than a little cheeky himself as he poured her a cup. Especially given that the man seemed to have woken up on the wrong side of the bed during the few minutes Cal had been alone with him.

Half an hour later, Cal was in complete awe of her. He didn't even need to be there. Lyssa told Westerbourne about her parents, how hard they'd worked when they were young, how they'd raised five sons, four of them foster sons, who'd grown up to work their fingers to the bone so that they could afford to move their parents out of that seedy Chicago neighborhood.

It turned out that Westerbourne had come from a similar neighborhood in London. Susan and Bob's story was remarkable, their generosity awe-inspiring, the Mavericks' story equally incredible. But it was the way Lyssa told it, her heart in each word, that Westerbourne fell in love with.

"Normally," he said, "I would never do this. But your story—and the foundation you're representing—both sound extraordinary."

He proceeded to send a *massive* wire transfer through to Lean on Us that very minute.

"Please, be my guests and stay here at my estate for the night," he said once he'd sent the money. "There's no need for you to drive all the way back to Harrington's resort."

"I so appreciate your lovely invitation," she said, "but all my things are at Dane's resort, and I would hate to impose."

Westerbourne looked a little gruff again. "You wouldn't want to disappoint an old man, would you?"

"Of course not," she replied with a grin. "Okay, I'll stay. But only if you promise to give me a personal tour of your gardens."

"You have a deal. And don't worry about your

things. I'll send my driver."

"That's so kind of you, Mr. Westerbourne."

"Please, call me Clyde."

It was no wonder she had him eating out of her hand. She was a million times more magnificent than any garden could ever be.

★ ★ ★

After an entertaining lunch during which Clyde told them stories of his youth that kept them laughing, he said, "Thank you for humoring an old man. Now it's time for you young people to go off and enjoy yourselves while I take a rest."

"Thank you, again, Clyde," Lyssa said. "For everything. But especially for making me laugh so much my stomach hurts." Though a little prickly at first, he was a sweet man, and he'd totally related to her parents' story. "And don't forget, you still owe me a garden tour."

He kissed her hand gallantly before he wheeled himself off, leaving Lyssa and Cal alone at last.

Seeing Cal again after what happened on Catalina Island had been a shock to her system. She'd felt a powerful jolt of awareness, remembering his kiss, the feel of his hands on her, his admission that he'd run away from her because he couldn't resist her.

But after that first instant, she'd shoved everything to the background and focused on her job.

Now that Clyde was sending them off, however, Lyssa was once again a bundle of nerves. Even repeating her mantra—*no matter how Cal reacts, everything will be okay*—wasn't helping.

"I should get back to the airport," Cal said after only a few steps away from the house. "I need to be in Miami for a meeting."

She gaped at him. She knew for a fact that he and Dane had budgeted enough time to do more than just talk business with Clyde, if they were invited to do so.

Heck no, Cal was *not* running away from this conversation. If she had the guts to start it, he was damn well going to have the guts to listen.

"First of all," she told him, "Clyde will be extremely disappointed if you leave. Not to mention how disappointed *I* will be if you run away from me again like you have too many times in the past weeks. Especially when it's beyond imperative that we talk. Not about the foundation, but about *us*."

He swallowed hard, but nodded. "You're right. Hopping on a plane is a bad habit I have when I don't want to deal with—"

He seemed to realize what he was saying and stopped himself. But it was too late. He'd already confirmed what she had come to know on her own: He didn't want to deal with *her*.

Which was okay, she reminded herself. She was a Spencer. She had it in her to take care of her baby on her own. Especially when she had a wonderful family to lean on if she needed help.

Knowing he'd made a misstep, Cal said, "Sorry, that came out wrong."

"It's okay." She waved away his apology, meaning it. She didn't want Cal to pretend to be anyone he wasn't. She certainly didn't want him to pretend to care about her beyond their employee-employer relationship. "Why don't we take a walk in the garden, where we'll have privacy to talk?"

She didn't want to build things up too much and make him nervous about what she had to say. At the same time, it was hard to downplay what she was about to tell him. Thankfully, some of her equilibrium returned as they strolled the wide path of flagstones through lush jungle ferns and exotic blooms, past fountains and a babbling brook, colorful birds calling out to one another from the trees overhead and lizards running beneath broad green leaves for cover from the sun.

As much as Lyssa was bursting to tell him about the baby, she figured easing into it was wiser. "I'm really pleased with how our meeting went."

When Cal nodded, she tried to ignore the fact that he was scowling slightly, as though he'd rather be anywhere but in a billionaire's Caribbean garden with her. "He's a nice man and very generous. It will be a pleasure to work with him as we put his donation to good use."

With the staggering amount Clyde Westerbourne had just donated, they could build and staff a complete facility in any city.

The path opened into a sitting area with a fountain surrounded by stone benches. It reminded her of the glade on Catalina. With the slight falter in Cal's step, she knew it reminded him too.

"It was the heartfelt story about your parents that touched him." Thankfully, Cal sounded more like his normal self. "You have a knack for connecting with people."

"Thank you." She was amazed that even after running away from her for weeks, he could still praise her abilities. "Let's sit for a minute, Cal."

"Lyssa—"

She held up her hand. "I really need you to listen. Just for a few moments."

He gave in, sitting on a stone bench. She sat next to him, wishing things could be easier. Then again, if *easier* meant giving up the life within her, she would never want to do that. She was keeping this baby no matter what.

"I'm pregnant."

He stared at her, clearly stunned, his mouth agape, his eyes suddenly wide. She couldn't read his expression when he finally spoke. "When we were on the plane?"

"Yes," she answered simply.

"But I thought… You said—"

"I thought I had it covered. And I didn't forget a pill or anything. But the pill is only ninety-nine percent effective. Which meant that my getting pregnant on the plane had a one percent chance of happening." She paused. "And the five pregnancy tests I took confirmed it definitely happened."

He didn't speak for several long moments. She couldn't seem to take in enough oxygen, her lungs about to burst, while she waited for his response.

"Say something, Cal," she got out.

Finally, he spoke. "Wow." Then a beat later, "Great."

It was her turn to stare at him, shocked right down to her tingling toes. "What do you mean, 'Wow, great'?"

A slow smile formed on his lips. "I mean it's great news."

She was sure she must be missing something. It didn't make sense. "Do you mean *great* with a sarcastic undertone? Or do you mean *great* great?"

"*Great* great." An emotion she hadn't expected gleamed in his eyes, one that mirrored her joy. "*Awesome* great!"

She'd absolutely, positively stepped into the Twilight Zone. Especially when a full-blown smile bloomed on his face.

Didn't he realize he'd just been hit with a life-altering revelation? Didn't he realize he was going to be a father in a little less than nine months, despite the fact that he didn't want to have a relationship with her, that he was her boss, and that he was twenty years older?

"But you've never wanted to get married or have kids," she blurted.

"Who said I never wanted marriage and a family?"

"If you wanted them, you would have had them already. You've always gone after what you want, so why would those things be any different?"

"For a long time, I thought my career was enough. But then, after watching your brothers start their own families, I began to see there's more to life than work. There's family, and I finally realized I want one of my own. On Catalina, I was *envious* of Evan and Paige, especially after they told us they were having twins." His smile was like the sun and the moon and the stars all rolled into one. "But I don't have to be envious anymore. Not with your great, *awesome* news."

Lyssa had been prepared for her news to turn him inside out, that he'd tear his hair out, but *she* was the one having trouble accepting his reaction. She'd given him the most shocking, out-of-the-blue news ever. And he was psyched about it?

Gazing at the ocean, reeling from his astonishing response, she spoke toward the water. "I'm stunned,

Cal." Gingerly, she put her hands to her head as if it might explode. "I thought you were going to freak out. I thought you'd even accuse me of trying to steal your freedom by getting pregnant on purpose, that you'd think I was trying to trap you into being with me."

She felt the warmth of his touch as he gently took her hands in his and pulled them away from her head. "I know you'd never try to trap me." His expression was as serious as she'd ever seen it. "This must have come as a huge surprise to you too, Lyssa. I can't imagine what it was like when you realized you were pregnant. I wish I could have been there for you when you took the test—"

"You mean instead of on a helicopter flying as far as possible from me?" She hadn't meant to spit out the words, but couldn't help herself.

He had the grace to look ashamed. "I've been a jerk. The biggest one imaginable."

For a moment, she was glad to hear him admit it. Then a thought hit her. "Wait a second. Are you just saying all of this *wow, great, awesome* stuff because you feel guilty for being a jerk? Or worse, because you think I can't deal with raising a baby on my own? Or because you're worried that my brothers will tear you apart twice—once when they find out that we were together and then again when you don't want the kid you've helped make?"

"No," he protested wildly. "That's not what's going

on. Not at all."

She didn't know what to believe anymore. "It wasn't your fault, Cal. You don't have to step up to any plate you don't want to. I told you I wasn't going to get pregnant because of the pill, and then I did. So this is on me, and I'm wholly capable of dealing with it on my own."

"You can deal with absolutely *anything*." His brow furrowed. "But we were equal partners together, both on the way back from London and again on Catalina Island. So your pregnancy is no one's 'fault.' And as for your brothers? It's true they're going to want to tear me to shreds, and that isn't my favorite part in all this. But even if they hate me forever, I'm positive they'll always love and support you. All that matters is that they're there for you and our child. I'll make sure to deflect any and all of their anger from you to me."

She shook her head vehemently. "No, we'll deal with my brothers together," she told him once she'd managed to catch her breath at everything he'd revealed. "That is, after we figure out exactly how we're going to deal with things. Then we'll present it as a *fait accompli*." Her head spun as she thought about all the details, all the changes, all the ups and downs that were sure to come.

"I hope you believe me when I say that hearing you're pregnant with my child—with *our* child—is the best news I've ever been given."

Warmth filled her at his solemn, heartfelt words. "I really want this baby too."

For a moment, she thought he'd kiss her. And in that singular moment, she desperately wanted him to. Until she remembered that his kisses always led to his disappearance—and to her playing the brokenhearted fool yet again.

Though it turned out they were both thrilled about the baby—thank God for that, given that it was a done deal—it only made things between them more compli- cated. It wasn't just about easy one-night stands anymore. It wasn't about simply having fun and ignoring the future. Neither of them could just up and disappear now. And she certainly wasn't about to let herself fall in love with him again. Not only would it make him uncomfortable, but she wasn't even the slightest bit interested in a lifetime of hiding secret, unrequited feelings for him while co-parenting their child. The truth was she could never trust him again with her heart.

"Lyssa, I know I've given you so many mixed sig- nals. But you're pregnant, and I really think we should—"

She put her fingertip to his lips, a touch so instantly electric that she yanked her hand back as though he'd burned her. "Please, don't say anything else."

Now that she'd finally told him, she felt drained in the aftermath of her worries about his reaction, topped by her shock at how he'd actually responded. And though she didn't know exactly what he'd been about to say, she was in no way up to hearing it now.

"I think that's enough big news and decisions for one day. I, for one, am totally spent. So why don't we take tonight off to enjoy Clyde's hospitality and grounds and then reconvene on the subject tomorrow when we're both feeling fresh? We can start figuring everything out then."

He lifted her hands to his lips and pressed a kiss to her knuckles. In a very soft voice full of wonder, he whispered, "Thank you for giving me the chance to be a father."

Chapter Fifteen

After spending the night at Clyde Westerbourne's estate, Cal and Lyssa left early the next morning to fly back to the Bay Area.

As they settled into the soft leather seats on his plane, Cal could hardly believe he was going to be a father. He wanted to hand out cigars to the pilots, old-school style. Boy or girl? Was it too early to tell? He'd have to read everything ever written about pregnancy, childbirth, and parenting. The more he knew, surely, the better everything would go.

At the same time, he felt deeply unsettled about the state of affairs between Lyssa and himself. They'd slept in separate rooms, but not because Cal didn't still desperately want her. If anything, he wanted her even *more* now.

But Lyssa was clearly still reeling from learning she was pregnant and then steeling herself to break the news to him. He wasn't sure she even wanted to be with him, now or ever. And why would she, when he'd acted like such a tool after the two times they'd been together?

Yesterday in the garden, overcome with joy about the baby, he'd been so close to giving in to the instinctive urge to kiss her. But she'd pulled away before he could, and he'd seen something new—and horribly heart-wrenching—in her eyes.

A wall.

A tall, thick wall she'd built to keep him out.

She'd always been so open, throwing herself into his arms without giving a thought to protecting her heart. Even after London, even after he'd done everything he could to outrun his desire for her, she'd still been so trusting.

But when he'd hopped on that helicopter from Catalina Island and flown away?

She'd obviously learned she couldn't trust him not to hurt her. And she'd raised her walls instinctively.

Even as he'd boarded that helicopter, hadn't he known he was making the biggest mistake of his life? No matter how many times he tried to tell himself it was just sex, his gut knew it wasn't. That it never had been.

No matter how fast or far he ran or flew, she remained in his every thought. He'd been going through the motions, barely able to pay attention in meetings or sleep at night without visions of Lyssa dancing in his head. She'd penetrated deep into his heart where no one had ever managed to reach him. She'd smiled and laughed and charmed her way in before he'd even realized what was happening.

But had he—stupidly—burned all of the bridges that led to Lyssa's heart?

Had his chance for a real family, for real happiness with Lyssa, been right there in his grasp? Only to slip away because he hadn't understood just how precious it really was?

At long last, he knew what he wanted—to be partners in a real family full of unconditional love and passion, not just co-parents who shared a child. Marriage might seem old-fashioned, but it was what he craved. With Lyssa and their child.

Lyssa hadn't let him say it, putting her finger to his lips to stop the words on the brink of spilling out of him.

She'd claimed to be too tired to discuss any details or options about the future. But was that really why she'd shut him down?

Could she guess there was still a part of him that couldn't quite see himself in a "happy family" picture, no matter how hard he tried? A part of him that didn't know if he could ever be good enough for her? A part of him that feared he'd eventually let her down the way his father had let them all down so badly in the end?

Cal had never doubted himself when it came to business. But when it came to forever love? He'd never believed real, lasting love was something he could have. Not when he'd seen firsthand just how destructive it could be.

All his life, Cal had run from emotion, finding it so much easier, so much safer, to throw himself into studying, then into work. But now that he and Lyssa were going to have a baby together, he couldn't run anymore. Hell, he didn't *want* to run from her, not ever again.

But how could he clean up the long-buried scars and emotions from his past when everyone he needed to confront was gone?

And did any of that even matter if Lyssa no longer trusted him enough to let him back in?

She shifted and made a sound that jerked his attention from his ruminations. Thinking she looked a little pale, he asked, "Are you feeling all right?"

She nodded, but even though she was one of the most honest people he'd ever met, he didn't believe her. "Do you have morning sickness?"

She shook her head. "Fortunately, I haven't had any morning sickness at all."

"Then is something else wrong?"

He held his breath as he waited for her answer, knowing *he* was likely the problem that had drained the color from her face.

"I meant it when I said I'm happy about the baby," she began. "I don't know any better way to describe it than to say that it's like having this little light inside me."

"I love that," he said, swearing he could actually see her light, centered right around her heart. And in his heart, as well.

"I love it too," she continued. "But at the same time, getting pregnant means my whole life has changed, just like that." She snapped her fingers. "Take my work at the foundation, for example—"

He interrupted before she could say anything more. "How is getting pregnant or having a baby going to impact your work at the foundation? You'll take maternity leave, sure, but I hope you aren't thinking about leaving. Neither Gideon, nor I, want you to go anywhere. And I can guarantee Dane and Mr. Westerbourne wouldn't want that either."

"I appreciate your saying that, Cal, but can't you see this changes everything between us? Look at how weird things got—" He heard what she wasn't saying: *Look how weird you got.* "—after we had sex. If it was awkward working together after that, I can't even begin to imagine how strange it will be when I'm in the next office growing bigger every day."

It won't be weird if we get married. If we wake up together, spend all day together building something great at the foundation, then fall asleep wrapped in each other's arms. If we build a family together, full of laughter and joy, it won't be weird, it will be perfect.

The words were on the tip of his tongue. But it was far too soon. Blurting out a marriage proposal in the skies over Texas wouldn't do a damn thing to convince her to give him another chance.

Whatever Cal wanted, he always got, even if it meant tackling difficult, complex problems and putting in exhausting hours of work to get to his desired outcome. Only, Lyssa wasn't a project at work. She wasn't a building to construct. She wasn't a profit to be made. She was a flesh-and-blood woman. And she deserved more from him than he'd ever given anyone or anything.

Somehow, some way, he needed to prove he was worthy of her. Worthy of her trust. Worthy of being with her *forever*. And if he could do that, then surely the scars from his past wouldn't matter anymore.

Realizing she was waiting for his response, he said emphatically, "We won't let it be weird. I know I said it yesterday, but I'll say it a thousand times until you believe me—I'm sorry I acted the way I did after we were together on the plane and then again on the island. I knew better than to run." He tapped his temple to show what an idiot he'd been. "Especially when none of it did a damn thing to get you out of my mind."

Her eyes grew big at his reminder of how much he wanted her. How much he'd *always* wanted her. How much he always would.

He could have sworn he saw desire mirrored in her eyes. Then again, the attraction between them had never been the issue. No, it was all of his nonsense. Nonsense that had all but kicked the doors to her heart closed.

"I appreciate your apologies for your stupid behavior," she replied, "but we can't ignore the hurdles we're going to face in all directions. In fact, as soon as my brothers find out…" She grimaced. "I guarantee they'll go out of their way to send you packing." *Send you packing* was a much more positive spin than *murder you painfully.*

"At the risk of sounding like a broken record, I meant it when I said I'm not afraid of their reactions. Even if they want to break business ties with me. Even if they need to pummel me to dust." Putting his hand over hers—even as he forced himself not to linger, no matter how badly he wanted to—he said, "Don't worry, Lyssa. Every step of the way, we're in this together." He paused before adding, "I understand you need time to wrap your head around this huge change in your life, but I want you to know that whenever you're ready to talk about our future, I'll be waiting and absolutely ready too."

★ ★ ★

Lyssa took a chocolate chip cookie from the plate that Cal had put out for them and shoved it into her mouth.

She was suddenly ravenously hungry. Because she was pregnant, of course. But also, without being able to sate her hunger for Cal, she needed to sate her hunger for food instead.

He'd been great about everything so far, especially giving her time to process before they made any big decisions about how to move forward.

Lord knew she needed that time. She was still upside down and inside out. Nothing this major had ever happened to her, and she desperately wanted to get it right. The child she was growing deserved that, but so did she. And even though she'd never again make the mistake of trusting Cal with her heart, she still believed he deserved all good things too.

She knew one thing for sure. Cal was this child's father, and she wanted him to be involved in every step of her pregnancy and childbirth, for the baby's sake. "I made an appointment with an obstetrician, if you'd like to go with me."

His whole face brightened. "Of course I do. When's the appointment? I'll put it on my calendar."

"In a couple of weeks."

"Two *weeks*?" He stared at her, aghast. "Shouldn't you go right away to make sure everything's okay?"

"I did five tests already at home to confirm that I'm pregnant, and given my age, being pregnant is in no way a medical emergency. Two weeks was the earliest opening they had. They said that timing would be perfect, in fact."

"Okay, if you say so. It's just that two weeks seems like a long time to wait to have the doctor confirm that everything is going well and is on track."

"Believe me, I want to confirm that too," she told him.

When she met his eyes, their connection was off the charts. Surpassing even the two times they'd come together.

But though the force of her feelings threatened to overwhelm her—especially with the new hormones racing through her veins—she'd never forget the devastation to her heart when he'd flown away from Catalina Island mere minutes after that beautiful, momentous interlude in the glade. Mere minutes after she'd been so certain they could overcome any hurdle preventing their relationship. She'd even *winked* at him.

It made her cringe, remembering that. Which was why, instead of allowing herself to foolishly get caught up in emotion and attraction, she slapped another layer on the wall she'd erected around her heart. Clearing her throat, she pivoted to something far easier and more clear-cut. Work.

"Gideon sent that proposal for the foster care house while we were in the Caribbean. He's waiting for our feedback." It would be the foundation's first project. Gideon had seen a house in San Jose he wanted the foundation to purchase and renovate.

Though Cal looked disappointed by the change of subject, obviously wanting to steer them back to the baby, he reached into his bag for his computer.

Despite pushing them into work mode, Lyssa had trouble concentrating. Whenever she glanced at his long fingers and strong hands as he turned a page, pointing out an issue, reading a phrase aloud, it was impossible to keep her thoughts straight. Not when she couldn't stop thinking how good his hands had felt on her, how amazing their hot quickie had been on Catalina. How sweet and luxurious the hours they'd spent in that bed back there had been. How much she'd wanted him last night at the Westerbourne estate, only a wall away, so close she could have tiptoed into his bedroom without making a sound to climb naked into his bed.

She wanted him again, right now, wanted to shove their computers aside, crawl into his lap, and beg him to put his hands and his mouth on her.

But everything was different now. All those weeks ago, when she'd naively jumped into his arms on this plane, she'd told herself it was simply about feeling good and having fun in bed.

Yet all along, the truth was that she'd secretly been hoping for the fairy tale.

With Cal playing the part of her prince.

It wasn't his fault he'd broken her heart and crushed her silly, secret dreams.

But she wouldn't dare risk it again.

Chapter Sixteen

The two weeks before Lyssa's doctor's appointment were interminable. Cal couldn't stop thinking about the baby and his desperate need to confirm that everything was all right with its growth. And Lyssa seemed determined to keep him at arm's length.

In a complete reversal from his always-on-the-road behavior of the previous weeks, he hadn't left San Francisco once, instead conducting his business by phone, text, email, and video calls. When his associates insisted on face-to-face meetings, he said no.

Lyssa and the baby were far more important than any business deal.

Lyssa, on the other hand, was out of the office more than she was in it. It was true that she had plenty of meetings about the upcoming gala, but she hadn't so much as let Cal take her to lunch or dinner since they'd been back. She always claimed she'd just eaten, or that all she wanted to do was sleep.

Cal spent his spare time reading every book, article, or blog he could find on pregnancy and childbirth. It was, he quickly realized, a bad idea. Between the pregnancy books and the firsthand accounts he found on the Internet, there were not only too many opinions, there were also *way* too many horror stories that gave him the cold sweats.

What's more, every time he tried to get Lyssa to talk about any of the elephants in the room—their relationship, telling her family, even baby names—she wriggled her way out of it with another gala setup, phone call, or meeting, or by claiming there was no need to rush. Of course they'd tell her family before she started showing, she insisted, and until then, they needed to give themselves time to figure things out.

He knew she was still processing the major changes in her life and future. He had to be patient and give her time. After all, it was her body, her parents, her brothers. Her stakes were so much higher than his.

But God, he wanted a stake in her and her baby's life. A big, real, solid stake. One that came with a ring and the word *forever* and Lyssa in his bed every night and in the sunshine drinking coffee with him every morning.

The day before the doctor's appointment, they had a meeting with Gideon and Dane in the conference room. They'd been keeping Gideon informed about the foundation's progress in bits and pieces, but it was time to review the big picture with him.

"I swear, Lyssa, you're glowing," Gideon noted

after he said hello and hugged her. "The news must be great, huh?"

Lyssa's eyes shot to Cal's, before just as quickly moving away. Right now, the two of them were the only ones who knew why she was glowing. Yes, the foundation was doing very well. But pregnancy suited her even better.

Once Gideon knew about the baby—and that Cal was the father—he wouldn't be grinning like that at Cal anymore.

Lyssa went through the numbers—the massive total of donations they'd already received, along with the various organizations they'd already begun to fund, the San Jose property they'd put an offer on for the halfway house. The more she tallied, the bigger Gideon's eyes grew.

"I had no idea we'd come this far. I know you've been working hard, but this blows my mind." He looked stunned. "I don't know how you guys have done so much, so quickly."

"It's not just us," she replied. "We've got agents in San Francisco, Los Angeles, and Seattle looking for facilities. We considered building our own, but with all the empty office space out there right now, it doesn't make sense. We're also researching equipment for the rehab centers. As for the fundraising, you can thank Dane for that. He's brought us the bulk of our major contributors."

Dane held up his hands to ward off the praise. "I handed over a list of names, but between the two of them, Lyssa and Cal are the ones doing the work of a staff of ten."

Gideon looked at them all, and Cal thought he saw tears in the big guy's eyes. "When I asked you to head this foundation, Cal, I had no idea it would grow into something like this, let alone in little more than three months. You and Lyssa have turned my vision into something extraordinary. I'll never be able to thank you both enough."

Lyssa smiled. "You don't need to thank us. Trust me, it's our pleasure."

"And we've still got a long way to go," Cal added as he tried to focus on the foundation rather than Gideon's anger coming his way in the very near future. "You can hold off on any big thank-yous until we get there."

"That's not going to happen," Gideon said with a shake of his head. "Like Dane said, you've been working your tails off. And I have an edict from on high—AKA, Rosie. With Christmas coming up in a couple of weeks, I've been tasked with ordering the two of you to take some time off."

"I don't need time off," Lyssa protested. "I love this job."

"I'm glad," Gideon said. "But the last thing I want is for either of you to burn out. Plus, Rosie will be furious with me if she hears I couldn't convince you to take time off for the holidays."

Though Lyssa hadn't had morning sickness, Cal was still concerned she might not be getting enough rest. Especially given that she seemed to be running twice as fast in her efforts to avoid him. He knew exactly how that was, because he'd done the same thing only weeks before, when he'd been trying to control his baser urges.

On his own, Cal would never have been able to convince her to take a few days off. Thank God for Rosie and Gideon.

"All right, Gideon," he said before she could protest again. "You're on. We'll both dial things back for a few days and do a little recharging."

"But what about the gala?" Lyssa appealed to Dane. "There's so much to do."

Dane didn't look the least bit worried. "I'll put my people on it. You're an amazing accountant and a business wizard, Lyssa. I never expected you to take on the role of event coordinator too. You and Cal have been going nonstop. Gideon's right—take a little break to have some fun. You'll come back even more ready and raring to go if you're fresh."

At last, she reluctantly agreed.

Cal hoped this would finally be their chance to figure out their future together.

Not simply as co-parents, but as so much more.

★ ★ ★

It was the big day they'd been waiting for. The obstetrician was a couple of blocks from the office, and they
decided to walk, pulling on winter coats against the
blustery day.

Once they were outside, Lyssa was surprised when
Cal put his hand on the small of her back to help direct
her through the heavy foot traffic in downtown San
Francisco. Despite her vow not to lose her heart to him
again, she couldn't fight how much she loved his
touch, the way he moved with her as though they
belonged to each other.

For the past two weeks, she'd been going out of
her way to avoid him. This was the first time he'd
touched her since that brief moment on the plane
when he'd put his hand over hers. The faint touch,
even through her clothes, fired up every one of her
senses. And reminded her not to let her lingering
longings for him tip her over to the dark side, where
she handed him her heart only to have it crushed all
over again.

A short while later, both Cal and Lyssa were ush-
ered into the doctor's office. They shook Dr. Sanjay's
hand and took a seat. The doctor was around Cal's age,
and Lyssa liked her friendly smile and the sparkle in her
eyes.

Fingers on the keyboard of her computer, Dr. Sanjay asked, "You're here because you believe you're pregnant?"

Lyssa nodded. "I took five different pregnancy tests. They all said the same thing."

The doctor laughed. "Not quite a record for my patients, but fairly close." Then she went through a list of questions about what Lyssa ate and drank and whether she or her parents had any medical conditions that should be noted.

Then she asked Lyssa to pee in a cup, and when she returned from the bathroom, the doctor dipped a stick into it. The stick turned blue.

"Congratulations, you're definitely pregnant. You also look to be in marvelous shape, so having this baby likely won't be any problem for you. I do want to mention, however, that while you've said you haven't had any morning sickness, it might still happen toward the end of the first trimester. Now, why don't you move to the exam table for an ultrasound? Since you're wearing a skirt, if you're comfortable with removing your underwear, I'll place a sheet over your lower body while I do the internal exam and take pictures using the ultrasound wand."

Nodding, Lyssa did as the doctor suggested, feeling herself flush as she slipped off her panties with Cal there watching. It made no sense to feel shy after everything they'd done together, but she still found that she was.

"We can usually hear the baby's heartbeat between eight and ten weeks. You're right on the cusp, so don't be disappointed if we don't hear anything. If not today, you'll hear the heartbeat at our next visit."

"I'm very hopeful." Cal grinned, so eager to hear his baby's heartbeat that Lyssa's knees went weak. Good thing she was already in the stirrups.

Lyssa felt more than a little awkward as the doctor slid the ultrasound wand inside her with Cal right beside her, holding her hand. But her slight discomfort with the situation quickly disappeared when the doctor spoke.

"Goodness, we're in luck today." She beamed at both of them as she briefly looked away from the ultrasound's screen. "It's always lovely when a couple are both here to witness the heartbeat together for the first time. In another ten weeks or so, we should also know the baby's sex—that is, if you would like to know."

Though a part of Lyssa's brain stumbled over the doctor's inaccurate use of the word *couple*, the faint but steady *ba-bump, ba-bump, ba-bump* coming through the machine's speakers quickly stole all of her attention.

Elation like she'd never experienced rushed through her. Her heart raced, thrill bumps covered her arms, and tears pricked her eyes.

She looked at Cal. His face was a mask of wonder, his lips slightly parted, his eyes bright with unfettered joy.

He took her hand, squeezing her fingers, and looked at her with awe. "We did this, Lyssa. We made a baby together," he whispered.

In his eyes, with her hand in his, she felt the most amazing connection she'd ever known in her life.

★ ★ ★

After the appointment, Lyssa couldn't stop staring at the sonogram the doctor had given them.

"Wow. It's so small, but with such a powerful heartbeat already."

Cal would never forget hearing that miraculous sound and seeing the picture on the screen—their child nestled inside Lyssa. It was awe-inspiring, mind-blowing, astounding, beyond wonderful.

"Marry me, Lyssa." They were standing on the sidewalk just outside the doctor's building, but he couldn't keep the words inside for another moment. "Come with me to City Hall. Today, if possible. We can tell your family afterward."

Lyssa had been floating on cloud nine with the echo of the baby's heartbeat in her ears. So had he. But all her joy seemed to vanish in a flash. "Are you kidding me? People no longer need to jump into marriage because there's a baby coming." She tucked the photo inside her purse, almost as if she thought that would make him see sense again.

"I know they don't." A voice in his head was saying he should stop talking before he made things even worse. But now that he'd seen the baby's tiny form on the ultrasound screen, he couldn't keep the words from bursting out of him. "But we have to think about what's best for the baby."

Her face turned stony. "What makes you think marriage is best?" She crossed her arms over her chest. "If a marriage isn't based on love, the baby will suffer." Her expression softened slightly as she added, "I saw all the love my parents had over the years, even through the bad times. And I want that. Not just two people who get a legal piece of paper and live together in the same house because they're having a baby. Can you understand that?"

"I do. I get it. Your family is great. Why wouldn't you want what they had?" He was afraid she'd ask about his family, and he didn't want to go there, especially not on the heels of the miracle they'd just witnessed via the ultrasound machine. He rushed on. "I have money. I have success. But when I come home from work after a long day, what I've finally realized I long for is family. I said it all wrong a few minutes ago. But if you'll let me try again—"

She shook her head. "Please, Cal. Don't make this harder than it already is."

He couldn't give up just like that. Not when their entire future—and all the happiness he longed for—

hung in the balance. "I know you must find it hard to trust me now, after the way I behaved these past weeks."

"You don't need to keep apologizing, Cal. What happened happened. Now we've just got to figure out a smart way to move forward. Keep our focus on the logistics of the situation."

"We can be so much more than logistics, Lyssa." As soon as he said it, he felt the truth of it with every fiber of his being. "I've tried to give you time, but time won't change what I want—and what I hope you'll come to want too."

"I already told you." Her nostrils flared as she breathed in, her teeth seeming to clench. "I want more than a loveless marriage. So if you want me to marry you, there's only one way that will work. You need to make me fall in love with you." She paused before laying down the ultimate gauntlet. "And you have to love me just as much."

She threw the words at him, as if she knew he would balk.

But couldn't she feel what was already rushing through his veins, heating his skin, making his heart race the way it had when he'd heard the heartbeat and seen the baby on the screen? He already wanted her with every cell in his body, the way he'd never wanted anyone or anything before.

But she was asking for more than just attraction

and friendship. She was asking—no, demanding—*love.*

He had to widen his stance to keep his balance, take deep breaths to steady his heart.

Could he do it? Could he give and accept love without the shadows from his past dragging him back into the cold, hollow place he'd lived in for so long?

He looked into her eyes, saw the challenge, saw her doubt. And he knew that if he didn't rise to this challenge, if he didn't do everything he could to love her and make her love him, he'd end up on the periphery of her life, only there for the baby's sake, his days and nights empty and bleak. It wouldn't even be half a life.

It would be the *barest shell* of a life.

Right here, right now, Lyssa was giving him one final chance to have and to hold everything he'd been so sure had slipped through his fingers.

"Mission accepted."

She blinked at him. "Wait…you're up for this?"

"I am." He felt his lips lift into a smile. "You're going to fall in love with me so hard you're not going to know what hit you."

"And…?"

He reached for her hand. "I'm going to fall just as hard in love with you."

As the feel of her hand in his resonated through every cell in his body, he realized he just might be there already.

Chapter Seventeen

Lyssa could hardly believe what she'd just done. Had she really challenged Cal to make her love him?

And worse, had she actually challenged him to fall in love with her too?

Oh. My. God.

The scared part of her—the one she'd always pushed away when she was younger in order to keep up with her big brothers—wanted to grab the words back. Wanted to say "just kidding" and laugh it off.

The hurt part of her—the part that had ached since he'd flown away from Catalina Island as if he couldn't leave her behind fast enough—wanted to deny it could ever happen, wanted to proclaim her heart immune to him and her trust in him obliterated.

But she'd been letting fear get the best of her for too long. From the moment Cal had put her into the cab at SFO and walked away, she'd been too scared to confront him. Until Catalina Island. And even then, she'd let him leave her again without calling him out on what he'd done. Until she'd realized she was pregnant and no longer had a choice about confronting him.

But now, putting all her fears and hurt aside, she knew what she wanted. The kind of love her parents had. The love all her brothers had found.

Could Cal be *the one*?

Was there any chance that a one-night stand and an accidental pregnancy could lead to a deep and lasting love?

And how would she ever find out if she didn't open up a tiny part of her heart to her own challenge? How would she ever know if she didn't take one last risk with Cal?

The potential repercussions were massive. The likelihood of heartbreak was at an all-time high. The possibility that she'd look back on this and realize it was the biggest mistake she could ever make couldn't be ignored.

And yet…

She was pregnant. With Cal's baby. Whenever she looked at him, whenever he was near, whenever he touched her, her heart cried out for more. She'd never imagined it was possible to *feel* this much yet find it terrifying at the same time.

"Do we have a deal?"

His words jarred her out of her head and back to the moment. Back to the sidewalk where businesspeople and tourists scurried around them as they stood in the middle of the city's bustle.

And she made the biggest, most important decision of her life.

"Yes." She looked into his eyes. "We have a deal."

His eyes lit, and he drew her close. "Can I kiss you to seal it?"

She couldn't look away. Couldn't stop longing for his kiss.

But she made herself pause, think. "Not yet."

Her unspoken words—*not until I can trust you not to run again*—hung in the air between them.

He didn't push it, simply nodded. "In that case, how about a burrito from our favorite restaurant to seal the deal?"

She almost laughed at the absurdity of it. They were talking about their future, their child's future. And he was thinking about food. Yet she loved that they had a favorite restaurant. It wasn't just the big stuff that counted in the long run. The little stuff counted too. And she was starving. "Sounds perfect."

They headed into Taqueria Bueno and placed their orders without needing to look at the menu. A chicken quesadilla for her and a carne asada burrito for him, with the unspoken understanding that they'd split the meals and each eat half of the other's.

She could practically see the wheels turning inside his head as they munched on chips and salsa. Her wheels were working just as hard.

As always, their food was delivered quickly, and after splitting their entrees, Lyssa dove in, taking a bite of quesadilla smothered in guacamole first and then a bite of the everything-on-it burrito immediately after. She was *famished*.

Cal was slower getting to his food. "Gideon's right. We've been working extraordinarily hard. Especially you. And the more successful the foundation becomes, the more work there'll be. Therefore," he said as if he were laying out a business plan, "it's important for us to get in the habit of unplugging on a regular basis. We'll be no good to anyone if we're burned out. Especially while you're still in your first trimester."

Though she didn't disagree with anything he'd said, lest he get pushy, she still reminded him, "Pregnancy isn't making me tired. If anything, I have *more* energy than usual."

"And I'm glad you do. But we're coming up on the holidays. Not only will we stop actively soliciting donations right now, but contracts won't get signed during the holidays, and big decisions won't get made. Everyone waits until the new year."

"Right," she agreed, "which is why I planned to use this time to tackle some of the projects that have been sitting on my back burner."

"Please." He held her gaze, his gray eyes pleading. "Please give me some time with you. Away from the office. Away from real life. Just for a while."

He was asking for a chance to spend time together outside of work, a chance for her to fall in love with him…a chance for him to fall in love with her too.

But no matter how much she told herself she had too much to do at the office, that it wasn't practical to take time off right now, that she should be blasting through as much work as possible before the baby came, the real reason she was tempted to say no had nothing to do with work.

It was fear, plain and simple.

And she *hated* giving in to fear.

She'd already agreed to the "fall in love" challenge. It was only fair that she give them both room to see it through.

She wasn't about to make things easy on him, though. There'd be no falling at his feet and telling him she couldn't live without him based on a few pretty words, or even his delicious kisses. But she couldn't stay completely locked down either. Somehow, she'd have to find a balance.

She finally said, "Okay. Let's take a few days off."

He whooped with joy, and the other diners turned their heads to see what all the fuss was about.

"But we have to be back by next weekend so we don't miss the housewarming barbecue for Mom and Dad."

"We can make that work," he agreed. "What do you think about a road trip? No real plans. We'll follow our instincts and have fun, just like we did in London with the street art tour."

Travel with no reservations? No plans set in stone? Lyssa had always grounded herself in spreadsheets and lists. She never felt more at ease than when she knew exactly what was coming and when.

But with Cal, nothing had been planned up to now.

So a spontaneous road trip fit right in.

She raised her lemonade to his in a toast. "Let's hit the road and find magic in whatever unexpected places we end up in and whatever unexpected things we do."

Something told her that with Cal by her side, even if they were in the middle of nowhere, they would always find magic.

Chapter Eighteen

They worked like mad to clear the most pressing items off their desks, and at nine on Saturday morning, Cal pulled up in front of Lyssa's four-story walk-up. After she'd buzzed him in, he jogged up the stairs. She met him outside her door with her computer bag and a roller suitcase.

He pointed at the computer bag. "We're not working, remember?"

"I occasionally do other things on my computer besides work," she said dryly, then smiled widely. "I might have a teeny-tiny addiction to Pinterest. Particularly pictures of puppies and fabulously delicious cakes and now baby stuff."

"Doesn't everyone use their phone for that?"

"Not me. I like to see it on a bigger screen."

She bent to pick up the roller bag, but he wrapped his fingers around the handle before she could.

"I'll get that. It's way too heavy. I don't want you to strain yourself."

"I always pack too much," she agreed. "And even

though I can carry my own bag, I'll take you up on your offer because I secretly hate lugging that thing around."

They made their way down, and he put her bag into the trunk of his fancy Mercedes-Maybach. After she got into the passenger seat, he asked, "Did you remember the vitamins the doctor wanted you to take?"

"Of course I remembered my vitamins. I didn't suddenly become incapable just because I'm pregnant." Then she threw at him, "Did *you* remember *your* vitamins?"

"Honestly, in my excitement to hit the road with you, I was halfway to your apartment before I realized I forgot to bring my bag."

Just like that, her defenses fell. It was so good to know he wasn't with her because she'd put a figurative gun to his head, but because he actually *wanted* to spend time with her.

They made it through city traffic in record time and headed out to Highway 1.

"Where should we go? North or south?" he asked. They'd agreed she'd lead the first day, and he'd lead the second.

"South."

They followed the coastal road through Pacifica and Montara and Half Moon Bay. Despite it being mid-December, it was a sunny day without a cloud in the sky. That was one of the best things about living in Northern California.

When they hit Santa Cruz, she said, "I'm hungry. I've heard about a great restaurant in town that specializes in bean sprouts. We're only a couple of blocks away, so go ahead and find a parking space." She waved her hand imperiously, enjoying herself far too much at his expense.

He shot her an incredulous look as he pulled into a spot. "How can you specialize in bean sprouts?"

"Easy," Lyssa said after she'd climbed out. "You can order a bagel with bean sprouts and avocado and cucumber. Or a pita with tomatoes and bean sprouts and cucumber. Or a pizza with sprouts. Or a quiche with sprouts. Or a smoothie with sprouts."

"Does that mean I can't ask them to hold the sprouts?" he asked right before they walked inside.

She laughed, loving his fantastic sense of humor. "I'd like to see you try," she said on a grin, marching through the door.

Lyssa was pleasantly surprised when Cal ended up liking the sound of so many things on the menu that he had to ask the guy taking their order what he'd choose for himself. Through her easygoing billionaire brothers, she knew not all billionaires were picky or difficult, but it was still nice to see how easily Cal adjusted to his environment. The restaurant floor was concrete, with huge couches and chairs, coffee tables between them.

Movie posters plastered the walls, featuring films made in Santa Cruz, such as *The Lost Boys* and *Sudden Impact*.

"Want half?" Cal asked once their food was ready.

"Of course," she said, "but only if you'll take half of mine."

"I was counting on it." He gave her one of his beautiful smiles.

Warmth unfurled inside her as they split their food, and they both tucked in.

Their pita—with lettuce, avocado, bean sprouts, red pepper, and a fabulous sauce—and bagel—with cream cheese, sprouts, cucumber, chives, and spinach—were delicious, and when they were done, Cal said, "Great pick, Lyssa. I never would have come here, and I would clearly have missed out."

"Thanks for being open to it." She'd been testing him, seeing how he'd react to something so out of his comfort zone. And he'd passed splendidly.

Was this one of his get-Lyssa-to-fall-in-love techniques? Do whatever she wanted and act like he loved it?

But no, she'd never seen Cal be disingenuous.

And she felt herself being irresistibly drawn to him. Drawn toward one of his luscious kisses she hadn't been able to stop dreaming about.

But she wasn't ready to open that door again. No, she'd need more than a drive down the coast and a nice lunch to get there.

"Ready to head to our next destination?" she asked.

A hint of disappointment darkened his eyes as they walked back to his car, as if he had been dreaming about one of *her* kisses.

"You bet. Should I keep heading south?"

She nodded. "I'll tell you when to pull off. Just stay on Highway One for now."

As they sped south toward Monterey and Carmel, the meal in her belly lulled Lyssa into a naplike state. She was still awake, but too comfortable to do more than enjoy the view of the coast out her window and listen to old Beatles tunes playing over the sound system. Thankfully, Cal wasn't someone who needed to fill every moment with words. On the contrary, she'd always been struck by how carefully he chose his words.

She perked up when she saw a sign ahead. "Take the next left."

"Are we going to explore the beaches of Big Sur?"

She just smiled. He didn't know it yet, but he was in for something special. Something wild.

Something *Lyssa*.

★ ★ ★

Cal was enjoying himself more than he could remember doing since he'd been a teenager, before he'd turned seventeen.

No, that wasn't quite right. With Lyssa, every

moment was better than the last. London had been fun from start to finish. Even in the office, when she was there, he never stopped smiling all day.

But when she directed him to pull onto a gravel road surrounded on both sides with tall eucalyptus trees, he looked at her in disbelief. "Axe throwing?"

She beamed. "I read about it on the Internet, and it sounds like so much fun. We're going to throw axes at tree stumps."

He actually felt himself gape. "Seriously? You didn't have someone plant a sign here as a joke? This is a real thing?"

"People go to a rifle range." She shrugged. "Think of this as an axe-throwing range."

It was cool and windy on the central coast, and only one other car sat in the dirt parking lot. Check-in was in what looked like an old-fashioned saloon, with rocking chairs on a long front porch and swinging doors. Racks of postcards and a variety of axes for sale packed the interior.

A shaggy-haired man in suspenders stood behind the counter. "Howdy, folks."

Cal couldn't help but feel like they'd stepped through a time warp.

"We'd like to do axe throwing for two." Lyssa smiled broadly.

"Have you thrown axes before?" the man asked.

"Nope," Lyssa said, smiling and shaking her head.

"But it sounds like fun."

"It sure is." He gave them a wide grin. "Here's how it works." He went through a long-winded explanation that involved never throwing your axe underhand in case you accidentally chopped into your thigh—underhand was obviously for experts—and never throwing your axe at your partner when their back was turned. Cal barely stopped himself from asking if that meant you could throw an axe at your partner when they were looking.

When Cal took out his credit card, Lyssa held up her hand. "My idea, my treat. And don't worry," she said in a reassuring tone, "you're going to love this."

He'd never have dreamed up anything like this on his own, but her enthusiasm was infectious, and no doubt her enjoyment would be just as infectious, the same way he'd ended up enjoying the sprouts.

"The axes are out by your lane. But remember," the man said, "no throwing when someone's down-range. I've got a family out there right now. If you hear a whistle, you stop throwing."

Out the back door, the range was a row of fence posts, almost like hitching posts, with the tree stumps twelve feet away. Cal felt the weight of one of the axes and immediately said, "We need to see if he has lighter axes."

She hefted one. "These aren't heavy at all." Then she shot him a look. "But if they're too heavy for you, by all means, feel free to ask for something lighter."

"I was thinking about you."

"Cal…" There was a clear warning in her voice, but he was only being logical.

"What if you strain something?"

She gaped at him, her breath a big huff. "You can't be serious."

He tried to explain the facts. "Now that you're pregnant, you can't do all the stuff you used to."

She advanced on him, fire in her narrowed eyes. "Do you know how many times you've done that today? You don't want me carrying my own suitcase. You need to make sure I've taken my vitamins. Now you think I can't throw an axe." She stood toe to toe with him now. "One of the things that made me happy about working for you was that you never treated me like a helpless little girl who needed to be taken care of. But now you don't seem to think I possess the sense to decide anything for myself."

"I just want to make sure you and the baby are safe," he protested.

"We're both fine," she snapped. "In fact, the only person who *isn't* going to be fine is you, if you don't start treating me like I'm a capable, intelligent person."

On the heels of her tirade, the manager gave them the signal they were free to begin, and Lyssa threw the axe as hard as she could.

It embedded itself deeply in the tree stump, quivering from the force of her throw.

Cal gazed at her as if he were seeing her for the first time. "Wow, you're bloodthirsty, aren't you?"

Her gaze glittered. "At this moment, I sure am."

He looked at the tree and then back to her, very impressed. "You hit it dead center."

"What can I say?" She shrugged like it was no big deal. "I've always had great aim." She handed him another axe. "Your turn."

Cal threw, the axe flying out of his hand. He didn't miss by a wide margin, clipping the side of the stump. But Lyssa was the clear winner.

She punched the air. Then she said softly, staring him down, that glowing smile on her lips. "Beat ya."

That was when he realized what an ass he'd been. Lyssa was amazing and capable, intelligent and funny, gorgeous and sexy. He didn't need to worry about either her or the baby. She could take care of it all.

He wanted to kiss her so damn bad that he burned with the need.

But he was already deep in the doghouse, and he wouldn't make things worse by overstepping her boundaries—not when she'd made it clear he'd have to prove himself worthy of her kisses from here on out.

But he could look, and he let his gaze travel over her face, from her gorgeous brown eyes to her kissable rosebud lips. Then he said softly, "You're the most capable woman I know. And you're going to make the best mom ever."

Chapter Nineteen

You're going to make the best mom ever.

Lyssa had heard the beautiful heartbeat. She'd stared countless times at the sonogram. She'd gone over and over how she'd tell her parents and deal with her brothers. She'd given so much thought to how her life might change and just where Cal might fit into it.

Yet his words suddenly made it more real than all her hours and hours of reflection.

And her heart seemed to stop beneath the weight of responsibility that becoming a parent carried.

"Do you really think so?"

He pulled back slightly, as if surprised by her question. "I don't have a single doubt."

She tried to find the words, though her mouth had suddenly gone dry. "Sometimes...like right now...I'm scared." Her voice was barely louder than the breath of wind that ruffled her hair.

He cupped her cheek in his palm. "I was feeling scared too. But then I remembered that you can do absolutely anything you set your mind to." The warmth of his hand filled her. "There's no one I would rather have a child with, Lyssa. No one but *you*."

The sincerity and depth of his words made her shaky. She wanted so badly to be an amazing mother. Just as her mom had been for her. She wanted to believe she could be.

On emotional overload, she couldn't say another word, couldn't ask for another ounce of reassurance. She could only focus on rebuilding her natural resiliency.

Picking up another axe, she funneled her concentration into throwing. "Let's see if you can beat me this time." She laughed as her axe flew so wide it didn't even hit the stump.

Cal beat her big-time, sinking his axe deep into the wood.

They spent the rest of the hour they'd paid for one-upping each other with the axes, and the time flew by, wonderful and carefree, as if they had nothing looming over them but a silly throwing competition.

Cal got better. Lyssa got worse. Then Cal got worse again. And Lyssa ended up trumping him in the end by hitting the tree right in the center, like a bull's-eye.

It didn't matter who won or lost. All that mattered was how blissfully good being with him felt right now.

* * *

They got back on the road, and a short while later, after taking a Big Sur turnoff, Lyssa pointed. And Cal eyeballed her as if she'd lost her mind.

"You want to go camping?"

"Not camping. Glamping.

"What the hell is *glamping*?"

"Glamorous camping. It's a tent, but everything is luxurious—a big bed, a fireplace, your own bathroom."

He raised one eyebrow. "Are you sure it's not an outhouse?"

She laughed. "You're going to love it." But she crossed her fingers at her side where he wouldn't see.

The reception office was in a cute cottage that looked like it had been built with reclaimed wood, chic despite its rustic nature.

The concierge was in her fifties, with curly hair she'd allowed to go a pretty silver shade that sparkled as she stepped out to greet them. "Welcome to Cypress Resort! Do you have a reservation?"

"No," Lyssa replied with a smile. "We're on a fun road trip down the coast, and when I read about your place, I absolutely knew we had to stop to see if you have room."

The woman's smile was as wide as Big Sur. "We certainly do. We've got the most luxurious tent cabins you'll see on the coast. Hot showers and outdoor bathtubs, hot tubs, you name it. Would you like a double, a queen, or a king?"

Cal looked at Lyssa, and as she looked in his eyes, the decision she'd been grappling with all afternoon wasn't even a question anymore.

"How big is your bed on the plane?" she asked him.

A blaze lit in his gaze. "King."

Her breath quickened, her skin heated, and she tried to hide her breathlessness as she told the woman, "A king would be great."

He'd enjoyed the axe throwing, and she would make sure he loved glamping even more.

With trying to find fun and unique things to do, the trip felt like a give-and-take between them, as if she was trying to get him to fall in love with her as much as he was supposed to make her love him.

She'd said the challenging words outside the doctor's office without thinking it through. Given how much he'd hurt her before, maybe it was crazy to feel compelled to follow it through. But they'd made a deal...and Lyssa wasn't a woman who went back on her word.

"Fantastic," the woman said. "It's off-season, so we're not crowded, and I can put you in number twenty on the end. You can take a hike in the woods right from there."

"Sounds perfect." Cal handed her his credit card.

As the woman went inside to run the card, Cal anticipated Lyssa's objection. "You paid for the axe throwing. Now it's my turn."

"But—"

He put a finger over her lips. "I know how capable you are. But it would mean a lot to me if you let this be my treat."

She could insist on paying her way. Or she could graciously accept his sweet gift and appreciate him for it.

She made the choice that felt the best. "Thank you. That's really nice of you."

The lady returned with his credit card and had him sign. "We don't have a restaurant on our premises, but if you drive five miles back along the road, you'll come to Nepenthe, which is world renowned. If you'd like, I'll make you a reservation for dinner."

"Sound good to you?" Cal asked Lyssa.

They'd need to eat at some point tonight, but… "Thanks," she told the woman. "But I'm not sure what time we'll be ready." She looked at Cal. "Okay with you?"

He nodded. And she thought, even hoped, he was thinking along the same lines.

Because it wasn't food that filled her with hunger right now.

It was Cal.

★ ★ ★

Their glamorous tent—Cal could barely believe there was such a thing—was at the end of the row. Impressively, the interior resembled a luxury hotel, the bed high off the wood floor and covered with a thick eiderdown and feather pillows. A woodstove stood in the corner, and the table and chairs sat by a tent flap that opened so you could sip your morning coffee overlooking the forest. A small, European-style refrigerator was tucked beneath a long counter occupied by a microwave, a two-burner hot plate, and a state-of-the-art coffee maker.

"Wow, check out the bathroom." Lyssa stood back to let Cal see.

The tub was big enough for two, with a showerhead and a curtain in a forest motif around it and two pedestal sinks beside it.

Lyssa whirled back to the room. "This is so great," she said. "And I, for one, will be very glad for the tub after we get back from our hike."

"A hike sounds good." But given that she'd asked for one tent instead of two and a king bed instead of twins, Cal could think of a hell of a lot better things to do besides hiking.

Especially since the clock was ticking on her challenge to make her fall in love with him. No question, he had to step up his game—and if she wanted to go hiking, he'd happily be a mountain man for the afternoon.

Hike twenty miles through the desert? Swim to Alcatraz? Bike the entire coast of California? Stand on his head balancing plates on the soles of his feet?

He'd do whatever it took to convince her he was worth falling in love with.

* * *

The hike in Pfeiffer Big Sur State Park was strenuous enough that, despite the cool air, Lyssa was soon tying her windbreaker around her waist.

"You're a trailblazer, so why don't you take the lead?" she'd suggested to Cal as they started out.

They walked in companionable silence, speaking only to point out a beautiful plant or a stunning view. And what a perfect setup it was, giving her ample opportunity to focus on Cal's muscles moving beneath his blue jeans. It was like studying one of Michelangelo's statues. A droolworthy masterpiece.

She entertained fantasies of jumping him the moment they got back to the tent, right down to the tactile sensation of stripping off his clothes, the salty taste of his skin, the earthy scent of his body.

Was it baby hormones making her feel so sexy? Or was it simply that Cal was, hands down, the most attractive man on the planet?

By the time they came to a fork in the trail and Cal had pulled out the trail map the woman at the registration cottage had given them, Lyssa was out of breath. "And here I thought all you did was work and fly around the world in your plane, eating scrumptious meals. But you're quite the hiker." Her breathlessness wasn't *just* the climb.

"I work out at Sebastian's gym."

She instantly had a heart-thumping vision of Cal on the elliptical, his muscles glistening.

Oh Lord, it was hard to think about anything except Cal's body. His touch. His kisses.

She managed not to shiver with need. "That's very different from climbing mountains."

He grinned. "On business trips, if I can squeeze in an hour or two to myself, I like to find a good hiking trail. And when I'm at home, I go to Muir Woods or even as far as the Fremont Hills. I do my best thinking while I'm hiking."

She loved knowing that about him. "I really love being outside too. I walk the San Francisco hills."

They grinned at each other, another potent moment that could have led to a kiss...were it not for another hiker appearing. He asked if he could look at their map.

Once the guy had hiked on, Cal turned to her. "We're here." He traced the map with his finger. "This trail along the ridge will eventually loop back."

She thought about his finger tracing lines across her skin, mapping the hills and valleys of her body, down into the canyons and all her hidden places.

This time, she couldn't help the shiver, as if he were actually touching her.

"Are you cold?" He rubbed her arms, sending tingles through her entire body.

She'd never felt so aware of a man, never felt this I'm-going-to-die-if-I-don't-have-you sensation. Her body was so alive and energized, so attuned to the sight and feel and scent of him.

Did he feel the same thing at all? Was he thinking about pulling her against him and kissing her senseless? Or was it just her?

But she knew, deep in her belly, it was true for him too. She'd felt it on the plane, she'd known it on Catalina.

And maybe their amazing sex was the place from which all things could grow.

"How far have we come?" she asked.

"A couple of miles."

"That's far enough to make sure we get back before dark." Before she jumped him in the middle of the trail and had her wicked way with him where any hiker could stumble over them.

"Agreed," he said.

It was crazy how badly she wanted him. She'd never felt like this before, so hot, so full of desire and delicious anticipation.

And she *loved* it.

★ ★ ★

Lyssa took the lead on the way down the mountain,

and watching her move was like viewing a heavenly body.

One tent. One bed.

Keeping his hands off her once they got back to the glamping site—if that's what she wanted—was going to be the hardest thing he'd ever done.

If her plan was for them to share the king bed and not touch each other, he'd have to sleep outside with the mountain lions. Because there was no way he'd be able to keep his hands off her.

She walked fast, her stride strong. It took only three-quarters of the time to get down the mountain. By the time they made it to their tent, he was beyond desperate for her. If he could convince her to skip dinner and feast on each other instead…

At the porch, Lyssa toed out of her sneakers, leaving them outside so their shoes didn't track the forest into the cabin. Cal left his next to hers.

The moment he closed the tent's door, she was on him—*thank God*—her hands fisted in his shirt, pulling him down until she planted the hottest, sweetest kiss on his lips.

Chapter Twenty

Cal loved her take-charge attitude. He adored the way she consumed him, tasting him, taking him—and giving just as much of herself in return.

She finally drew back, her hand still fisted in his shirt and her eyelids half closed. "You can't possibly know how badly I wanted to do that."

"Oh yes, I can. It's all I've been dreaming about too." He wrapped his hand around her nape, hauling her close for another soul-shattering kiss, her body soft and pliable against his. His heart was pounding when he finally set her on her feet.

He'd had his fair share of casual liaisons. Sex for sex's sake. But what he'd done with Lyssa wasn't mere sex.

Being with Lyssa involved all his emotions.

Being with Lyssa consumed him.

Being with Lyssa was making *love*.

And he wanted more of it, more of her. He tugged the windbreaker off her waist, let it fall to the floor. Their breath, slightly quickened, mingled in the now steamy air of the tent.

"It's just about dinnertime," he said, his gaze tracing her features, her arched eyebrows, her long lashes, her slender nose, her full lips. "We could drive to Nepenthe and eat some world-class food."

She smiled the seductive smile that always turned him inside out. "I'm not hungry for food right now." She looped her arms around his neck. "I'm ravenous for your hands on me."

He loved that she wasn't afraid to say what she wanted. He loved that no matter what she'd said earlier about sometimes feeling scared, the honest truth was that she wasn't afraid of *anything*.

Bending to her throat, he tasted her salty skin. "I'm hungry to taste every inch of you."

She laughed softly, the sound vibrating against him. "It was all I could think about hiking up the mountain." She grinned wickedly. "And all the way down too."

He wanted to take his time, wanted to give her pleasure a thousand times over. He pulled her T-shirt from her jeans, slipping his fingers beneath the material and slowly pulling it up, his fingers skimming across her skin.

Closing her eyes, she tipped her head back. "Catalina was so delicious. I loved how fast it was, how crazy, how wild." She looked at him again, capturing him completely with her gaze. "But I loved the hours and hours we had on your plane too."

As she opened herself up to him again, his heart beat harder, his blood geysering through his veins. He loved that she was telling him what she liked.

And that she trusted him to give it to her.

"Fast and hard on Catalina really was amazing, wasn't it?" He skimmed her breast through her lacy bra.

She sucked in a breath in blissful reaction to his touch. "I couldn't stop thinking about taking you hard and fast in the woods while we walked down the mountain."

Her words—and the visions that went with them—were an exquisite turn-on, close to torture.

"Do you have any idea what you do to me?" he said, barely finding his next breath.

Gaze locked on his, she slipped her hand between them, cupped his erection. *"Yes."*

He couldn't wait another moment to get her naked. Moving fast, he stripped her shirt over her head and popped the clasp of her bra, losing his breath all over again at the sight of her gorgeous breasts. He unzipped her jeans and shoved them to the floor, leaving her standing before him in only her panties.

Her grace and splendor made his heart stop for several beats.

"You are so beautiful." He couldn't hide the reverence in his voice.

Wonderfully comfortable with her near nudity, she

stepped away from him, then sat on the bed and leaned back on her elbows like a goddess waiting to be painted.

"Get naked for me, Cal," she whispered.

God, he loved hearing his name on her lips. With her eyes locked on him, he stripped down to his boxer briefs. The atmosphere was sultry, heavy with the heat of her gaze on his skin.

She crooked a finger. "Come here."

He moved between her legs, spreading them, as she trailed one finger down the hard length of him through the cotton.

"I want you so much, Lyssa," he murmured.

"I want you more."

She caressed him with her palm, sending a jolt of electricity through him. Swiftly as a cat, she hooked her fingers in the waistband of his briefs and pulled them down, leaning forward until her face was so close, he could feel her breath on his hips.

He twitched with need.

Every time with her was unique, bringing out fresh emotions and never-before-experienced sensations. He shrugged off his briefs a beat before she licked him like a lollipop, up one side, down the other.

He groaned, answering the instinctive call to haul her higher onto the bed, then crawl over her on his hands and knees.

He took her lips, kissing her deeply, his tongue

melding with hers. When they were both breathing hard, he worked his way down—her chin, her throat, her breasts, her belly.

His heart swelled with the knowledge that their child nestled right *here*. He lavished her skin with attention, tasting, teasing. Until finally she put her hands on his shoulders and begged, "Please."

He gave her what she wanted, falling between her legs, burying his face against her, savoring her. She was the sweetest ambrosia, the most decadent wine. Her skin heated, a flush spreading over her, her belly quivering, her breath fast, her fingers fisting in the comforter. Her eyes closed, and she was lost to sensation.

Entering her with two fingers, he grazed that perfect spot inside. She cried out, her body bucking as she tossed her head on the pillow. Her hair flung over her face as, with his fingers and mouth, he rode out her quakes, her spasms, her contractions, drank in the glorious sounds she made.

When she finally collapsed on the bed, he crawled up her body, taking her mouth again. Her arms went around him, holding tight. He was desperate to be inside her, but even more, he wanted her to ride the edge for long, exquisite minutes before he took his pleasure.

He pulled the comforter from beneath her, shoving it to the bottom of the bed. They lay against the crisp, cool sheets, their bodies overheated, as he took her breasts with his mouth, sliding his fingers down her body to find her core. It seemed to take only a few moments before she hit the peak again, thrashing against him.

He loved her cries. He loved that she lost herself, riding the pleasure he gave her for all it was worth. He loved that when she was with him, she had no inhibitions.

He loved *her*.

Chapter Twenty-One

"Take me, Cal. *All* of me."

They needed no protection, not when she was already pregnant with their child. And when he moved inside her, skin on skin, with nothing between them?

There was nothing like it in the world. Nothing so good. Nothing so sweet. Nothing so perfect.

Only this.

Only *Cal*.

Lyssa felt as if she were in another dimension. Cal's movements were slow, almost agonizing, yet so perfect. She wanted it faster, wanted him to pound into her, and yet his measured thrusts seemed to touch everything inside her like nothing ever had before. The sensations turned her mindless, stole her breath, quickened her heartbeat.

When he held her face in his hands, she opened her eyes, and he nipped at her lip, shooting a jolt of hot pleasure through her.

"Don't stop," she whispered. If he stopped, she'd die.

"I'll never stop."

There was meaning in the word *never* that she wasn't ready for, not yet. All she could focus on was the beauty of his features as he brought her such pleasure. His pupils were wide, his eyes almost taken over by the black. She felt herself falling into their depths, felt his heat surrounding her, his strength taking her over.

An ocean of sensation built, bigger, harder, higher, until she detonated from the inside out. Her body clenched around him, her cries wrenched from her, and then—*finally*—he took her hard and fast. She loved his weight and the power of his body as he slammed into her.

She gripped his face between her hands and demanded, "Come with me."

His arms shuddered, his body quaked, and he throbbed inside her, his eyes on hers until the very last moment when he closed his lids, threw back his head, groaned from deep, deep down, and shook with the force of his pleasure, taking her over the edge with him.

Later, she didn't quite remember how it had happened, but he'd pulled the comforter over them, their bodies flush together as their skin cooled and their breathing slowed.

A part of her wanted to tell him how good it had been. But another part—the bigger part—couldn't.

It had been *too* good, *too* perfect. The power of what they created when they touched, when they kissed, when he filled her was too overwhelming. Was it the out-of-this-world connection between them that could make her fall for him all over again? And make him fall for her?

Or was it simply the synergy of their bodies? Was it the baby inside her, connecting them? Or something even bigger and far more intense?

Something that her heart was still afraid to acknowledge in the wake of the two times he'd deserted her.

She stretched against him. "*Now* I'm hungry for food."

He chuckled softly, the sound vibrating lusciously through her. "I could make you change your mind," he said in a low voice that made her want to start at the beginning and do it all again. "But you're going to need food to keep up your strength, so we should definitely eat."

Cal slid off the bed and padded to the small refrigerator. She enjoyed the view of his flexing hips, the play of muscle across his back as he squatted by the fridge. She wanted to drink him in, and watching him, she could get drunk on the sight of him alone.

He stood again, giving her the full magnificent picture, beautiful and amazing as he glided back across the floor, a real-life sculpture.

Stuffing a pillow behind herself, she leaned against the headboard, eyeing the sparkling glass he offered her. "But I can't drink champagne." She patted her stomach. "The baby."

He smiled. "I brought sparkling apple cider for us instead."

Then he went back to the tiny kitchen and brought out a plate of cheese and crackers, which he set between them. The man thought of everything. She remembered that he'd brought in a small cooler, but hadn't paid attention when he was unloading it.

It was so sweet, so incredibly thoughtful that her heart swelled in her chest.

Setting his glass of sparkling cider on the side table, he climbed in beside her and pulled up the covers. She savored the cheese on a cracker, took a grape as a chaser, and sipped the apple cider. "This is perfect."

He smiled. "And you will note these are all pregnancy-approved cheeses."

Clearly, he'd been researching and discovered that Bries and blues were off the list for the next nine months. She wouldn't be surprised to hear that he'd already read every pregnancy book there was. He'd done this for the baby. And for her. What other man would ever have thought to look? It wasn't just part of making her fall in love with him. It was his innate caring.

"This is a smoked Gouda." He pointed. "And the

Jarlsberg will be delicious with a little apricot jam."

"Mmmm," she said around a mouthful of deliciousness. "Who would have guessed you're a cheese connoisseur, on top of your other talents?" And he had so many talents, not just the way he touched her or the pleasure he gave her, but the way he made sure to notice and compliment her abilities, building her up.

Cal chuckled. "Will had a variety of cheeses he wanted me to try one night. We ate cheese until we nearly popped."

Her brother Will was in imports and exports, and he'd come across the most amazing goods, everything from wine and caviar to Persian rugs and porcelain teacups. When Will introduced a product, it nearly always became a new fad.

"He didn't ask me to taste-test," she groused.

"That's because you've buried yourself in work since you joined the foundation."

"Tell me more," she said. "Tell me something else I don't know about you." Suddenly, she wanted to know everything. "Start with where you went to college."

His face changed, an infinitesimal adjustment of his features that slightly flattened his expression. "Back East."

"Where back East?"

He looked as though he didn't want to tell her. Finally, however, he said, "Harvard."

"Wow." She raised her eyebrows. "That's very impressive. And not at all surprising. Why don't you seem happier about it?"

"I wanted to be a lawyer, following in my dad's footsteps." He huffed out a breath, as if it was painful to remember the past. "But I changed my mind and went to Harvard Business School instead." He finally looked into her eyes. "It was the right move. I like what I'm doing. A lot. I like working with the Mavericks. And I like buying and selling companies on my own too."

"We've never really talked about that," she said. "I mean, I know that's what you do, but we're always so busy with the foundation when we're together that sometimes I forget you even have another focus."

"I've been doing it a long time," he told her. "And I have a great team who've been executing my vision so well, for so many years, that I'm pretty peripheral at this point."

"I doubt that," she said with a smile. "You could never be peripheral to anything or anyone."

Especially to her, she realized. Somewhere along the way, she didn't even know how, Cal had become the very center of her universe. It was kind of scary. And kind of wonderful too.

"That's why you fly all over the world?" she asked. "Because you're checking in on all the companies you're managing?"

"I wouldn't say managing. More like advising.

When we were in London, I visited a textiles manufacturer. They'll show a profit by the end of the year, and the owner can buy me out if he wants. It's a win-win for both of us. I buy only what people want to sell. Sometimes they don't have capital, so I invest, help turn them around. Other times, people are just tired and want out. So I take the company off their hands."

He didn't do hostile takeovers. He made sure a merger helped both sides, that they both received benefits. And he was modest about it all too.

He leaned in to kiss the tip of her nose. "Now it's my turn to ask you some questions." Though she got the sense he was deliberately pivoting away from himself—the way he always did, she suddenly realized—she couldn't help but laugh when he said, "How many hearts have you broken in high school, college, and after?"

"I never broke any hearts," she said with a shake of her head.

"I find that impossible to believe."

"It's true. I guess it's just that I never met anyone who measured up to my brothers and my dad. Everyone I've dated—" She shrugged. "—paled in comparison." She looked up at the ceiling fan. "The guys in high school and college all seemed like such boys. And when I graduated, I wanted to concentrate on my career. I wanted to get on with my life." She thought about Gary, her last date before she'd flown down to see Cal. "Even now, the men I've dated all seem so immature."

"Your brothers and father are very difficult to measure up to," Cal agreed.

But you do.

As soon as the thought popped into her head, she knew it was true. Regardless of what had come between them before now—specifically his repeated post-sex disappearing acts—she had no doubt whatsoever that Cal was a good man.

The question was *why* had he disappeared on her?

Their sex was so powerful, so all-consuming that it was clear he was attracted to her. So it wasn't that he'd been trying to let her down easy.

He was genuinely over the moon about the baby, so it wasn't that he didn't want children.

And once he'd known she was pregnant, he'd become intent on persuading her to marry him, so he wasn't marriage averse.

But why had he held back initially? And why, even now, did she feel as though he was still keeping a part of himself hidden from her?

Was it because he knew she was still weighing all the pros and cons? Or could it have something to do with his reaction when she'd asked him about his past, even something as innocuous as where he'd gone to college?

Mired in her own emotions about his leaving and

the baby, she hadn't been able to see the forest for the trees where Cal was concerned. But now, she could start to see things more clearly. To see *him* more clearly.

Only one thing was absolutely certain thus far: Cal never liked to talk about his past.

Which begged the question yet again. *Why?*

★ ★ ★

They rose late after that wonderful night of loving and climbed down the cliff path to walk along the narrow strip of beach. Surfers were out there catching the waves.

Cal had made love to Lyssa again in the early hours, the night so dark he couldn't see her. It was so damn sexy, their touches and sighs and kisses and bodies coming together.

He wanted Lyssa and their child with everything in him. He wanted the kind of family he'd never had. He hoped the day, and night, they'd just spent together had tempted her at least part of the way along the path to loving him.

Especially since he was *all* the way there himself.

He took her hand as they walked, enjoying the ease between them, the romance of a walk along the shore.

Lyssa pulled her jacket tighter around her with her free hand. "It's gorgeous out here."

"Absolutely gorgeous," he said, seeing only her.

"Look at those mind-blowing waves."

As she said it, a monster wave crashed down on a surfer, throwing his board high in the air, tossing him around like a blender might, until he eventually popped up.

There was a lot more Cal could have told her about his life, beyond going to Harvard and pivoting from law to business. He rarely talked about his younger years. The Mavericks knew, because they'd deliberately plied him with alcohol to pry out a few secrets. They each had enough dark secrets of their own that they could accept his history without so much as a blink.

But what would Lyssa think?

"Where should we go next?" She looked at him with a glow on her face, the inner light Lyssa always possessed. "I chose axe throwing and glamping. That means it's your turn."

He was glad he had a great idea to throw her way. "What do you think about heading to Cambria to watch the light show in Paso Robles after dark?"

"You mean like a laser light show?"

"Not quite." He pulled out his phone and brought up the website. Turning the phone toward her, he watched her face as she scrolled, her eyes growing wider, her smile bigger.

"This looks incredible."

The site displayed a field of flowers made of solar lights that charged in the sun all day. At night, they were brilliant, creating shapes and waves across the landscape for a dazzling light show.

"I've always liked outdoor art and the way it not only uses the elements, like how this guy is using solar to power the lights, but the way it actually becomes part of the elements."

"What other outdoor art have you seen?"

"In Palm Springs, there was a display of giant metal babies crawling around a huge sandbox. They had no faces, just a stripe down the middle like a bar code." He raised an eyebrow. "I believe it was supposed to represent the dehumanization of society. But I just thought it made them look soulless." He pursed his lips. "And I don't believe we're a soulless generation."

Lyssa snorted. "I bet Charlie would have a field day with babies." Sebastian's fiancée would not make them soulless. "All of her work is so upbeat."

Cal wrapped his arm around her and pulled her close, holding her tight against him. "That's why I liked the London street art so much. It brightened my mood with all the brilliant colors."

This time, she was the one raising an eyebrow. "As I recall, you liked the street art other people made, but hated your own."

"You're right. I didn't like the idea of doing my own art. But I've found myself looking at the pictures of it more than once. And I have to admit...I actually kind of like what I did now."

She hugged him hard. "I'm so glad. What you made was *brilliant*. And even if it wasn't, I still would have loved it, simply because *you* made it."

Did she know how much she'd just revealed to him? That she'd told him something mattered to her because he'd imagined it? Did that mean she was closer to loving him than she knew?

Clearly, he needed to make a point of revealing himself to her. Take the street art—all this time, she'd thought he hated what he'd done, when the truth was he'd cherish their day in London forever. It had been one of the best days of his life.

In all the years since his family had fallen apart, nothing surpassed the time he'd spent with Lyssa.

"I loved dancing on the London Eye," he told her, wanting her to know it all now. "I loved the street art. I loved glamping. I even loved axe throwing."

"Thank you for telling me that," she said, laughing in his arms.

The way her happiness bubbled up and out so freely made him want to make love to her right on this narrow strip of beach.

All he wanted, from now until forever, was to make Lyssa Spencer happy.

The question remained. Could he do it through sheer determination and depth of love?

Or was he bound to fail the same way his father had?

★ ★ ★

"I haven't relaxed into a vacation like this since I got out of college." Lyssa leaned back in her seat with a happy sigh as Cal maneuvered the car along the coastal road's winding curves.

"I'm glad you're enjoying yourself," he said as he reached out to put his hand over hers.

Being with Cal felt so good, was so much fun. He made her feel so safe. And at the same time, he respected her mind, her ideas, and the way she could take care of herself.

She looked at his gorgeous profile, then out at the ocean's breathtaking waves. Being with him was at once calming and incredibly exciting. Especially when she thought about all those deliciously wicked things they'd done in bed. And that sexy interlude on Catalina, too, even if it had ended badly.

When her stomach rumbled, it was a good thing they'd just rolled into Ragged Point, a small coastal town with a few cute shops, a resort, and a couple of restaurants.

"Hungry?"

She rubbed her stomach. "Hungry times two."

His eyes lit the way they always did when they talked about the baby. It warmed every part of her that he truly wanted to be a father.

Suddenly, she spied the perfect place. "Let's eat

there. Frank's Fish Market."

He slowed in front of the restaurant. "The line is a mile long."

"That means the food has to be amazing." She glanced at Cal. "You don't wait in lines much, do you?"

"Nope. Only with you, it seems." He smiled as he pulled into a parking spot. "Fortunately, you're more than worth it."

His words—and his smile—were like a warm caress.

They waited in line on the sidewalk for half an hour, talking and laughing. He grilled her about why she hadn't liked her last job, and she told him about the boss who never recognized her skills.

It struck her that while she wanted to know everything about him, there were so many things he didn't know about her. If he was to fall for her, too, then revealing herself was as important as learning more about him.

"Have you always wanted to be an accountant?" he asked.

"Yes, but mostly because I know it's a great pathway to my ultimate goal. Accountants know a business inside and out," she explained. "It's a stepping stone to being CEO of my own company someday."

He tipped his head, as though looking at her in a new light. "I see you doing whatever you set your mind to."

He continued with the questions until he finally leaned in close. "I know you think I hired you because your brothers wanted me to. I'm not going to deny they applied some heavy-duty pressure, but I hired you because you're smart and hardworking." He brushed his fingertip over her lips. "And because you made my heart beat faster."

"You never even noticed me," she scoffed. "I was just the Mavericks' little sister."

His gaze was suddenly deep. "That's what I tried to tell myself. I didn't want to admit what you did to me." He curled a lock of her hair around his finger. "But you had my heart in the palm of your hand, Ms. Spencer, from the moment we danced the funky chicken at Matt and Ari's wedding."

She laughed, turning heads, and she knew she was glowing. She'd gone wild and crazy that day, miffed when Daniel had tried to tell her how to live her life and who she could and could not fall for.

Was Cal saying that what happened between them on the flight back from London had been inevitable?

A big part of her longed to tell him he'd won the challenge—that her heart was his. But there was still enough sting left over from the way he'd hurt her that she held the words inside, saying instead, "You only like me for my funky chicken."

He didn't let her turn it into a joke. Instead, he lowered his lips to hers and whispered, "I like you for a hell of a lot more than that."

Then he kissed her, and she almost forgot about trying to guard the last sliver of her heart still holding on to the pain. It was only a nudge from the people in line behind them that kept her from dropping her final walls and blurting out three little words in the middle of a sidewalk in Ragged Point.

Chapter Twenty-Two

The fish at Frank's was worth the wait. Especially now that Lyssa found herself thinking about food far more than she had before she'd gotten pregnant.

Afterward, they found a darling inn in Cambria, a small midcoast town near Hearst Castle that she'd heard of but never had the chance to visit. Their room was cozy, with a queen-size bed and a plush rug by the fireplace.

Lyssa was hugely tempted to rip off her clothes and pull Cal down with her in front of the fire. But despite her momentary lapse in line, when she'd almost declared her feelings to him, she knew that to truly get all the way to *love*, she needed to know him better outside of either work or sex. He was amazing at both. Naturally. But though her heart was falling more for him with every passing second, there was the opposite side of the coin too. She needed Cal to fall for her just as much. It was mutual love that counted. He needed to want her for more than her work capabilities, her funky chicken, and everything she made him feel when she touched him.

Building a life together was so much more than just work, or sex. Or even the inescapable pitter-patter of her heart where he was concerned. It was about knowing, and trusting, and supporting each other through thick and thin, good and bad, up and down, no matter what. Building a life together was about unconditional love. And that, she sensed, came only when both people had completely let down their guards.

Her guard hadn't fallen all the way yet.

And, if she wasn't mistaken, neither had his.

Hoping tonight might be her chance to make inroads on uncovering Cal's hidden parts, she grabbed his hand. "Let's go for a walk by the ocean. I saw a boardwalk across the road."

They walked to the end, stopping on their return trip to watch the elephant seals.

"It's a satellite pod," he told her. "A much larger group heads up to Año Nuevo."

She'd heard of the preserve just south of Half Moon Bay, where tourists could view the elephant seals' nursery. They were huge, lumbering creatures nestled together along the rocky beach below the railing. Two males rose up in open warfare, pounding their chests violently against each other, causing the females to slither out of the way. The tiff was over in a moment, and they settled again.

"They're magnificent," he said. "Especially up

close. I was lucky enough to win a lottery ticket to see them at Año Nuevo. They're their own art form. Two great bulls got into a major conflict, probably because one was poaching on a female, and he chased him across the beachhead. They can move unbelievably fast. It was like watching a dance."

He spoke so lyrically. There was so much more to him than she'd ever imagined. And she certainly couldn't imagine any of the women she'd seen him pictured with on glossy society pages trekking over the dunes to see elephant seals.

Before London, she'd thought of him mostly in a business sense, as if he had no life outside his business and his ventures with her brothers, because he wasn't married, he didn't have kids, and he never seemed to date a woman for more than a month or two. It had been silly of her to think he was so one-dimensional.

In the same way her brothers still thought of her as the little sister who needed to be taken care of, she'd done the same thing to Cal, pigeonholing him into a slot made for an untouchable, unemotional business-man.

"Why do you always let me pick the music in the car?"

To his credit, he took her out-of-left-field question in stride. "I'm interested in what music you like."

She tilted her head. "What have you learned?"

"That you like everything from New Age to sixties

rock to classical to musicals to big band to old standards like 'Unforgettable.'" He grinned. "I think it's great
that you're impossible to stick into a box."

What a lovely thing to say. And even lovelier that
he had taken the time to notice.

"Now I want to know what kind of music you
like."

"Will you think badly of me if I say I don't really
listen to music?" He grimaced slightly, as though he
was a little embarrassed. "There's always news to stay
abreast of or a podcast to listen to or an interview to
learn from." Then he paused. "But I like how your
music makes me feel."

He put a hand over his chest, and her heart swelled
at how sweet he was. She went up on her tippy-toes
and pressed a soft kiss to his lips.

"I like the way being with *you* makes me feel," she
said softly.

He pushed the hair away from her face, tucked it
behind her ear in a sweet, intimate gesture. "It's the
same for me, Lyssa."

He lowered his mouth to hers, and this time their
kiss went on far longer than just one beautiful moment. It would surely have led them back to the inn
and forgetting all about seeing the light show, had her
stomach not chosen that moment to growl. How could
she possibly be hungry again after Frank's seafood?

Cal laughed as he drew back and laid a gentle hand

over her stomach. "If we head over to Paso Robles now, we'll have plenty of time to get some dinner before the light show begins."

Though she nodded, they stood for a few moments longer as the glow of the setting sun frosted the elephant seals in shades of pink and purple and gold. The wind against her face was sharp and elemental. But with Cal's arm around her and his breath sweet against her face, she felt warm all over.

* * *

"This has to be one of the most amazing things I've ever seen," Lyssa said as they gazed at the field of multicolored lights installed by artist Bruce Munro, who was renowned all over the world, from the U.K. to Australia to South Korea to the U.S., for his nature-based light shows.

It was crisp and cold in Paso Robles, and they stood hand in hand as the blues and purples and pinks and reds, all the colors of the spectrum, seemed to dance across the wide-open space. This was how Cal wanted things to be—Lyssa by his side, her hand in his.

Not only was she beautiful and sexy as hell, she was also someone with whom he could drive in the car for hours and listen to music, saying nothing at all and being completely comfortable with it. She was a woman with whom he could gaze at elephant seals and watch the sunset, wait in line at a fish shack, and hold hands with on a beach.

When it was over, they drove back along the two-lane road to Cambria, not even listening to music, simply reveling in the wonder of what they'd experienced in the open field of lights.

She turned to him. "Thank you. It was beautiful."

"I agree." Even though *she* was the most beautiful thing of all. "Your parents would love it, wouldn't they?"

She nodded. "We should bring them down here."

It was the *we* that burrowed deep inside him, as though they were bonded now in a way they hadn't been before.

He'd previously believed that women in their twenties were always on their cell phones or social media, that they needed to be plugged in, that they were always angling to attract outside attention.

But Lyssa was like no one else.

He lifted her hand to his lips, kissing her skin, breathing her in.

And waited with breathless anticipation for the moment he could hold her in his arms again and make her his.

★ ★ ★

The field of lights had been dazzling.

We should bring them down here.

The words had slipped out of her mouth before

she'd realized they were coming. It felt right, but it was also scary. It meant she was already making plans for the future, though neither of them had said the L-word yet, or even made a formal commitment to one another.

That was what this trip was about, of course. By the end of it, they'd both need to make a big decision about what they were going to be to each other...and then tell her family.

But for right now, for a few hours longer, she wanted to exist only in the moment. With Cal. And as he closed the door to their adorable cottage with the soft rug and crackling fire, she didn't want to think at all. Didn't want to wonder if he could make her fall in love. Or if she could get him to love her. Or if their amazing physical connection could lead to a future.

"Let's sit by the fire," Cal suggested, crossing to the bed for a couple of pillows and throwing them on the rug.

She took his hand, and together they lay down, her back nestled to his chest, the warmth of the fire on her face, the heat of him melting her on the inside. Resting her head on his arm, she watched the flickering flames. Though she could feel that he was hard against her, there was no clothes-tearing. Simply a sense of contentment and peace and the knowledge that they had all night to love each other with their bodies.

He slipped his hand to her belly, and she instinctively placed her hand over his. And, with a smile on her lips, she closed her eyes.

★ ★ ★

She didn't know who woke whom, whether she kissed him first, or he kissed her awake. All she knew was that it was *perfect*.

Deep darkness lay outside, and she had no idea how long she'd slept, or if he'd slept with her. But time ceased to matter as his hand caressed her slowly, rising up to her breasts, palming her, then squeezing lightly. He teased her through the lace bra until the peaks hardened into sensitive nubs. He moved his lips from her mouth to her ear and blew a warm breath until she shivered inside.

They didn't share a word, complete silence in the darkened room, except their breathing, their sighs and moans of pleasure, and the crackle of flames. It was sexy and seductive, and she'd never known lovemaking like it. Only with Cal.

He kissed her hair and the tender flesh of her neck as he circled his fingers under her breast, then finally pulled the lacy cup aside to tease her bare flesh. Everything turned hot inside and out, and then, as though reading her mind, he moved his hand to the waistband of her jeans.

He popped the button and unzipped her, slipped his hand inside, skimmed the lacy thong, glided under the material until he found her sex. Wet and hot and so incredibly ready for him. She hooked her leg over his, opening herself to him. He touched her in the room lit only by firelight, without words, without looking at each other, and it made it all the sexier, all the hotter.

She moaned when he found the apex of her pleasure, circling, teasing. She turned her head slightly and gave his bicep a love bite. She loved the seductive sound of his groan.

Together, they shoved down her jeans, then she silently gave herself over to him, to his touch, to his kisses, to his need.

It was bliss, it was ecstasy. His touch built a fire, searing her body as though the flames were licking at her skin. She searched for the peak, felt the quivers and quakes moving through her, building moment by moment, until the pleasure was so intense it flung her off to the stars.

Even then, instead of crying out her pleasure, she let the silence of the night wrap around them, making the sensations even more delicious and powerful.

He undid his pants, pushing them down so he could slide his hard shaft over her sensitive flesh, again and again, pushing her to the edge until she was gasping, her fingers clutching the rug.

Finally, he thrust home, hard and hot and deep and fast. At last, she cried out as pleasure tore through her yet again, lost to everything but Cal.

★ ★ ★

Lyssa's climax was the most exquisite sensation he'd ever known. He tried to hold out, wanting her pleasure, and his, to go on forever. Wanting *her* forever.

But he was no match for her obvious need to haul him into the bliss right along with her. To be with her in need, and beauty, and what he knew deep in his bones was love.

Afterward, he held her tight. They didn't need words. In this moment, with her heart beating against his, they were so close, closer than he'd ever been with anyone else.

True communion and connection, he'd finally realized, didn't need words.

I love you, he said, silently speaking from his heart to hers.

And even as he sensed she still wasn't ready to hear the words aloud in the light of day, he hoped she could hear them as she lay in his arms tonight.

★ ★ ★

Lyssa woke the next morning sheltered in Cal's arms. In tacit agreement, neither of them spoke about the night they'd shared.

Or maybe she was the one who didn't want to talk about it. A few times, she thought he might say something. It was in the way he looked at her, with a hopefulness he couldn't quite hide. She knew what he wanted.

He wanted her to say that the trip had worked, that she loved him. And if she was completely honest, she wanted the same thing from him.

And yet...

She couldn't shake the fact that she didn't have all the puzzle pieces that made up Cal the man. Until then, how could she possibly risk the last piece of her heart she was still shielding out of sheer self-preservation in the wake of the pain he'd caused before?

She'd never been shy. Never been afraid of asking for what she wanted.

But she'd also never faced something this big. This life-changing.

She would ask him about his past, she vowed. As soon as the perfect moment presented itself.

They packed up just before checkout, then headed to the boardwalk to say good-bye to the elephant seals and gaze at the ocean as the sun sparkled on the waves.

Her fingers wrapped in Cal's, she said, "What a gorgeous day."

His answering smile was as brilliant as the sun. "I've never seen a better one," he agreed.

Before either of them could say more, her stomach growled, loudly, crying out to be heard.

"I've got a brilliant idea." Cal pointed to a diner

that boasted the best hot dogs on the coast. "I'm thinking we can't leave town without finding out if their claim is true."

Lyssa laughed. "They've got to be better than the hot dogs Matt always burns on the grill."

Nodding his agreement, they headed to the restaurant. It was cute, with a green and white checkerboard floor, red-cushioned benches, white Formica tabletops, an old-fashioned jukebox in the corner, and the delicious scent of hot dogs sizzling on the grill.

When their dogs arrived, the waiter, who was also the cook, slid them onto the table, saying, "Bon appétit." Then he skip-jumped back to the kitchen. Which was amazing for a guy who had to be six foot four and had the muscles of Arnold Schwarzenegger.

Cal grinned as he prepared to pick up his massive everything-on-it hot dog. "Man, I love that smell."

"I never would have guessed you were a hot-dog guy."

Before he took a big bite, he said, "When I was a kid, my dad would take me fishing really early in the morning. We were done by noon. And on the way back from the lake, there was this little diner where we always stopped for hot dogs."

"It sounds like you were really close to your dad."

"Yeah, when I was a kid, we were." A frown replaced the happy light in his eyes.

This was her moment. The perfect opportunity to

ask him to share more of his past with her, even the difficult parts. Especially those. "Did something change when you became an adult?"

He was silent for a long moment. Long enough for her to wonder if he would finally divulge something of his secret past to her.

But all he said was, "He died a long time ago." Then he shook his head, as if he was letting the memory go rather than telling her more.

When he took a big bite, she realized the moment had already slipped away, without his actually answering her question.

But she had to tell him, "I'm sorry you lost him."

"Thanks." He took another bite of his hot dog as though the death of his father was nothing serious.

Her chest clenched at how quickly he'd shoved aside his emotions. If she decided to be with him in the long term, would he do that with her? With their child? Just shove every feeling down deep where he never had to look at it, never actually feel it?

She couldn't live with that. But she had to believe he would eventually trust her enough to open up to her all the way.

When he did, she could finally open herself up to marriage and, far more important, love.

Chapter Twenty-Three

After their hot dogs, as they drove farther south, Lyssa gasped and grabbed his arm. She held out her phone. "I just found a haunted hotel. We have to go!"

Cal had never thought he'd find someone who could introduce him to so many new things. And get him to enjoy them, too, taking him out of a rut he hadn't even known he was in. He wanted to soak up every new surprise she came up with like a sponge. He felt like the two of them were on the same wavelength, the same plane of existence. He could hardly believe he'd found a woman so unique and yet so perfect for him.

But could he convince her to stay? That was still the unanswerable question...

While Cal had waxed nostalgic over hot dogs, he'd stopped short of telling Lyssa about the ways his dad had destroyed the family.

He'd told himself he wanted to keep only good memories of their road trip, not mire them in the bad. He tried to convince himself that his father's sins had no bearing on his relationship with Lyssa. He didn't want to dwell on the fear that he was just like his father—good old Dad, who couldn't resist his much younger secretary and had blown the family apart. Just as Cal's need for Lyssa might blow apart their relationships with the Mavericks and Lyssa's parents.

Her voice pulled him out of the past and back to the present. "I'm so excited. I can't wait to see a ghost. Will you be there to hold me tight if I scream?"

"You're going to be the one holding me tight," he said, his humor bubbling up. That's what Lyssa did for him, always seeing the brighter side.

Laughing most of the way, they arrived at the haunted hotel an hour and a half later.

The town was barely more than a dot on the map, with all-American streets named D and E and F one way and Fifteenth, Sixteenth, and Seventeenth the other. He wondered what had happened to A, B, and C and First through Fourteenth.

The hotel was straight out of the 1800s, with a wide wooden front porch and a long balcony along the second floor. The lobby resembled the sitting room of a bordello, with sofas and chairs upholstered in plush red fabric. The reception desk might once have been the oak bar of a saloon. And surprisingly, there was quite a large crowd waiting in the lobby.

At reception, the concierge was a tall, thin woman in her early sixties, with the name Dorothy emblazoned on her name tag.

"Dorothy, we're hoping to book a room." With a pleasant smile, Cal leaned on the counter.

"Well," she said, eyeing the crowd taking up most of the lobby's seating, "you've come in the middle of one of our ghost-hunting conferences. However, I just got a last-second cancellation, so I have a room with a street view and its own bathroom if you want it."

"Sounds perfect," Lyssa said.

Dorothy leaned in conspiratorially. "There's one hitch. That pesky varmint Wild Bill McCutchen was killed in the bed in Room 8." Her tone was suited to the deep, dark midnight of a scary haunted house.

Cal had never heard of the *varmint* Wild Bill McCutchen. "Wouldn't a ghost hunter want that room? It could be a wild night." Beside him, Lyssa stifled a laugh.

Dorothy explained solemnly, "It's our most terrifying room. Over the years, we've had guests almost frightened to death." She leaned closer to whisper, "One even thought he'd had a heart attack."

Lyssa put a hand to her chest. "Oh my."

With the hint of a smile, Dorothy added, "It's also our most expensive room, and this crowd is a thrifty bunch."

Cal handed her his credit card. "We'll take it."

She smiled, showing her teeth like a shark who'd trapped a big one. "Right next door, you'll find our world-famous restaurant serving the best steaks west of the Pecos." Then she cackled. "We're also the only game in town, so even if you don't like the food, it's all you've got."

He signed the register, and Dorothy rang a bell. A man as tall and thin as the concierge but much, much older rushed over.

"Abel," she called in a loud voice. "Take this couple up to Wild Bill McCutchen's room."

The entire lobby fell silent, every eye on them, mouths agape at what audacious spendthrifts they were.

Lyssa couldn't quite hold in her laughter this time.

"I'll get your bags." Abel bent down, his back creaking.

"It's no problem, I can carry them," Cal said.

Abel allowed the help, taking them up wide wooden stairs to a narrow hall that led to the front of the hotel, where the dimly lit corridor opened on a large public area filled with tables. Unlocking the door to Room 8 with an old-fashioned skeleton key, Abel waved them in.

A crocheted coverlet enveloped the big brass bed, while the hardwood floor was covered in braided rugs. Two rocking chairs with needlepoint cushions sat by the long front window. The bathroom sported a claw-foot tub and a toilet topped by a hanging cistern with a chain to flush.

Lyssa clapped her hands. "I love it!" She pointed to the bed. "Did Wild Bill actually die right there?"

Cal hoped not, or the ancient mattress would be very uncomfortable.

Abel turned animated. "He sure did, ma'am. But don't you worry, those sheets aren't the ones he died on."

Lyssa couldn't hold back a smile as she asked, "You wouldn't happen to have a ghost tour we could join, would you?"

"Well, ma'am, we don't have an official tour." Abel affected an Old West drawl. "But I'd be happy to give you the lowdown." His eyes twinkled. "Dorothy can ring the bell real loud if she needs me."

They spent the next hour with Abel. A couple had been murdered in Room 12. Room 2 had seen a wife murder her husband. And Room 16 boasted a deadly squabble between two cowboys over a saloon girl. Evidently, the ghosts of them all haunted the hotel, day and night, along with Wild Bill McCutchen.

They were chilling, thrilling tales. Lyssa asked question after question, giving Abel ample room to embellish his stories.

"So tell me, Abel, have you seen any of these ghosts in person?" Her eyes bright, it was clear she hoped the answer was yes.

"Why, no, ma'am, I've never seen a thing. That's why I can work here, because I don't have sensibilities.

People who can see spirits are far too sensitive to the emotions of the ghosts who wander these halls to stay on for more than a night or two. But there will be a séance in the parlor outside your room tonight. And you might get some knocks on your door from people asking if you've seen Wild Bill McCutchen's ghost."

Once Abel left them alone in their room, Lyssa threw herself at Cal. "This is going to be so much fun." Standing back, she deepened her voice. "Is it just me, or do you feel an icy cold in this room?"

"Now that you mention it, I'm suddenly feeling bony fingers down my spine."

Lyssa collapsed on the bed in giggles. "We absolutely have to watch the séance."

God, how he loved the way she enjoyed life. Until he'd met her, he'd forgotten about having fun.

Now, all he wanted was to laugh with her—and love her—for the rest of his life.

★ ★ ★

They had dinner in the hotel dining room crowded with ghost hunters, all jabbering excitedly about tonight's upcoming séance. The menu featured Wild Bill McCutchen 16-ounce Steak, Butch Cassidy Prime Rib, and Wyatt Earp Beef Stew.

Upstairs, the parlor outside their door had been readied for the séance, set up with six round tables, each with a candle and a Ouija board in the center.

After dinner, as they made their way to their room, they were accosted by two white-haired ladies dying to see the bed in which Wild Bill McCutchen had died. Cal gave them a tour of the room, letting them touch the mattress.

"Last night," one of the women told them, "we were assailed by a series of moans and groans and cries and sighs from the spirits in this room. There was even a bit of wailing. And I do believe the headboard was banging the wall too."

Lyssa, who was sitting in the rocking chair before the window, had to look away to control the burst of laughter struggling to get out. Clearly, the couple who'd been in the room the night before had been having an extremely good time.

After that, they had a steady stream of visitors, most of whom were in costume, with dresses suited to bygone ages, low-heeled pumps, and suits tailored to the Old West.

As Cal entertained each and every one, making them titter and gasp with his tall tales, Lyssa felt something shift inside her, a new emotion capturing her heart. She couldn't put a label on it, but he was amazing and wonderful, so sweet and kind to the flow of elderly men and women.

She'd always known he was hardworking, smart, determined, and ambitious, not to mention handsome, sexy, seductive, and beguiling. But yet again, he showed her another side—an adorably sweet one. Just the way, she realized, he'd been when playing in the pool with Noah and Jorge, or dancing with the boys at Ari's wedding.

Cal Danniger was a kind, wonderful man, with just enough of a naughty glint in his eyes to charm every person who walked through the door.

Just the way he'd always charmed Lyssa.

She liked to think she was offering something, too—fun experiences, new ways to look at things around him. She loved how he'd come around to enjoying street art, axe throwing, glamping. And now haunted houses. She wanted to share his love of hiking and the outdoor art he appreciated, but she also wanted to share things with him that she delighted in. If the deal was to make him fall for her and vice versa, then showing him new pleasures, and not just in bed, had to be part of it. Her parents had taught her the joy of life, and she wanted to share that joy with him.

When it was time for the séance, Lyssa asked the man who seemed to be in charge, "Do you mind if we watch?"

Short and stocky, he almost had to look up at her as he said, "You're welcome to watch, but please…" He shook his finger dramatically. "No talking."

They leaned against the wall outside their room, and Cal held her hand, murmuring, "Just in case you get scared."

The lights were dimmed, the candles on the tables lit.

"Join hands, please." The medium sat at the front of the group, his chair on a dais so he could look out over them all. "Is there anyone who would like to speak with us tonight?" His big baritone boomed across the assembly.

"Do you feel it?" one of the women asked. "There's a cold wave in the room. Someone is with us."

A door in the back was open, letting in the cold air, but Lyssa was as happy to ignore that fact as everyone else in the room.

A woman wearing a turban out of the 1920s raised her hand. "Oh, please, could you talk to my Wilbur? He's been gone these past twenty years. I miss him so."

The medium seized on the request with gusto, his voice resounding. "Is there a Wilbur in the house? Please, Wilbur, come into me, speak to your beautiful lady through me."

His body went rigid, his face a rictus of pain or glory, before his head suddenly fell forward, his chin hitting his chest. The entire room was silent except for the honk of a horn from the road below. When he raised his head again, his eyes were closed, his features softened.

"My darling Imogen, it is I."

Imogen cried out, "Wilbur! Is that really you?"

"Yes, my dear. Do you remember our first kiss out

in the apple orchard on your father's farm?"

Imogen clapped her hands to her mouth. "It's really *is* you, Wilbur."

All the guests' mouths hung open, with Imogen's face beatific in the low light of the flickering candle.

★ ★ ★

The medium went around the room, giving each person exactly what they'd come for.

Giving Cal a lightness that encircled his heart, as well.

Grabbing Lyssa's hand, he pulled her into their room. Listening to the elderly communicate with their long-lost loves, their dearly departed parent or sibling or beloved pet, moved him. It made him think that anything was possible.

And he wanted to make *everything* possible with Lyssa.

He closed the door and pushed her up against it. Outside, a voice called, "Did you hear that? It came from Wild Bill McCutchen's room. Do you think he's angry?"

The medium's voice rose above them. "Ladies and gentlemen, there are no malevolent spirits here. Not in this room. You're safe."

"So safe," Lyssa whispered at she pressed her mouth to Cal's, letting him feel just how much she wanted him.

When they finally came up for air, he whispered, "Should we be quiet? Or should we give them a huge thrill thinking it's the ghost of Wild Bill McCutchen?"

She giggled. "When all along it's actually Wild Lyssa and Cal."

With that, he picked her up and laid her on the bed, the brass rails knocking the wall, the bed springs squeaking.

He climbed over Lyssa. "The more you cry out and sigh—"

"—and the more you moan and groan—"

"—the happier everyone at the seance will be knowing they must surely be hearing real live ghosts, just a wall away."

Scrambling with each other's buttons and snaps and zippers, they didn't even get fully naked before they came together.

The bed squealed, and the brass rails banged the wall. And outside, the ghost hunters chanted, "Wild Bill McCutchen is here! Wild Bill McCutchen is here!"

Cal was damned glad he'd locked the door, just in case. Then he lost himself in Lyssa's kiss, in her scent, in the sweetness of her skin, and the heat of her body around him.

In his own head, he repeated the words he still didn't believe she was ready for: *I love you, I love you, I love you.*

★ ★ ★

Maybe Lyssa should have been embarrassed at the way the headboard had hit the wall and the bed springs had creaked with a room full of people just a wall away. Instead, she'd relished every touch, every sigh, every kiss.

Down in the restaurant for breakfast the next morning, the other guests in the hotel crowded their table, dying for every detail of what they'd experienced in Wild Bill McCutchen's room.

"Cal was terrified," Lyssa told them, her tongue firmly in her cheek. "But I protected him, no matter what Wild Bill threatened."

There was a chorus of *oohs* and *aahs*.

After checking out and saying their good-byes, Cal was still laughing as they got in the car.

"You're a really good sport," she said, humor infusing her words. "I already knew you were good with kids, since I've seen you with Noah and Jorge, but now I know you can knock it out of the park with the older crowd too."

"I really like people," he told her. "All people, no matter their age."

"Me too," she said. "I think it's because I grew up in such a big family. There was always someone to talk to, always someone with a perspective different from mine. That's why I want a big family—because I loved growing up in one." She looked at him. "What about you? What do you think about having a big family?"

He must have felt the earnest turn of the conversation, because he looked at her for a moment before returning his attention to the road. "I was an only child and didn't have any aunts or uncles either. The closest I've come to a big family is the Mavericks." His expression shifted, his smile fading. "You've probably guessed by now, but family is a pretty complicated subject for me."

"I have guessed that," she said slowly, "but I don't know why."

If he wanted to tell her more, she wanted him to do it in his own time, rather than her having to drag the information out of him. She braced for a change of subject, the way he'd always handled it before.

They were close to a freeway exit that led to an ocean overlook when he said, "Why don't we pull over for a minute so we can talk without worrying about what's going on in traffic?"

He parked, then stared out at the water a few moments. "I've told you how my dad and I used to go fishing, then out for hot dogs on the way home. Back then, I wanted to be just like him. He always had time for me, no matter his caseload. He seemed like the best dad in the world." He paused for a deep breath. "Until I found out that was all a lie."

She watched him closely as he spoke without looking at her, staring out to sea. His muscles were more tense now, as though he was bracing for impact, even though they were parked.

"I was seventeen and applying to universities that also had good law schools when my father left my mother for his secretary."

She felt his words like a punch. "Wow, that must have been a blow to her. And to you." Lyssa knew how lucky she was that her parents had always had a solid marriage, with none of the huge relationship upheavals other families suffered.

"It was as if a bomb went off, blowing our family to smithereens. I stood by my mother, even after she turned into an angry, bitter person. All because my father couldn't live without a woman who was twenty years younger." He forced out a harsh breath. "Once upon a time, I idolized my dad and believed in everything he stood for. But from that day forward, I lost all respect for him."

Twenty years younger.

No wonder he'd fixated on their age difference. She put her hand over his, and he finally turned to face her. "Thank you for telling me about your father. Do you know how much it means that you opened up to me about something I'm guessing you've only ever told a handful of people? I bet you never told another woman the truth about your past."

He regarded her with a gaze as deep as the ocean.

"I never felt enough for any woman to go there. But with you, I *have* to."

This was what she had been waiting for—the day when Cal opened up about the things that had shaped him. The really important things.

Which meant she could finally trust him with her really important things, especially the heart she'd been afraid to risk on him again.

"Any chance you want to go to a baby store with me?" she asked suddenly. "I'm thinking we should start looking for a crib and bedding and a chest of drawers we both think will look good in the room we turn into the baby's bedroom at your place."

"My place?" He blinked at her as though she were giving him the moon, the sun, and the stars. "Does this mean you'll move in with me?"

"Your place has quite a bit more room than mine," she said with a smile as she threaded her fingers through his. "And I can't imagine sleeping anywhere but in your arms. Or waking up without you beside me."

Chapter Twenty-Four

This trip had started out as a challenge to make her fall in love with him so they could marry, and he could be a father to their baby. But it had become a burning need for her to fall in love with him because he couldn't live without her.

Did wanting to sleep in his arms and wake up beside him mean she wanted forever? Did going to a baby store mean she was finally seeing him as a man she could depend on, a man she wanted as the father of her child?

A man she could love?

He kissed her long and deep, there in the front seat, until they were both breathless and aching for more. Until they could feel the stares of the people in the car parked beside them.

"I guess we'd better move on and find that baby store," Lyssa said, her cheeks rosy with the heat of their kisses.

On the freeway, she directed him several exits down to another coastal town that had a baby boutique. He'd been in stores like this before to buy gifts for business associates who were expecting.

Today, he was here for his own child. It blew his mind.

The store was filled with baby clothes and lots of colorful, delicate things that made him realize just how small a baby was. He could hardly imagine what it would be like to hold his child in his arms.

"Cal, you've got to take a look at this." Lyssa held up a green…thing.

"What is it?"

She was laughing as she said, "It's an avocado suit. The baby's head goes right here in this circle like it's the avocado pit."

He knew even before she said it. "You want one for our kid, don't you?"

"Who wouldn't?" she replied, a teasing glint in her eyes.

Still laughing, she stuck it back on the rack with the flower petals and dinosaurs and puppy outfits.

A sales clerk approached them. "Can I help you find something?"

Lyssa looped her arm through Cal's. "We're having a baby. It's our first, and we wanted to stroll around your store to get a feel for everything we're going to need."

The woman's blue eyes twinkled. "How exciting! Congratulations. I'm more than happy to let you wander without hanging over your shoulder." She smiled. "If you have any questions about breast pumps or car seats or bassinets, just call me." She returned to the register, busying herself with sorting receipts.

"Look at these darling dresses." Lyssa fingered frilly things in a multitude of colors.

"Are you hoping for a girl?"

She gestured to the boys' rack filled with sailor suits and cowboy outfits and rompers. "Either one would be perfect." Then she turned her gaze to him. "What do you want?"

He was suddenly so choked up he couldn't speak, could barely breathe. The sonogram and the heartbeat had made everything real. Yet, somehow, this was more.

Because Lyssa wanted him not only to be a part of the baby's life, but part of *her* life too.

"Are you all right?" Her hand on his arm, she leaned up to look into his face.

He finally got his voice to work. "I'll be deliriously happy either way."

"Me too," she said, giving him a quick hug before pulling him deeper into the store.

They found cribs and mobiles and bassinets, changing tables and tiny little bathtubs, car seats and diaper bags, baby bottles and changing kits for traveling. He couldn't believe how much paraphernalia went into taking care of a baby.

"This is cute." He pointed to a mobile of twirling dinosaurs. "But I like this one too." It was a mobile of flowers and figures of baby animals.

He suddenly had such a clear vision of the baby's room. A white crib, an old-fashioned rocker, walls painted with animals or clouds. "I want to paint the baby's room. Whatever color you want."

"I don't want pink or blue." Her eyes lit up as she decided. "How about seafoam green?"

"That sounds great."

"And a border around the top," she said, tapping her finger on her chin as she saw the vision too.

"I can paint animals. Or clouds." There were stencils. And what could be hard about painting a cloud freehand? After all, Lyssa thought his street art was a masterpiece. "How about clouds on the ceiling, and the sun, moon, and stars on the border?"

"I love it!"

He wanted to haul her into his arms. He could see it all. Seafoam walls covered in suns and clouds, the stars and moon over the crib as the baby slept.

And Lyssa right beside him, in his home. In his bed. In his life.

Forever.

They were standing in the middle of a dozen different strollers when she said, "My parents' housewarming party is this weekend. How would you feel about telling everyone about the baby—and us—

during the party?"

He took her hands and drew her close. "I'd love that, Lyssa."

He wouldn't worry about the Mavericks. They'd freak out when they heard the news, but he and Lyssa were a team now, and he felt deep in his bones that they could weather whatever came their way.

There was no longer a reason to hide the truth about how she made him feel. "And I love you."

★ ★ ★

"Let's not go home yet," Lyssa said as they climbed into his car. She was still on the high of hearing him say, *I love you.*

He raised her hand to his lips. "Just being with you wherever you want to be is enough for me."

She hadn't yet said those three little words back to him. The moment had to be right. The place had to be just right. "Let's look for a place by the ocean."

As if it had been waiting just for them, they found a darling waterfront cottage on a cove so small with cliffs so high that the beach was completely private. Normally, it was rented out by the week, but since it was unoccupied, the owner let them have it for the night.

They ate takeout Chinese, then Cal lit a fire in the metal ring on the beach, and they sat on a blanket to watch the sunset, his arm wrapped around her.

The clouds and sky were lit with streaks of pink

and yellow as pelicans flew by in formation.

"This is perfection," Lyssa said, feeling happier than she could ever remember feeling before.

"Yes, it is," he agreed, his lips against her hair.

And the moment was exactly what she'd been waiting for to give him her heart. "I love you, Cal."

"You do?"

"Of course I do."

"But I was such an ass, and I hurt you with all my foolish attempts to run away from my feelings for you."

She stroked her fingers along his jaw. "Yes, I was hurt. But I forgive you. I understand more now, that you were afraid of making the same mistake as your father. Afraid of taking advantage of me or ruining my life. But you never had to worry about any of that."

"I know that now. And I loved you from day one even if I couldn't admit it. I love how smart you are, how capable, how kind and caring, how dedicated, how determined. How very loving you are with your family. I love what a wonderful mother you're going to be." He tipped her chin to kiss her softly. "And I love how beautiful and sexy you are."

She cupped his cheek. "I love everything about you. How wise you are. How clever. I love the way you work for the foundation for free. I love how much you already love our baby. I love that you know something about everything and that you read all those books about pregnancy. I love that you're willing to try anything I ask you to. I love how great you are with Noah and Jorge and how good you were with those old ladies at the haunted hotel. I love how much you care about people. And I love how you make me feel." She put her hand to her chest. "In my heart as well as everywhere else."

He kissed her then, a long, sweet, deep kiss that touched her heart, reached into her soul. Together, they lay back on the blanket as the sky darkened and the stars began to shine.

She drew his hand to her breast. "Make love to me, Cal."

"Here?" he murmured against her throat.

"Right here. With just the moon and the stars above us."

He took her lips again, undoing her buttons and trailing his fingers over her sensitive skin until she moaned. She lifted when he pulled her jeans down and cried out softly as he found the heat between her legs.

And when he filled her, he filled her whole heart, her whole soul.

She wrapped her arms around him and pulled him deeper. "I love you with everything in me."

★ ★ ★

"God, I love you." She was his everything. Without Lyssa, he was only half a human being. And it was a miracle that she loved him back.

He steeped himself in her scent, her taste, the feel of her around him.

"I love you. I love you." His voice echoed in the night, and she filled him up with her cries of pleasure, with her words of love.

He vowed that nothing would come between them now.

Chapter Twenty-Five

Saturday arrived, and Lyssa and Cal drove down to Susan and Bob's newly renovated house in Portola Valley. Since they both lived in San Francisco and worked at the foundation, no one questioned their walking in together.

The Mavericks had done an amazing job with the remodel. They'd installed hardwood floors, painted the walls, remodeled the kitchen from top to bottom with new appliances, and redone every bathroom. There were three new decks, one outside the kitchen door, stepping down to another deck with the barbecue, then up to a third deck outside the dining room. The backyard was full of newly planted flowers and bushes. The pool had an in-ground hot tub at the far end, and the sauna was just inside their parents' bathroom, with a door that led out to the pool and hot tub.

Everyone was in the backyard admiring the new landscaping.

"Are you ready for this?" Cal asked as they set out their Gouda cheese and artisan bread offering on one of her mother's platters.

It had been two days since their trip, and though they'd agreed the party would be the best time to tell the family, Lyssa couldn't ignore the quivers in her belly.

Still, she put on a brave smile, knowing that she and Cal would have each other's backs, no matter how anyone reacted. "I'm sure some of my brothers will have a momentary freak-out when we tell them about us…and the baby. But they'll all be okay with it in the end."

Cal didn't look so sure. "Your parents, maybe. But the Mavericks?" He shook his head. "They're not going to like our being together—or my getting you pregnant—not one bit."

She lifted her hand to his cheek. "Don't worry, I'll talk them around. I'm good at that, remember?"

He smiled into her eyes. "You sure are. You have a particular knack for sweet-talking billionaires."

He leaned in, giving her a soft, deliciously sweet kiss.

Then they squared their shoulders and prepared to break the big news to her family.

★ ★ ★

Daniel finished a quick check of the household, making sure everything was in place, no tools left behind, every finishing nail concealed with putty, all excess tile grout wiped away.

He was about to enter the kitchen when he saw that Cal and Lyssa had arrived, their soft voices clearly audible in the empty house.

A word caught his attention, and though he shouldn't have, he listened.

"I'm sure some of my brothers will have a momentary freak-out when we tell them about us...and the baby."

His heart stopped beating entirely. Lyssa couldn't be saying what he thought she was saying. Could she?

What else could sound like the word *baby*?

Maybe it was something to do with the foundation. Yeah, they had to be talking about a huge donor. Or maybe one of Gideon's facilities. Or a social club for veterans.

But then Cal said, *"They're not going to like our being together—or my getting you pregnant—not one bit."*

The blood started to roar in Daniel's ears, rising to a crescendo when he saw Cal lean in close and kiss his baby sister.

That was when he knew for sure: Cal had seduced his sister and gotten her pregnant.

And Daniel was going to kill him.

* * *

Everyone was standing by the pool. Francine, Charlie's mom, had turned her walker around and was sitting on it, a beatific smile on her face. She loved being with family even if she lived in an extremely nice care facility.

"Can me and Jorge go swimming?" Noah asked his dad.

"We haven't heated the pool yet, guys. It's freezing in there. And it's not all that hot out today, even if the sun is shining."

It was warm in the December sun, but the shade was cool. Lyssa wore a fluffy sweatshirt.

Noah turned a pleading face to Ari as if he could get the answer he wanted from her. "What do you say, Mom?"

She ruffled his hair. "I say you should listen to your dad. That pool probably isn't even fifty-five degrees."

Lyssa was just wondering where Daniel was when the back door slammed open, banging on its hinges, and her brother barreled out.

He ran full tilt at Cal, shouting something Lyssa couldn't understand. Until Daniel's fist connected with Cal's face, and blood spurted from his nose.

"You got my little sister pregnant!" Daniel yelled.

He smashed his fist into Cal's shoulder, pushing him back. "Deny it, you asshole."

He landed another punch, this time to Cal's jaw, though Cal turned slightly, lessening the force of the blow.

"You can't deny it, can you, asshole? I heard what you said in the kitchen, and I saw you kiss her. Now you're going to pay for what you've done."

It all happened so fast no one had time to react. Especially when it was clear that no one could believe what Daniel was saying.

No one except Lyssa, who realized too late that Daniel must have been in the house and overheard their conversation. And as predicted, he'd gone crazy.

Then Cal was defending himself in any way he could. He'd let Daniel get in those first three punches, until he clearly couldn't take it anymore.

They went at it like two fighters in a ring, smashing their fists into each other, crushing, cracking, excruciating blows, punching each other onto the new grass, tearing out tufts of sod.

Good God. This was her brother. This was her lover. They'd been friends and co-workers for years. And now they were trying to kill each other. At least, Daniel was mauling Cal as if he wanted to destroy him.

Daniel dragged Cal up by his shirt and hit him full in the face again, but this time Cal hit back just as hard, splitting Daniel's lip, blood gushing. *Pow! Bam! Smash!*

With a huge splash, they stumbled into the pool, arms and legs flailing, both of them coming up spluttering and still throwing punches again and again.

"Somebody stop them!"

Even if it didn't feel like her mouth was moving, it was her voice. Lyssa was beyond scared, coming unhinged just like Cal and Daniel had.

Her father shouted, "Get the boys inside. Now!"

Will and Sebastian dived into the pool, each of them grabbing one of Daniel's arms. Gideon jumped in on the other side, getting his hands on Cal, keeping them apart.

"Sebastian and Will have them." Charlie folded Lyssa and Tasha into her arms.

She was surrounded by her family, her best friends, her loved ones, but terror clogged her throat. Her eyes seemed to bleed tears. The water in the pool was pink with fresh blood, floating out like a red sea.

Gideon hauled Cal to the other side of the pool, clearly trying to calm him down, while Cal's eyes searched the horrified crowd. Searching for *her*.

When he looked into her eyes, there was such pain and remorse in his gaze that it tore her apart. Blood dripped from his nose, his broken lip, the cuts on his face, and one eye was swelling shut.

On the other side of the pool, even with Will and Sebastian pinning him down, Daniel was still growling and shouting and struggling.

An arm slipped around her, and her mother's floral scent enveloped her. "Come with me, honey. You don't need to be here while they finish this. We need to talk."

Lyssa let herself be led away. The look in Cal's eyes had been so bleak, her own pain worse because she'd blown off his fears, saying the family would get over it, that they'd come around.

She'd been so wrong.

Chapter Twenty-Six

Cal ignored Gideon's outstretched hand as he climbed—every muscle screaming—up the shallow steps and out of the cold water.

Daniel's words pierced his gut: *You got my little sister pregnant... You asshole.*

Sebastian's voice rang out as the other guys hauled Daniel out of the pool. "We haven't seen action like that since we were fifteen years old."

"Well, none of you are fifteen anymore." Bob's voice was gruffer than Cal had ever heard it. "You're all going to hurt like hell in the morning."

Their voices echoed around Cal, but what stabbed him was the look on Lyssa's face. Pain, anger, anguish.

It was never supposed to be like this. The day she told her parents she was in love and pregnant should have been beautiful. It should have been a memory she would hold close to her heart forever.

Instead, she'd gotten mixed up with him, and that memory would forever be horrific.

Cal hadn't only let Lyssa down. He'd let the whole

clan down. He should have taken the beating he deserved without throwing a single punch.

And yet, as the hits had kept coming, he'd wanted to fight back—not just for himself, but for all the times Lyssa had felt as though her brothers hadn't respected or valued her.

Someone handed him a baggie of ice from the cooler, and he put it to his face. Water streamed from his clothes all over the pristine new deck.

Will turned to Cal and asked what they all wanted to know now that the fight was over—at least for the moment. "Is it true, Cal? Is Lyssa pregnant with your baby?"

He was glad Susan had taken Lyssa into the house. He didn't want her to see him face the Mavericks, the men he'd called friends for so many years. The men he'd let down.

Daniel's face was battered and bruised, and next to him, Will's features were stony, a dark flare of betrayal in his eyes as he waited for Cal to respond. Evan stared at him, his features bleak, clearly hoping it wasn't true. Matt's expression was that of a man seeing the real Cal Danniger for the very first time and sickened by the sight. Sebastian wore a grimace of disgust. Beside Matt, Gideon crossed his arms over his chest. All of them were waiting.

Cal couldn't bear to look at their loved ones, especially fragile Francine, gripping her walker, and Jeremy, his face stricken. He could only thank God that Rosie and Ari had spirited the boys away.

"Yes." The word gritted from his throat, raw from the punches Daniel had landed there. "We didn't mean for it to happen, but yes, Lyssa is having my child."

Sebastian growled, "What the hell were you thinking?"

Before he could reply, Matt barked, "She's twenty years younger than you!"

Evan's indictment was the worst. "She worked for you. She trusted you. *We* trusted you."

Cal's heart shrank to the size of a pea in his chest. His face ached along with his whole body, but it was nothing compared to the ache squeezing his heart.

There were so many reasons he could have given them. That he'd felt so drawn to Lyssa it had been impossible to turn away from her. That she was everything he'd ever wanted—bright, beautiful, sweet. That the baby was a dream come true.

Then Daniel dealt the blow that nearly brought him to his knees. "You're just like your father."

The words were garbled through Daniel's swollen lips, but they pierced Cal's soul.

The guys were the only people who knew the real story about his past. A story he'd told during nights of friendship, drinking a little too much, talking a little too much, telling them about his father and how he'd always made sure never to follow in good old Dad's footsteps. He'd refused to be a lawyer. And he'd certainly never messed around with his employees.

Until Lyssa.

Until he couldn't resist an affair with the gorgeous, beautiful, fabulous, amazing woman.

A woman who worked for him.

Then he'd gone a huge step further than his father.

He'd gotten his best friends' sister pregnant.

He wanted to apologize, to ask for forgiveness just the way his father had asked for forgiveness from him. Forgiveness he had never given. Forgiveness he'd refused to even consider giving.

Knowing how futile it was to say he was sorry, he told them the only thing that really mattered. "I'm in love with her. And I want our child. More than you can possibly know."

When he turned away—to the house, to find Lyssa—he heard Daniel spit on the ground behind him. Making it perfectly clear what they thought about the value of his love for their sister.

And making it equally clear that forgiveness would never be in the cards.

Cal had done the unforgivable.

He'd ruined their sister's life.

★ ★ ★

They'd known they'd have to face the music, as the old saying went, yet Lyssa had never imagined this—Cal's face broken, bloody, and swollen—and that the damage would be done by her own brother!

"Is it true, Lyssa?" Susan asked.

She turned to her mother. "Yes." She lifted her chin and pushed her shoulders back. "I'm having Cal's baby."

She spoke defiantly. Proudly. Her pregnancy might have been an accident, but during those beautiful, glorious, wonderful, amazingly fun days with Cal, she'd learned that he and the baby were the best things that had ever happened to her.

"We were going to tell everyone today, but Daniel must have overheard us talking in the kitchen."

"You work for him," her father said gently. "Please tell me he didn't—"

"God, no!" she exclaimed, jumping to Cal's defense. "Of course he didn't do anything wrong. He's not that kind of man. He's honorable. Everything that happened was mutual."

Suddenly, between her parents' stunned reactions and the threatening stances of her brothers all lined up against Cal, she was angry. *Beyond* angry. She'd hoped for so much more from them. Hoped they'd be happy for her. Hoped they'd know she was more than capable of taking care of herself, of fighting her own battles, if need be.

She pointed outside. "Look at them. All ganged up like this is some battle, them against him. Why can't anyone see this isn't just about Cal? It's like they think I had nothing to do with it. That I'm not strong enough or smart enough to make my own decisions." She turned to her parents. "And now, both of you in here, worrying that Cal took advantage of me." It was only by sheer force of will that she didn't crumble as she realized that all her fears about her family and what they thought of her were true.

"No, honey," her mother protested. "We're just surprised by the news, that's all."

But Lyssa wouldn't let her parents deny the truth anymore. "You still think I'm a little girl who needs to be protected. But I'm not. I'm a grown woman. I make my own decisions. Maybe I made a mistake, and I understand if you all need some time to process what happened, but that doesn't change the fact that all of you need to learn to *respect me.*"

"Is that what you really think, honey?" Her mother's features drooped in a profound sadness. "That your brothers, that your father and I don't respect you?"

Lyssa's throat clogged with emotion. "They still see me as the little sister they have to protect from the big bad world. As if I can't take care of myself. And you and Dad…yes, sometimes I'm afraid you don't know how capable I am."

"Oh, honey, that's never how we think of you." She threw her arms around Lyssa, hugged her tight. "We love you. We're so proud of everything you've accomplished. And we know you're capable of handling whatever life throws at you. Even this."

Lyssa stepped back. "Then why did you wait until I left Chicago before you decided to move out here?"

Her mother lifted her shoulders in a helpless shrug, shaking her head. "Because Chicago was our home, and we loved having you with us. But when you came out here, suddenly Chicago didn't seem like home anymore."

"And your brothers made it so easy for us to stay there," her dad explained. "They bought us the house. And your mom loves the white Christmases." He heaved a sigh, looking at Lyssa. "We love you, sweetheart. But we didn't come out here to look over your shoulder. We wanted to be here for Paige and Evan's baby, especially now that we know they're having twins."

Her mom cupped her cheek. "Forgive us. We never meant to make you feel incompetent. And we love you, more than words can say."

"Thank you for saying all of that." Then she and her mom were enveloped in one of her dad's big bear hugs.

Finally, her mother stepped back and wiped her eyes. "What about the baby, Lyssa? What are you going to do?"

Lyssa put a hand on her stomach and turned back to the window, as though looking for Cal was automatic and necessary. He was turning, his face bleak, and it wasn't just the pounding he'd taken. All the life seemed to have leached out of his features as he walked away from her brothers.

Gazing out at him, something tender broke open inside her. "I love him. And even though my pregnancy wasn't planned, we both want the baby. So very much."

"I'm so glad," her mother said, her father nodding beside her.

Lyssa gave her parents another hug, then said, "I'm glad you respect my decisions. But since my brothers clearly don't, I can't be around them right now. And I need to help Cal, so we're going to have to leave before I say or do something none of us can come back from."

The crush of that blow turned her mother's face pale. "We're family, honey. We'll always come back to each other, no matter what."

Normally, Lyssa would have believed that. But after what had happened out by the pool, she was no longer sure.

Chapter Twenty-Seven

Tasha took Daniel's hand, leading him to the house. "We need to clean you up."

His whole body was on fire, his mind still roiling. If Cal was still in the kitchen when he walked in, Daniel would go at him again. He wouldn't be able to stop himself.

"Those cuts need peroxide." Tasha bent close to examine his swollen eye. "Do you know if there's any here?"

He shook his head and realized his brain hurt. He didn't know how he looked, but if it was anything like Cal, he was a freaking mess.

As she wet a clean towel and dabbed his bloodied knuckles, Tasha asked, "What was that all about?"

Damn, it hurt, but he didn't complain.

"Didn't you hear? That asshole got my little sister pregnant." His voice was a rasp through his split lip. Even talking hurt. But not as much as knowing what Cal—a man he'd trusted with his life—had done with his sister. The one person he'd always made sure to keep safe from harm. Only to realize that he'd failed her by trusting the wrong man.

Her dark hair fell over her face, and he couldn't see her expression as she said, "Yes, we all heard. Cal and Lyssa are going to have a baby. But you lost your mind out there, Daniel."

As she worked on his hand, he almost welcomed the pain as if it were some sort of release.

"He deserved what he got." His voice was a low growl in his throat.

She looked up with despair in her blue eyes. Or maybe it was disappointment. "You could have really hurt him. Or yourself. Especially when you ended up in the water."

She was right. For those few minutes, Daniel had completely lost his mind. If Sebastian thought it had been like when they were fifteen, he got it wrong—this had been so much worse.

All Lyssa's life, he'd looked out for her, protected her from all the terrible things that lurked in the shitty neighborhood they'd lived in.

Then he got cocky, took his eye off the ball, thought she was safe with his friend Cal.

And Cal had done *that* to her. Instead of protecting Lyssa, it turned out that Daniel had handed her to the big bad wolf.

All the anger, all the insanity welled up inside him again. "You don't get it," he snapped. "She's my baby sister. It's always been my job to take care of her. I mean, we *asked* him to give her that job because we thought she'd be safe. And look what he did. He took advantage of his position. He took advantage of *her!*"

Tasha stared at him as if she didn't even know him. "Do you even hear yourself? The idea that you asked Cal to give her that job is nuts. It's like you think you have the right to manipulate her life."

He shook his head, releasing another spike of pain. "We've always taken care of Lyssa. And we always will."

She made a sound of disgust. "I can't believe I need to tell you this, when you should be able to see it with your own eyes, but you don't need to take care of her anymore."

He growled, "You don't get it."

"Of course I do. You're her big brother. You love her. But *you* don't get that she's an adult now. She can do whatever she wants with her own life."

"Well, he's damn well gonna marry her." Although the thought of having Cal as his brother-in-law made him see red all over again.

She wiped at the blood on his chin with a little more force than before, and he winced.

"What century is this? Whether or not they get married is up to them. And so is where they want their relationship to go. Lyssa is perfectly capable of being a single mom if that's what she chooses. I get that protecting her was your job when she was a kid," Tasha went on, torturing him with her cleanup methods, torturing him even more with her words. "But you need to get that she can make her own choices." She tipped his chin, making sure he was looking at her, even if he could see her beautiful face out of only one eye. "Lyssa is a funny, smart, amazing woman."

He opened his eye wide enough to see her undistorted. Every time he looked at Tasha, he fell more deeply in love with her.

For one second, he wondered if that was how Cal felt about Lyssa. And for that same brief second, he hoped it was. Until instinctive, protective fury rose up in him again.

"And," Tasha added as if he needed another *and*, "she sure as hell doesn't need you beating up her boyfriend because you think he stepped out of line by falling in love with her."

He heard footsteps in the living room over the ringing in his ears.

"Oh good, Susan," Tasha said to his mother. "I'm glad you're here. I've just had round one with Daniel over his behavior. He's all yours now for rounds two through nine."

With that, his fiancée walked away and left him at the mercy of his mom.

Out of his one good eye, Daniel made out her flushed face, the rigid set of her jaw, and the anguish in her eyes. She'd always been formidable. Even now, with her cap of steel-gray hair, she was fearsome to behold.

He tried to remember when he'd seen her this angry. Probably the last time he'd gotten in a fight. Although this fight had been far worse than any he'd ever had. He understood that, even if he felt that avenging his sister had been justified.

She glared at him, standing close enough for him to see how wide her pupils were, her lips pressed into an uncompromising line, and every muscle in her body tensed.

"Your behavior was unacceptable on every level." Each word seemed to be its own separate, furious, disappointed sentence. "Not only did you step over every possible line with a man you've always called your friend and upset your sister right when she needs you most, but you also traumatized two little boys. Right now, back in the bedroom, their mothers are trying to calm them down."

Okay, that was bad. He'd forgotten all about Noah and Jorge. The rage had risen up to cloud his vision before he could stop it.

"I raised you to be better than this. I don't care what you think of what Lyssa or Cal has done." She stepped closer, and the look in her eyes made him flinch and nearly take a step back. "You have the right to your own emotions, Daniel, but what you did out there is beyond protectiveness. It's just plain *idiocy*." That word was as close as she'd ever come to swearing, because she was too kind to ever call anyone an idiot. Until now. "You owe Lyssa an apology. And you most definitely owe Cal an apology. You owe *everyone* an apology."

It was on the tip of his tongue to say he'd go to hell before he'd ever apologize to Cal Danniger.

But his mother glowered at him, clearly reading his mind. "Don't you dare say it, Daniel." Then her tone softened, saddened. "I'm so disappointed in you."

For the second time, he felt that spike of pain, just as he had when he'd seen the disillusioned look in Tasha's eyes. His mother's words made him feel…

Ashamed. He felt ashamed, despite the righteous fury still roiling in his chest.

The back door opened, and all the Mavericks stomped in.

His mom turned on them. "I thought I'd seen you all at your worst, but this takes the cake. I told Daniel, and I'll tell you too. I'm beyond disappointed in your behavior. And you all owe Lyssa an apology."

"But we broke up the fight, Mom," Will said.

She rounded on him. "I cannot believe you're trying to weasel out of what you did. You might have broken up the fistfight, but you all tried to break Cal down with your words. I never thought the day would come when I would be this upset with all of you."

Their wonderful, warm, loving mother all but growled the words. "I want an apology to your sister and Cal, do you hear me?" She flashed them all a glare like Daniel had never seen as she added, "This is your sister's *life*. None of you have the right to step into the middle of it. Just like she never stepped into the middle of any of your relationships. She respected you and your choices the way you'd better start respecting her and her choices."

With that, she spun on her heel, leaving her sons gaping after her.

And feeling like they were the lowest of the low.

Because deep in their hearts, no matter how much they tried to justify what they'd done, they knew she was right.

Chapter Twenty-Eight

With Cal's eye swollen shut, Lyssa had taken the keys to his car. He didn't say a word on the long drive from Portola Valley to San Francisco. It was a beautiful, sunny Saturday afternoon, even if it was cool, and the traffic into the city was horrendous as they headed toward her apartment.

She sensed every muscle in his body shutting down, every pore closing up, shutting her out. Suddenly, they were right back where they'd been when he'd run away from Catalina, with Cal holed up inside himself.

Finally, she couldn't stand the silence another minute. "I'm sorry for what Daniel did."

They'd crawled another quarter mile before he answered. "He was right to do it."

She whipped her head to the side to look at him. "Are you kidding me? How could he possibly have been right to attack you like that?"

"They only want what's best for you," he said with a lisp through his cut lip. "And they're right that I'm not good enough for you. They're right that I never should have touched you. They're right that I've derailed your whole life."

Lyssa couldn't believe what he was saying. It was as if their glorious road trip had never happened, as if they'd never confessed their love, as if they'd never lain on the beach in each other's arms and exchanged what she'd felt were vows.

Was he suddenly rethinking everything, the baby, wanting to be a family with her?

When he'd finally opened up to her about his past, she'd believed they could deal with anything that came their way from now on openly and honestly. Was she wrong about everything?

Scared and mad and confused all at the same time, she pulled up outside her building, her voice sharp as she said, "You need the blood cleaned off your face. Come inside."

In her apartment, she had Cal sit down on a kitchen chair. Retrieving the first aid kit from under the kitchen sink, she grabbed a bag of frozen peas and wrapped it in a towel. "Hold this on your eye." Then she went to work on his cuts and bruises. "You probably think I should be grateful that you defended my honor, or whatever the hell you thought you were doing."

He shook his head, wincing as she hit a tender spot. "I wasn't being chivalrous. I got you pregnant. I deserved every punch Daniel threw at me."

"*We* got me pregnant, Cal. We did that *together*."

"I'm older. I'm your boss. I didn't do right by you. I should have known better."

She let out a long, incredulous breath. "You were the one person who treated me like I could take care of myself," she said in a low voice full of all the anguish and loss his words punched out of her. He was repeating all the same arguments he'd had in the beginning. "The one person who respected me to make my own decisions." And now, he was acting like their relationship had never been anything but a one-way street. Whatever lines had been crossed, they'd *both* crossed them. And it was good, it was love, it was everything.

Over the last three days, she'd been planning how to rearrange his home for the baby. And for her. Her apartment was the size of a postage stamp. The bedroom barely fit her bed, let alone all the things a baby would need. But in her heart, moving in with Cal—living with him, making love with him, sleeping with him, waking up with him—was the only thing she wanted. She'd never wanted anything more.

Until that damned terrible fight changed everything all over again.

She wanted to shout and scream and break something. Except that her brothers and Cal had already done that, and the fight, the violence, the anger had all been wrong. So very wrong.

She refused to make that same mistake herself,

clenching her teeth to stop herself from hurling angry, bitter, unforgivable words at Cal as she cleaned his face, his cuts, his bruises, his hands.

She'd nearly finished when the downstairs buzzer rang. Assuming it was one of the girls coming to check on her—she and Cal had left before they'd had a chance to talk with anyone but her parents—she pressed the buzzer. "Hello?"

"Honey, can you let me in?"

Her mother. They'd already spoken about Cal and the baby. But Lyssa wanted, *needed* her comforting presence again. Especially when it felt like her entire world had slid off its axis.

As she buzzed her in, Cal finally spoke again. "I won't leave you to deal with this on your own."

"I've already spoken with my parents." Which he would have known if he'd been able to communicate like a normal human being during the past hour, instead of a self-recriminating idiot. "There's nothing to *deal* with."

Her mother rapped on the door, and Lyssa was surprised to see she was alone.

"Where's Dad?"

"I wanted to speak with you on my own." She actually smiled at Cal. "I'm not sure who looks worse, you or Daniel."

Even with the swelling and cuts and bruises, Lyssa saw the heat rise in his face as he stood politely. "I apologize for ruining your housewarming party, Susan. And I'm sorry I hurt your son."

Without even a moment's hesitation, Susan crossed the kitchen and took the big man in her arms. Then, stepping back, she held him at arm's length, surveying the damage. "It's not the first time passions have run high in my house. And I'm sure it won't be the last." She started to pat his cheek, thought better of it, and patted his shoulder instead. "Now, I wonder if I can have a bit of time alone with my daughter?"

Nodding, he said to Lyssa, "Could you walk me to the door?"

"I'll just make some tea," her mother said, giving them privacy.

Lyssa had a bad feeling about what Cal intended to say. In a low voice her mother wouldn't overhear, she said, "You're running again, aren't you?"

She couldn't read his expression, and it wasn't just the bruises on his face or the swollen eye. "I have some thinking to do." He spoke just as softly. "And you need room to think too."

"Don't tell me what I need." She narrowed her eyes. "If you want to go, go. But don't you *dare* try to make it about me. This is all you, Cal." She took a breath so deep, it shook her chest. "I've made it clear to you in a million ways that I know you're a good man. A wonderful man. I accept you just the way you are and love you for the man you are. But if you can't believe it, then it doesn't matter what I think or how many times I say I love you."

He stared at her for a long moment, started to reach for her. But before he made contact, he pulled his hand back. "You need your rest, especially after today. I'll be bad company, so I'll stay at my place tonight."

She refused to let him see how badly he'd hurt her once again. Far worse than the blows he'd landed on her brother. "Do whatever you need to do," she said. Then she turned and walked away from him. If he wanted to leave so badly, he could let himself out.

Crushed by his behavior, Lyssa was happier than ever that her mother had come. Along with two cups of tea, she'd put out some cheese she'd found in the fridge, as well as some crackers and cookies from the pantry.

"Sit, honey. Eat. I figured you might be hungry, since you didn't get to eat at the party."

Despite the ache in her chest, Lyssa realized she was starving. "This is great, Mom." Her voice felt wobbly despite her best efforts.

Of course, Susan picked up on her distress right away and opened her arms. Lyssa sank into the warmth of her mother's embrace.

They finally broke apart, sitting down at the tiny dining table. "I'm so glad you're here, Mom. Your hug was just what I needed."

"I needed it too, honey." Her mother, who was

never a nervous fidget, seemed to fidget a little. "I want you to know that after you left, I had a talk with the boys and let them know how disappointed I am in their behavior. We taught them a long time ago that fists don't solve anything. I don't believe Cal intended to hit your brother back, but it was self-defense on his part, pure and simple." Her mouth was set in a firm line as she spoke of her sons, so different from the way they usually made her smile. "I also told them they should be happy that you'd found a man who's your equal in heart and mind. He laughs with you and respects you. And he looks at you as if you're the most precious jewel in the whole world."

A sweet shiver coursed through her at her mother's words. Still… "How can you say that when you just saw him leave that way?" So distant, so disconnected. "After what Daniel did and what the others said to him, he told me that he needs some time to think. Time away from me." She blinked away the tears that threatened.

Her mother put a hand over hers. "Over the years, your father and I have sometimes needed to take a few hours, or even a couple of days, to process big events and emotions. But it doesn't mean we love each other any less." She squeezed Lyssa's hand and gave a little sigh. "In fact, this is a good time for me to tell you my secret. A secret I should have told you a long time ago. You're not the only woman who's had an accidental pregnancy, honey. It happened to me too."

Chapter Twenty-Nine

Lyssa blinked at her mother, beyond stunned, but trying to come up to speed. "Are you saying you were already pregnant when you married Dad?"

Her mother nodded. "Although it wasn't quite that clear cut." She sipped her tea as if she needed something to do. "As soon as I found out I was going to have a baby, I left your father."

"You left Dad?" Lyssa felt her world turn completely upside down. Her parents were the perfect couple. She couldn't imagine a world in which they would ever break up—not then, not now, not ever.

"I wanted him to have the life he'd dreamed of," her mother explained. "I wanted him to have the chance to go to college and forge a better path. I didn't want to saddle him with a child he hadn't planned on. I intended to keep Daniel, no matter what, and letting your dad go his own way felt like the best choice for everyone." She gave a small smile. "Or so I thought at the time."

Lyssa tried not to gape at her mother, although she

wasn't succeeding in the slightest. It was the oddest thing, suddenly seeing her parents as people with a history so different than she could ever have imagined.

"But in the end, you did marry him."

Her mother's eyes filled with lightness and love. "Your father wouldn't let me go, no matter now noble I thought I was being in setting him free. And he wanted the baby, too, just as much as I did. We chose that special path instead of the one we'd planned." Her smile widened, a sunbeam on her face. "Neither of us has ever regretted our decision to be together and start a family on an accelerated schedule." Her mom put her hand, still warm from the mug, over Lyssa's. "So you see, I would never judge you for loving someone and having a child with him, even if it wasn't intended."

Lyssa blinked back tears. "But what if I'm judging myself?" she asked very softly.

Her mother's arms came around her. "All of us make mistakes, honey. We're all beautiful and flawed at the same time. But deep down in our bones, we always know what the best thing is, the right decision to make. You're a smart, loving, caring, loyal woman. You've worked hard, and you have a bright future ahead of you. I promise you, this baby will only make your life brighter." But her mom frowned. "I know you're upset with your brothers for babying you, for not seeing you as an adult and always thinking they have to protect you. But it was your father—and especially me—" She put a hand to her chest. "—who started it." Before Lyssa could protest, Susan said, "When you were a little girl, I always told them, 'Take care of your little sister. She's your responsibility too.' You were so sweet and so young, and all we wanted was to keep you safe and well. But I see now that we never stopped trying to protect you, even when you were so clearly capable of taking care of yourself. And that was both wrong and unfair to you. I hope you can forgive all of us." A sheen of tears misted her mother's eyes. "I hope you can forgive *me*."

"Mom," Lyssa protested. "There's nothing to forgive."

"We both know there is," Susan said softly. "What I really came to say, honey, is that I'm so proud of you. You've grown into exactly the kind of woman I always knew you would be. You're going to be a wonderful mother. And Cal is going to be a wonderful father. Whatever you decide about your relationship and your future, your father and I support you one hundred percent."

Lyssa threw her arms around her mother for a long, tight, heartfelt hug. "Thank you for sharing your story, Mom. I love you."

"I love you too, honey."

Her heart felt full to the brim, and she absolutely had to share. "Would you like to see the sonogram?"

Her mother gasped, hands to her chest, eyes shiny

with tears and love and hope. "More than anything."

Lyssa pulled out her phone. "I was planning to show it to everybody after we told you all about the baby. But then…" Pushing away the painful memories of how wrong everything had gone at the housewarming-party-that-wasn't, she handed the phone to her mother, who held it reverently in her palm, touching a finger to the tiny form.

Tears streamed down Susan's face. "Oh my. He or she is already so beautiful." She sniffed, dabbing at her eyes. "I can't wait to hold the baby in my arms."

"Me too." Lyssa grabbed a box of tissues off the counter.

After wiping her eyes and blowing her nose, Susan asked, "How have you been feeling? Give me all the details."

"You won't believe it, but I don't feel sick at all. My mind is so sharp, and I feel energized instead of tired."

Susan's smile was as wide as her love. "You're exactly like me. I never felt any morning sickness. Although I did occasionally have what your dad called 'foggy baby brain' and I forgot things."

They chatted awhile longer, comparing notes, and right before her mother left, she said, "Everything is going to work out, honey. I know it will."

As she kissed her mom good-bye and closed the door, Lyssa wished she could be as sure. Especially since Cal hadn't texted or called or even emailed to say good night. She hadn't heard a single ping. She even checked her phone just in case she'd missed the sound. Nothing.

He loved her. She knew he did. She felt it in his touch, in his kiss, heard it in his voice, in his words. So what the heck was going on? Okay, she knew it had to do with his past. But she thought they'd talked that through.

Men. They were so damned complicated. Cal more than most.

And she was suddenly so exhausted, she collapsed in her bed without even washing her face.

She was awakened by the ding of an incoming text, and her heart leaped as she thought it might be Cal. She grabbed her phone.

But it was Kelsey.

She swallowed her disappointment. He was *still* acting like a lone wolf. What on earth would it take for him to realize it didn't have to be that way anymore? They were meant to be together, no matter how difficult her brothers might try to make it.

She read Kelsey's short message.

We're coming to take you out for brunch. After what happened yesterday, we need some woman power and bonding. You have fifteen minutes to get ready.

Good Lord, it was morning. She hadn't woken even once.

After jumping out of bed and taking the world's quickest shower, then throwing on a stretchy wrap dress, Lyssa heard the honk of Ari's minivan out front. It did her heart so much good to see the whole assembly of Maverick ladies, including Chi, as she squished into the backseat.

Next to her, Kelsey said, "We invited your mom too, but she said she'd talked to you yesterday, and she thought you needed the younger generation's perspective."

"Not that your mom doesn't always have great advice," Harper said.

Harper didn't know how right she was. Lyssa had a whole new vision of her mother after yesterday's revelation. She'd been in almost exactly Lyssa's position. Except for the brothers.

"She sure lit into Daniel yesterday," Tasha told her.

"She lit into *all* of them," Charlie confirmed.

"And every single one of them deserved it," Ari agreed as she drove down the steep hill. "We've got a reservation at that fancy tearoom on Union Square. We're going to eat tiny sandwiches and cakes until we pop." And she beamed.

Rosie leaned forward to see around Kelsey. "Gideon apologizes for not stepping in sooner, but we were all so stunned by how quickly it went down and spiraled out of control."

"I appreciate what he did," Lyssa said. "Are the

boys okay?"

Rosie nodded. "We had to explain to them that fighting wasn't the way to resolve an argument. But they're fine."

Ari found space in the underground parking, and ten minutes later, they were seated around the table with pots of tea already steaming.

"Let's get the deluxe," Tasha said. "Daniel can pay the bill for all the trouble he caused."

Harper added, "Will deserves to pay part of it, too, for the things he said to Cal."

"They all do," Ari added.

"At least he jumped in the water to pull them apart," Paige said. "Evan just wrapped himself around me as if he thought I'd be injured in the flinging of limbs and fists."

"He was right to watch out for you," Ari said. "Those guys were crazy. Who knows what would've happened if one of us had gotten in the middle of it?" Her eyes were wide, her tone harsh.

"I appreciate that Sebastian jumped in," Charlie said. "But I'm still angry with him for the way he lashed out at Cal afterward."

"Suffice it to say," Kelsey said, "all of the men are in the doghouse right now. Even Tony. I can't believe he got into it too."

Chi coughed dramatically. "I agree they shouldn't have done it, but you have to admit that was one hell of a fight. Cal might be ten years older, but he sure as heck held his own."

Her words seemed to ease all the tension, and suddenly they were laughing. It felt so good to laugh. As though her worries, her fears, her anger were finally lifting away.

"How is Cal?" Tasha asked. "He looked pretty bad."

"No worse than Daniel," Ari proclaimed.

"He deserved it," Tasha huffed. "But Cal was defending you." She held Lyssa's gaze. "He really cares about you."

Lyssa felt speechless and more than a little teary-eyed at the support of such wonderful, amazing women. "Thank you," she said, her lip trembling.

"Oh, Lyssa." Kelsey wrapped her arm around Lyssa's shoulders. "It's going to be okay. You and Cal will figure it out, and the boys will get over it, and we'll all be one big, happy family again. Very soon. We're all here for you."

"I'm not crying about my brothers or Cal or how we're going to resolve everything that's gone so wrong." Her voice was shaky. "It's that I'm so glad I have all of you as my family and my friends and my soul sisters. You're the absolute best."

And just like the soul sisters they were, they didn't push her about her plans with Cal. They didn't bombard her with opinions on what she should do. They simply ate sandwiches and cake and took a few precious moments to relax together.

When they were stuffed to the gills, Lyssa asked, "Do you want to see the sonogram?" She dug in her purse for her phone, and everyone wooted with joy.

"I'm so glad we're pregnant at the same time," Paige said, her eyes shining.

Lyssa reached across the table to hold tight to Paige's hand. "Me too." Then she laughed, feeling a sudden joy. "Anyone else who wants to join us in this baby-making thing is absolutely welcome."

Ari winked, Rosie smiled...and was that a sparkle in Harper's eyes?

They were a club, they were family, they were Mavericks. They supported each other, and they'd support her no matter what happened with Cal.

Their love gave her the strength to know *exactly* what she had to do.

Chapter Thirty

Cal hadn't been able to sleep since the moment he'd left Lyssa. He'd worn a path in the carpet, pacing back and forth all night and on through the sunrise. He wanted to call her. He wanted to rush back to her apartment.

But he knew it was futile if he couldn't change. It was the only way he could ever have her back.

He'd been like this since his father had blown the family sky high. They'd never been able to put the pieces back together. At that point, Cal's life had become all about books and spreadsheets and business mergers. If he had a problem, he tackled it by learning, gaining knowledge, analyzing all the angles, working through every possible solution. Thinking his way through, never feeling his way. And in all that, he'd forgotten how to feel with his heart. His decisions were based on logic and ethics, not on what his heart felt. He'd never actually let his heart *feel*.

Until Lyssa.

But even with her, he'd let his fears and his demons

rise up over everything, even his heart.

He finally threw himself on the couch, scraping his hands through his hair, his bruised fingers aching, his head throbbing. Outside, the sun had climbed higher and higher in the sky. Time was running out.

And his demons were still running amok.

The only way he'd win her back was by facing down those damn demons. By facing what his father had done. By facing how he himself had dealt with it in the aftermath.

There was a box somewhere. In a closet? In a drawer? In a filing cabinet?

He found what he was looking for in a folder filed under *F* for Father. Or *F* for Failure. Or maybe it was for Family.

He didn't look inside the folder until he was seated once more on the couch. Then he opened it slowly, so slowly, as though whatever was inside could mortally wound him.

The first was a Polaroid of his parents. His mother had the big hair of the early eighties, and his dad was still wearing glasses. They were laughing.

He spread the rest of the photos across the coffee table. He found another Polaroid of the family in which he'd been six or seven. And he saw the happiness shining on their faces, especially his.

The Polaroids gave way to printed pictures, and somewhere around the beginning of his teens, the faces changed. There were fewer photos of them all, more of him with just his mom or his dad, and their faces were grimmer, their smiles smaller. Especially his mother, as if she'd begun to lose her joy in life. And his dad just started to look old.

He'd always thought his father's defection had been a surprise, something out of the blue, but he could see here, in these pictures, that it had been coming for a while. Years.

He picked up a photo of himself and his dad that someone had taken on one of their fishing trips when he was maybe thirteen or so. He wore a toothy grin, holding up a string of fish, his dad's arm around him. Examining it for a long time, he noticed the grooves around his father's mouth, the shadow in his eyes, the smile that didn't look completely real, as if he were putting on a good face for his son.

"What happened, Dad?" he asked the two-dimensional image. "Why did you want to leave us?"

The image had no answers. But for the first time, Cal wondered if he might finally have an inkling. He'd always seen his dad as the bad guy, a terrible human being who'd deserted his marriage and his family, a man who would coerce a much younger subordinate. But that wasn't the man in the photo. This man was just…sad. And trying to put on a happy face for his kid.

"Were you just lonely and unhappy, Dad? Is that why you did it?"

He'd been so hurt and angry that he hadn't wanted to look at the reasons why. He'd just wanted to blame his dad for everything, the way his mom had. He'd demonized his father. Cal had wanted to be a lawyer just like him, then suddenly, he'd hated the very idea of doing anything his dad had done.

But maybe there was another side. Maybe his dad wasn't a terrible man, just a man who'd made a mistake. He'd wanted to come back after his girlfriend left him, but Cal's mother had slammed the door in his face. Cal's father had never recovered—not from the affair, not from the divorce, not from his wife's wrath. He'd died of a heart attack.

Or maybe it was a broken heart.

"I don't condone what you did," he said softly, as if his father were sitting on the couch beside him. "But I can't hate you anymore. I know the power of love now, and maybe you did too. Maybe you really did love that woman. Maybe you thought she was the answer to your unhappiness. I'm sorry you were so broken. I'm sorry you were so sad. I'm sorry for the shitty things I said to you." He looked up as if he could see his dad. "You wanted me to forgive you, and I refused. I know it's late coming, but I do now, Dad. I realize now that you were just a man doing the best you could, and you screwed up. But I forgive you. And I hope you can forgive me for the pain I caused too."

Cal had spent his life trying never to make an emotional mistake, trying never to follow in his father's footsteps. And in his fear of being like his father, he'd never listened to his heart. He'd allowed himself to wound Lyssa, the woman he truly loved with all his heart.

"I love you, Dad," he whispered, hoping his father would finally hear him.

And when he dropped the photo back on the table, it landed beside one of his mom. Before the divorce. Before the affair. Even then, her eyes mirrored his father's misery.

"I wish I could have done something for you, Mom. Helped you with the pain, before and even more after. I'm so sorry I didn't see until it was too late. Not that I could have done anything except be there for you." Instead, he could only be there as the cancer ate her up, hold her hand, tell her he loved her. "I hope you're at peace now."

He understood the power of love now. *Love heals, love saves, love is strength.*

And he'd almost thrown Lyssa's love away. He understood, too, why Daniel's words had sliced him into a thousand pieces. Because he'd always believed he was capable of the worst things his father had done. And now he saw that he *was* like his father—a man who could make mistakes. But he was also a man who could admit when he was wrong. He hadn't given love enough credit. He hadn't given *Lyssa* enough credit.

And he had to tell her, right now, this minute. Where the hell was his phone?

His doorbell chimed. Praying that just thinking of Lyssa had called her to him, he all but ran for the door.

And there she was, beautiful and sweet and everything he could ever want.

He wanted to stroke her cheek, but he didn't, not yet. "How did you know I was thinking about you and wishing you were here?"

The hint of a smile lifted her lips. "It's our connection, Cal. It's so strong that nothing can ever break it." She reached for his hand. "Or us." She raised an eyebrow. "Even when you act like an idiot over and over again."

He dragged her into his arms. "Thank God you're not going to kick me to the curb." Drawing back, he drank in her beautiful face. "Even though we both know I deserve it."

She didn't say anything to that, simply raised her hand to his battered face. "Why don't you let me inside and tell me what's going around and around inside that big, brilliant head of yours? That is, if you're ready to talk."

"I am. Beyond ready. I know I shouldn't have left again, but it turns out there was something I really needed to do, even though I hadn't realized it yet."

She came inside and stopped at the sight of the old photos spread across the coffee table. Then she reached for one, lifted it, a Polaroid that had gone a little blurry with age. "Is this your mother and father? And you as a little boy?"

He nodded, an ache tightening his chest. "I've hidden my past away for too long. Not only from you, but also from myself." He drew her down to the couch with him. "I told you about what my father did, but I didn't tell you how much I worried about becoming like him. I didn't tell you how I vowed never to be a liar like he was, never to do the awful things he did. And that vow has shaped my life for the past thirty years." He dragged in a breath, let it out. "After your brother called me out for sleeping with you—a woman who was not only my friend, but also my employee, and twenty years my junior—he tapped right into the part of me that's always been afraid I'd end up being just like my father. A man who was capable of harassing someone he worked with."

"Cal, you didn't harass me."

"I know that now, and I know for sure that what we did was mutual. Just as I've finally come to understand that my father didn't harass his secretary either. He truly loved her, and that's why he left my mother and me. I never even tried to understand his reasons for breaking my trust and my mother's heart in such a terrible way. Because I never wanted to accept that love had anything to do with it."

He held out his hand, and when Lyssa curled her

fingers around his, he didn't even feel the ache of his bruised knuckles. There was only her warmth, her love.

"He was never the same after that," he told her. "Neither was my mother. And the ironic twist is that once he confessed and blew apart our family, the secretary left him, telling him she'd never had any intention of living the rest of her life with an old man. I'm not sure what killed him—losing her or his family or his self-respect—but he died of a heart attack not long after that. And then cancer took my mother, the bitterness eating her up inside until there was nothing left of her."

"I'm so sorry for all the pain you and your family went through," she said softly. "But I still can't help but wonder if your father was really a bad man, or if he was just a man who made a mistake, a big one, falling in love when he shouldn't have, and with the wrong woman who didn't care about him. His actions destroyed your family, Cal, but I can't believe he ever stopped loving you."

He nodded, leaning down to kiss the back of her hand. "You've just said everything I realized last night." He laughed softly. "More like this morning."

"I know it without a doubt," she said. "How could anyone stop loving you?" He was still reeling from the wonder of her words when she added, "Maybe it's time you forgave him. Once you do, you can stop worrying that being like him is a bad thing, or that you won't be a good father. Especially when I know for certain you're going to be the best father ever."

He breathed in deeply, as if he could breathe in her belief in him. "How can you know that for sure?"

"Because you're the first person who really saw *me*." She fisted her hand against her chest. "You believed in me before anyone else did, even my parents and brothers. That's what you'll give our child, Cal. Unconditional love and support, and the belief that they can do anything."

He shook his head slightly. She was twenty years younger and twenty times smarter than he was.

"What you see so clearly is something I understood for the first time only in the last few hours. I realized it was finally time to end the pain, once and for all. To make peace with my parents and the past." He gave her a small smile. "I actually have to thank Daniel for what he did. The moment he started whaling on me, it highlighted the way I instinctively assume my father's mantle of guilt and succumb to the subconscious fear I've lived with all my life. All along, I've secretly believed that, given the chance, I'd end up being just like him." He shook his head. "I don't know if it was getting hit over the head so many times that finally knocked some sense loose, but I finally see that I can no longer base all my decisions on what my father did or on what I thought was behind his actions. It was so automatic to think the worst on all counts—of him and myself."

Her gaze held his, and the love in her eyes made him lose his breath. "I know you're a good man, Cal. An honorable man who would never leave me high and dry. Even if I didn't want to have a relationship, you would always be there for our child."

"You still believe that even after I betrayed you by running away? Not just once, not just twice, but all over again last night?" His voice cracked with emotion.

She smoothed her fingers across his bruised and scraped knuckles. "Everyone has a little wobble. Or lots of little wobbles," she amended with a tiny smile. "And it didn't help that throughout those early weeks, I kept insisting it was just sex, when the truth is that what we did was *never* just sex. That's not who I am—I would never sleep with a casual stranger. But even though being with you meant so much, I was afraid to admit it."

"You're not afraid of *anything*, Lyssa. It took a hell of a lot of guts to confront me on Catalina. And even more to go all the way to the Caribbean to tell me about our baby."

"And it took guts for you to finally forgive your father, after all these years."

"I finally listened to my heart, and I understood he wasn't a bad man. He was a good father. He just made a bad mistake. Maybe because he was already unhappy.

I don't know. But I had to forgive him. Or I was going to lose you. That's the worst thing that could ever happen."

"You're not going to lose me, Cal. No matter how wrong you might get things sometimes. I get things wrong too. It's called being human. And that's what unconditional love is all about—not just loving despite people's imperfections, but loving them *for* their imperfections."

He slipped his hand beneath the fall of her hair. "What could I possibly have done to deserve you?"

"All you ever needed to do was be yourself. Right, wrong, confident, scared, strong, shaky. You're perfect just the way you are, Cal. Perfect for me."

"So are you, Lyssa. Perfect just the way you are, and perfect for me." He pulled her into his lap and held her tight despite the ache in his ribs. "When I left you after London, I was running from my feelings. But they never changed, even when I wasn't near you. I thought you were the one woman I could never have, the Mavericks' younger sister I could never dare touch. Never dare admit how much I cared for—beyond friends, beyond co-workers." He put his hand to her cheek. "But I don't care how off-limits you are. I don't care if Daniel beats the crap out of me every day, or if your brothers never speak to me again. You are the only woman for me. And if that's what it takes, I will happily brave your brothers' wrath forever to be with you."

She wrapped her arms around his neck. "Will you marry me, Cal Danniger?"

His heart swelled a million times bigger in his chest. "There's nothing I've ever wanted more."

Chapter Thirty-One

It was more than he could ever have dreamed of, that this beautiful, amazing woman would love him, that she would brave the Mavericks' disapproval to be with him. Lyssa would not only be the mother of his child, but also his lover, his wife, his everything. And there was no question that he would ever betray her the way his father had betrayed his family.

He pulled her right next to his heart. "I fell in love with you that unforgettable night we danced on the London Eye. I was already falling before, even if I couldn't admit it to myself, but with you in my arms that night, I was lost."

"Maybe you were found," she said, her eyes shining. "Because I'm pretty sure I fell in love with you at Matt and Ari's wedding, when I told the girls you had my name written all over you in lipstick."

He laughed. "You told them that, huh?"

"I did," she said with a nod. "Except I couldn't admit to myself I was falling for you either."

He couldn't keep his hands off her for another

moment, pulling her close until their lips met. For the first time, he kissed the woman he was going to marry.

She tasted so sweet and fit against him so perfectly that he barely felt the pain of his split lip or his swollen eye or his bruised ribs.

"Have you ever seen my bedroom?" he asked.

"Not yet. Is today my lucky day?"

"It's *my* lucky day." He led her down the hall to his big bed. On another day, he'd carry her, but his ribs weren't up to it right now. "Although I do believe I'll always be partial to Wild Bill McCutchen's big brass bed."

She laughed the way he hoped she would for the rest of their lives. "Do you have any idea how much I love you?"

She was still laughing when she climbed onto his bed, tugged her shirt over her head, and popped the snaps on her jeans. All that sweet, smooth, tasty skin was a feast before his one fully open eye. He wanted her so badly that his heart ached.

As he crawled over her, she put a hand to his face, stroked his broken lip, beneath the tender skin of his eye. "Are you sure you're up to this?"

"Nothing could tear me away from you. Especially not a few cuts and bruises." He shrugged out of his shirt and jeans, throwing them on the floor on top of hers. Any ache or pain would be worth having her in his arms.

She lay there, gorgeous in a skimpy bra and panties. He wanted to eat her up, but she got to him first, tracing her fingers over the bruises on his chest and abdomen, her touch easing away any ache.

"Have I ever told you how sexy those boxer briefs are on you? Tight in all the right places."

Her words, her touch, her eyes on him, made the ache coil tighter inside him. She tugged on his briefs, set him free, and suddenly she was sliding him into her mouth.

There had never been anything like Lyssa's mouth on him. She toyed with him, pushing him to the edge of ecstasy, then pulling back, only to drive him wild again with her hands and her lips and her tongue.

"You make me crazy." His voice was a harsh rasp. "But I need to be inside you."

She looked up at him, her eyes sparkling. "I've heard older men can keep going for a very long time."

God, she made him laugh. And groan with pleasure. "If you're laying down the challenge, I can promise you, I'm up for it. Five, ten, fifteen times. However many orgasms you need, I'll give them to you."

"Go ahead," she teased, throwing herself back against the pillows. "I'm counting."

He fell on her, snapping the clasp on her bra. As the lace fell away, she arched, begging for his kiss on the tips. He sucked her into his mouth, making her shiver with pleasure.

"Mmmm, you are definitely on the right track."

He trailed kisses down her abdomen, over the slight swell of her belly where their baby grew, their miracle child, everything he'd ever wanted. Then he moved down between her legs and made love to her with his mouth, kissed her, licked her, touched her, stroked her, and entered her with his fingers. Until she shuddered and cried out and clenched around him.

Crawling back up, he said "Number one," kissing every inch of her skin, until finally he reached her mouth.

Then he took her to the heights once more with just his fingers, starting slow, faster, circling until she moaned against his lips.

"Number two." And he started again.

She laughed and wriggled beneath him. "I changed my mind. Two is enough. I want you inside me."

"Oh no. I'm an honorable man." He dropped a kiss on her lips. "At least ten is a point of honor. Although I'm more than up for fifteen if you want."

She made it to five before begging, "*Please*, I just want you inside me. I need you so badly."

"I need you too." At last, he took her—hard, deep, fast. "*Forever*, Lyssa. *Forever*."

★ ★ ★

It had been two days since Saturday's disastrous

barbecue.

"You're not going to work today?" Tasha asked Daniel as he stood in the doorway of her office.

Since she'd moved in with him six months ago, he'd rearranged things in the San Francisco flat, creating a workspace for her with a desk, shelves, and cabinets he'd lovingly crafted himself. A brilliant web designer, she'd created an innovative app for Top Notch that allowed customers to interactively design furnishings for the entire house. Every day, he couldn't believe he'd been lucky enough to find her.

Daniel shrugged, and even that hurt. "I'm working from home."

She tipped her head, her dark hair falling over her shoulder. "You're ashamed to let your employees see you looking like you've been in a barroom brawl, aren't you?"

He wanted to say it was Cal's fault. He'd been trying to convince himself of that for two days.

It wasn't working.

Especially when he'd shown Tasha a side of him that he was deeply ashamed of.

"I blew it, didn't I?"

"Big-time."

She'd had brunch with Lyssa and the girls yesterday. But she hadn't revealed a word his sister had said. The need to know whether Lyssa would ever forgive him was an ache burrowing under his ribs that had nothing to do with the punches Cal had thrown.

He'd had two days to consider everything Tasha had said, everything his mom said. He'd wanted to stay angry at Cal and thereby justify himself.

But the truth was he hadn't been justified at all. He hadn't stopped to think, he'd simply lost control. Now he had no idea how to fix it. "I called Lyssa, but she won't answer."

"I'm not surprised," Tasha said.

At last, it all came spilling out. "You were right all along. It's Lyssa's life. I had no right to criticize her actions." It hurt to talk through his split lip, but it hurt even worse to recognize how wrong he'd been. "She's not a little girl anymore. She's an adult. An adult who can not only take care of herself, but who's also been doing a damned good job of it." He grimaced slightly. "Even if she ended up getting pregnant by a guy nearly twice her age."

Tasha finally rose from her desk and came to him, putting her hand on the relatively undamaged side of his face. "I know how hard it is to change the view you've always had of someone you love."

Tasha understood. She'd idolized her big brother Drew. Until the day she'd had to view him through different eyes.

"The way I reacted was unacceptable," he said in a low voice. "I had no right to judge either of them. I would do anything to rewind and undo it all."

Tasha went up on her toes to kiss his broken lip, and he almost staggered beneath the weight of her unspoken forgiveness.

"You can fix this, Daniel."

With her belief in him, he believed he actually could.

But how?

* * *

Lyssa and Cal left the office early, at five o'clock instead of seven or eight, and picked up a curry because neither of them felt like cooking. They went to her apartment so she could pack a bag. Because they didn't want to spend a single moment apart.

"Daniel's been calling me today," she said as they ate at her tiny kitchen table. "But I'm not ready to see him yet."

"You will be." Cal raised her hand to kiss her fingers. "He's your big brother, and you love him."

"Yeah. I love that big ugly lug. But I still need time to think about what to say to him so he understands he can never, ever treat me—or you—like that again."

Cal pushed his plate away. "I'd like to speak with him first, if that's okay with you." He held up his hand before she mistook his meaning. "I'm not under the delusion that I need to avenge you. You're more than capable of dealing with your brother."

"I certainly am." She gave him a soft kiss. "You're

going to talk with him about your relationship, aren't you?"

He nodded. "Before I ever met you, I had a business relationship with Daniel, then a close friendship. Not only is all of that in jeopardy, but now that I'm your husband-to-be, Daniel will also be my brother-in-law. I need to fix things with him just as much as you do." He cupped her cheek. "And this will give you extra time to figure out what you want to say to him."

"Thank you," she whispered. "I love you."

"As I love you. Always."

Chapter Thirty-Two

After letting himself out of the apartment, Cal jogged down the stairs. And almost ran into Daniel coming up.

The left side of Daniel's face was a mass of purplish bruising. His lip was split, and his eye was swollen shut like Cal's. The two of them were mirror images.

Cal studied his friend. The man he'd fought like a bear a mere two days ago. "Do I look as bad as you?"

"Worse." Daniel stepped onto the landing, his shoulders slumped, his head dipped in defeat. "Lyssa won't take my calls. So I tailgated someone coming in the building to get past the locked entry." He held up a small stuffed animal, a dog. "I came to bring her this."

"Like she's a little girl you can mollify with a toy?" Cal asked in utter incredulity. Had the man learned nothing?

"Not because I still think she's a little girl. Because it'll help me explain." He held up the toy, his expression almost sheepish. "There's a story."

Cal had intended to tell his own story. But now he

needed to hear Daniel's. "I'm listening."

Daniel huffed out a sigh. Clearly, he didn't want to tell Cal. But just as clearly, he seemed to realize that if he didn't talk now, on the landing between two floors, the two of them might never talk again.

"It's not just a stuffed animal. When Lyssa was about six, she wanted a puppy. But of course the apartment was way too small, and we didn't have any money to feed it or take it to the vet. So all of us—me, Will, Matt, Evan, Sebastian—each went in search of stuffed animals, something to make her feel better. And we all came back with something different." With his face so wrecked, his smile was hard to recognize, but his voice had gone soft with memory. "Will got her this ridiculously huge Saint Bernard she could actually sit on like a horse. Sebastian found a stuffed dog with a missing eye. Matt came back with three he'd won at an arcade. Never challenge that guy to an arcade game. Evan brought some cute stuffed toy that he managed to get for a huge discount at a fancy store. And I hit the thrift shops up in Wicker Park, where the rich kids gave away stuff they'd never even used."

It was such a Maverick thing to do. They'd only ever wanted Lyssa to be happy.

"That's how we took care of her. We found ways to make sure she never had to face the big bad world. We didn't want her to realize the apartment was a dump, albeit one Mom kept spotless. We always wanted her to feel safe and protected, even if we were dirt poor."

"That's where it all started, when you were kids." Cal got where his friend was coming from, finally. "When Lyssa needed to be taken care of, you were all there for her, her loving big brothers, making sure nothing bad happened to her. Believe me, I applaud that." He paused for a beat. "But you have to understand that she doesn't need you to protect her now. She's a grown woman. She's brilliant and funny and caring and wonderful, and she's completely capable of taking care not only of herself but also her child. She's the most capable woman I know." He smiled. "Other than your mother."

"Yeah," Daniel said with a nod, "she's so much like Mom. I was wrong not to see that. I was wrong to lash out at you." He hung his head. "I have no excuses. And honestly, I'm not sure Tasha's ever going to forgive me."

"Of course she will."

Daniel shook his head. "If you heard the way she tore a strip off me Saturday, you wouldn't be so sure. And she was right—even if I hated your guts in the moment, I shouldn't have attacked you the way I did."

"I had no right to beat you up either," Cal said. "Especially in front of the kids."

"You were defending yourself. I was the one who lost control. It was my fault."

"It wasn't. Not entirely." Now Cal had his own explaining to do. "You were blindsided by something you never dreamed would happen. But I need you to know that I love your sister with everything in me. I'll be there for her in every way she needs me. And I already love this baby more than I can express. I'm going to be a good father." He believed that now. And he'd learned it from his own father, who'd been a great dad, until that one huge mistake.

Cal stopped short of saying he'd be the best husband. That was Lyssa's news to share with her brother.

Daniel was silent for a long moment. "I know you will be." Then he cracked a smile with that broken lip. "Or I'll have to beat the crap out of you again."

Cal saw the joke in it, happy to see Daniel had finally accepted that his sister wasn't a little girl anymore.

"I'm glad Lyssa found a man who loves, respects, and values her. That's all I've ever wanted for her. You understand her in a way I never allowed myself to. But I do now." Daniel held out the stuffed dog. "I brought her this today as an apology, because she wouldn't take my calls." He flicked something tied to its collar, a bit of paper Cal hadn't noticed. "It's a note telling her I know how badly I screwed up. That I'm sorry, and I hope she can forgive me. Maybe she'll talk to me again someday." He held it up to Cal. "Would you give it to her for me?"

"You need to give it to her yourself." Cal nodded

toward the stairs. "Go knock on the door. She'll let you in."

It was the only time Cal had ever seen Daniel Spencer unsure of himself. "I'm scared down to my bones."

"I have faith in you, man."

Cal slapped him on the back, a gesture of forgiveness. Then he jogged down the stairs, leaving Daniel to march himself up to his sister's door.

* * *

Lyssa was putting away the leftover curry when she heard a knock. She opened the door, about to ask Cal why he was back so soon. The words died on her lips.

Daniel stood in the doorway. "I know you said you needed time to think. But I couldn't let any more time pass knowing you hated me."

Of course she didn't hate him. At the same time, she wasn't ready to let him off the hook that easily. She also wasn't interested in hiding anything from him anymore, so she deliberately looked past him into the hallway. "Cal was just here. Did you see him coming up?"

Daniel nodded, blinking with the only eyelid that worked. "I did. And we talked."

She put a hand on her hip. "With fists or words?"

"Words." He tried to smile, but his swollen mouth wasn't cooperating. "We had a really good talk, Lyssa.

Then he left to give you and me time to talk. He said he'd be back."

Ah. If Cal was giving them space, whatever Daniel had told him must have convinced Cal that she'd want to hear what her brother had to say.

And it would be churlish to leave Daniel standing in the hallway. "Come on in."

Truthfully, he looked even worse than Cal. One half of his face was black and blue. Cal had obviously gotten in some very good right hooks. Her brother's left eye was barely open, and she was surprised he could talk through that swollen lip.

She stood, her arms folded, waiting.

Daniel held up a stuffed animal with both hands, like an offering. "I was going to give this to you, like that time we all got you the stuffed animals." His nostrils flared as he breathed in, as if something was swollen up there too. "But you're not a little girl who needs stuffed animals to make her feel better." It was hard to tell with the colors marking his face, but she thought his features softened. "So I'm giving you this as an early gift for your baby. My niece or nephew." A slip of paper was tied to its collar, and Daniel tore it off, shoving it in his pocket. "I wrote you a note, because I thought for sure you wouldn't let me in. But if you'll listen, I'll tell you what it said."

"I'm listening," she said softly to her very big brother.

He looked more contrite than she'd ever thought possible. "I'm sorry for not giving you and Cal a chance to tell everyone yourselves. I'm sorry for not trusting you to know what you were doing. I'm sorry for thinking that I had the right to judge you. Or Cal. I don't have an excuse. Like Mom said, what I did was totally unacceptable. That's not what this family is about." He swallowed, and she thought it went down hard. "I've asked Cal to forgive me. But I need to ask your forgiveness even more."

She took the fluffy dog, holding it against her belly, against the baby. Then she held out her hand to Daniel. "There's something I want to show you."

She led him to the bedroom, stepping aside so he could enter.

The bed was covered with well-loved stuffed animals, the Saint Bernard standing sentinel at the foot. Surprise lit his features—at least she thought it did.

"You still have them all." His voice was soft, low, as if he couldn't believe it.

"Of course I do. They've gone with me everywhere, from the old apartment, to the house you bought Mom and Dad, to here. They've always been my most precious possessions."

She held up the dog he'd just given her. "And I know this will be one of my child's most precious possessions too."

Something shimmered in his eyes, and though it

could have been just the pain of his injuries, she felt certain they were tears.

"I have no excuse. I lost control completely. You've always been my little sister. And I'll always be the big brother who wants to take care of you. But I got it all mixed up in my head, feeling like you still needed me to step in and make things right. I didn't think, I just acted. And I acted badly." He looked at her with such grief in his one open eye. "When you moved out here, I urged Mom and Dad to come with you, told them we all needed to look out for you. I just didn't want to see that you'd grown up. I wanted you to be my little sister forever. But I've finally figured out that you don't need us to take care of you, because you're a strong, amazing woman. I made so many mistakes along the way, trying to get Cal to give you that job because I thought you'd be safe. But you don't need me to protect you. And you don't need me to arrange jobs for you. You can do it all on your own. You can do *anything* on your own."

She hugged the stuffed animal. "I can take care of myself. But in your misguided wisdom, you ended up giving me the chance to know Cal better. I might never have seen the truly wonderful man he is if I hadn't been able to spend all this time with him."

Daniel touched her hand. "Do you remember at the wedding, when I told you that Cal wasn't for you?"

She nodded, allowing herself a small smile. "It was

a really bad idea to say that."

He snorted a soft laugh. "Yeah, probably. I've never been more wrong in my life. He's *exactly* the kind of man I want for you. I see the way he shines when he talks about you." He waved a hand down her face. "I see the way you glow. And it's not just the baby you're carrying. It's the two of you together. It's the love between you. If only I'd taken fifteen minutes to cool down and see what was right in front of me. But I never gave you a chance. I just let this red mist cloud my eyes. Of all the mistakes I've made in my life, that's the worst. Because I truly support you in every decision you make. And I will love your baby with everything in me."

Her heart melting for her big brother, she threw herself into his arms. "I love you and forgive you." She stepped back, hands on his arms, still clutching the baby's first gift. "Uncle Daniel."

* * *

Cal returned after Daniel had gone, helping her pack some of her things to take over to his place. She was so glad that she and Daniel had mended the rift between them. But there was still an ache inside her when she thought about the rest of the Mavericks. Tomorrow morning, she'd go to each of them and hope they'd also come around.

Yes, she could take care of herself, but she still

wanted her family—her *entire* family—in her life.

She'd only just decided to call her mom to tell her about their marriage plans, to let her know they weren't planning to rush off to Vegas or Tahoe for a quickie wedding, when she heard the stomping and snorting of what sounded like a herd of buffalo outside her apartment.

She opened the door to find six Mavericks standing outside. "What are you all doing here?"

"As soon as I left," Daniel said, "I called an emergency meeting, only to learn the other guys all had the same idea and were calling one too. But before I turn it over to them, I want to say again that I love you, Lyssa. I believe in you. I support you." Then he turned to Cal, who was standing in astonishment behind Lyssa, and smiled as widely as his sore mouth would allow. "You know you've always been a Maverick, and we're proud as hell to count you as one of us."

Though Cal simply nodded, Lyssa saw the softening of his features and knew how much this meant to him.

Will elbowed Daniel out of the way, the tiniest bit careful of his ribs. "Jeremy is so excited about the baby." He pointed at Cal. "And he's excited to have you as a real uncle." Then he reached for Lyssa's hand. "I have no excuse for my behavior. I should have supported you both. Believe me, I'll do everything in my power never to blow it like that again with either of you, or the baby."

Matt stepped forward. "I believe in you, Lyssa, even if sometimes I screw up and act like an idiot." And to Cal, he said, "I love you like a brother. We all said some rotten things on Saturday that should never have come out of our mouths. I hope you can forgive us."

Cal nodded. "Of course I do."

Then Sebastian moved up front. "First, I have to thank you for the best damn fight I've ever witnessed." All the brothers laughed. Then he got serious. "Lyssa, you're the bomb. You always have been. I swear I never questioned your judgment, even though sometimes it may have seemed like it." Then to Cal, he said, "We know you'll make Lyssa happy. We see it in your eyes now, and we saw it on Saturday. It was one of our biggest mistakes that we didn't acknowledge it."

He held out his hand, and Cal shook it despite the bruises and cuts on his knuckles.

Evan simply opened his arms wide, and Lyssa gladly walked into them. "You're an amazing woman, Lyssa, in every way. I'm so glad you've found your happy place in your business. And in the rest of your life too." He stepped back, holding her shoulders. "Paige is ecstatic that our babies will be so close in age. We can't wait to watch them all grow up together." Then he let her go and looked at Cal with a bit of trepidation and a lot of remorse. "Forgive us if you can, Cal. We acted like—"

Lyssa finished before he could. "Like a herd of buffalo trampling everything."

They all laughed and nodded. Even Cal.

Then Gideon pushed his way through, having stood silently at the back. "You know I think the world of you both," he said in his strong, quiet way. "And I'm glad you've found one another. I know you're going to make it. Forever."

She held out her arms to encompass all the Mavericks. And when their hugfest was over, she caught Cal's eye. When he smiled and nodded, she said, "I'm glad you're all here, because this way I can tell you all at the same time." She reached for Cal's hand. "We want you all to know we're getting married."

Every single Maverick in the whole darn place cheered.

It might even have been louder than a herd of stampeding buffalo.

Epilogue

The New Year's fundraising gala at Dane Harrington's Napa resort was a rousing success. By eight o'clock, the ballroom was crammed with beautifully dressed partygoers. Drinks were flowing, appetizers were abundant, and Dane had released hundreds of black, silver, and purple balloons, which now floated against the high ceiling. The walls were draped in matching tinsel foil, and silver tablecloths draped thirty tables with seating for ten, the chair covers and napkins all in black. Crystal glasses sparkled and silverware glittered, ready for the sit-down gourmet meal. Dane Harrington had graciously donated everything—the venue, the food, the staff, and the drinks.

Lyssa stood with Cal near the edge of the dance floor, looking out over the party. With his arm around her, Cal surprised her by capturing her mouth in a quick and sizzling kiss.

She loved being with him like this—no more hiding, no more dashing into secluded glades for a little nookie, no more worrying about what the family would think. Standing next to Cal, Lyssa felt the wonder of being with him all over again—the heat of his arm around her, the warmth of his body, the beguiling scent of him—and knew their love would always feel fresh and thrilling and new.

"This fundraiser is amazing," she said, once she'd gotten her breath back in the wake of his second, then third impromptu kiss. She'd worked on some of the planning, but as far as she was concerned, most of this was down to Dane.

"Harrington sure knows how to throw a party," Cal noted.

And Cal knew how to dress for it in a tailored black tux. He was drool-worthy, as always. And he was *hers*.

Lyssa wore a classic black, flirty cocktail dress. She'd been thrilled to have the chance to wear it one more time before she'd no longer be able to zip it up. "Do you know how much money this event will bring to the foundation?" She named a seven-figure amount that would all go to Lean on Us. Everyone who was anyone in Silicon Valley was here tonight, plus all the Mavericks, of course, who were mingling with the guests.

"Have I mentioned recently how much I love your accounting mind?"

She grinned, pulling him in for a kiss this time.

Then Gideon spotted them across the room and made a beeline for them, Rosie's hand in his. She wore a beautiful red dress with a pencil skirt, and Gideon was no less dashing in his tuxedo.

"This is amazeballs." Rosie was breathless with awe.

"Harrington is definitely an asset," Gideon acknowledged with a wide smile.

"Where's Jorge?" Lyssa asked.

"We've got a sitter, and they're deep into Legos, so Ari and I decided the boys should stay in the room."

"Smart. You wouldn't want to lose them in this crowd."

Lyssa had already lost sight of the other Mavericks. But wait, there was Tasha in a burgundy strapless number and Daniel wearing his tux, though he looked ready to tug off the tie and cummerbund. He'd called her every day to see how the baby was doing, and even though she was still a little bit mad at him for trying to drown her fiancé, she loved her brother's excitement over his growing niece or nephew.

Lyssa had seen her mom and dad fifteen minutes ago, her mother gorgeous in a floor-length royal blue gown and her father surprisingly comfortable in a new tailored suit.

She spotted Sebastian seating Francine at a table so she didn't have to lean on her walker. Charlie's silver chiffon matched the décor.

Jeremy was by the appetizer table, happily wolfing down food, while Harper, in a lovely teal dress with a flared skirt, was probably warning him not to spoil his dinner. Will looked snazzy in a gray tux as he rounded out their trio. It was actually Will and Harper's anniversary, and they'd all celebrated with them earlier in the day. A lot had happened in a year.

"There's Ari and Matt." Lyssa waved, but she didn't think they saw her in the crush.

"She always looks so good in cream and lace." Then Rosie looked at Lyssa. "Have you seen Kelsey?"

Lyssa nodded. "She came with Evan and Paige." Which meant Tony and their mother were somewhere in the throng too. "They also picked up Chi."

Gideon glanced at his watch and turned to Cal. "Should we gather up our guests of honor?" He grinned. "That way we can get to dinner."

Cal asked Lyssa, "Are you sure you don't want to join us behind the mic? After all, none of this would have been possible without you."

"I'm sure." She kissed him again before sending him off. "Now go. Gideon's not the only one who's hungry." To prove her point, her stomach growled loudly enough to be heard over the music and chatter.

Watching their men go, Rosie told Lyssa, "Gideon's ecstatic about the gala and all the donations for the foundation. But most especially that he'll be able to honor his old friends."

Earlier in the day, before the gala, there'd been a small reception where everyone had been introduced—the Mavericks, Dane's family, Gideon's guests.

Gideon truly seemed to have reached a new level of peace and happiness. It was Rosie's and Jorge's love, of course, but it was also finally feeling like he was achieving something important.

The lights dimmed, signaling everyone to quiet down and look toward the dance floor, where a small dais had been set up with a lectern and microphone.

Cal stepped into the spotlight. "Ladies and gentlemen, I'm Cal Danniger of Lean on Us, and thank you for coming tonight. We're glad you all seem to be having such a wonderful evening so far."

He had such a strong presence and was so handsome and kind. His deep voice was like a caress along Lyssa's skin. She put her hand on her belly and wondered how she could be so lucky. Not only had she found this incredible man, but she was also making a family with him.

"The foundation would like to thank Dane Harrington for providing this venue for our New Year's celebration." He saluted Dane, who was flanked by his brothers and sisters, a very attractive and compelling family group.

"We're here tonight to dedicate the Lean on Us Foundation to the memory of Karmen Sanchez, a daughter, a nurse, a friend, a soldier, who lost her life in defense of her country and while rushing to the aid of her wounded comrades. I've asked Gideon Jones to tell you more."

Rosie's face glowed with love and pride as Gideon stepped into the spotlight beside Cal.

Gideon and Cal leaned in for a manly, back-slap hug. But Lyssa could see the emotion on Cal's face. Lean on Us wasn't just his job or responsibility. It was a duty and an honor, and something he believed in as much as Gideon did.

As Gideon took his place at the microphone, Cal left the dance floor, coming back to her, taking her hand as though there was nowhere else he'd rather be.

Gideon's voice rang out. "This foundation is possible because Karmen Sanchez took a chance on me. She gave me a very special painting and trusted that I would do the right thing with it. It took me ten long years, and it was through my beautiful fiancée and her son that I finally understood what I had to do in Karmen's name."

His gaze rested on Rosie, and all eyes followed his, even without the spotlight. Lyssa saw the tears of love in her friend's eyes. Ari and Matt had joined them, too, and Ari's adoring gaze was riveted on her brother.

Gideon cleared his throat before he choked up. "Karmen Sanchez was a medic first and a soldier second. Her job was to save our lives. And that's exactly what she did when she gave her life for us. She was one of my best friends. What you have to understand is that the friends we soldiers make overseas are our lifelines." He looked and sounded every inch a soldier, his back ramrod straight, his voice strong and compelling. "When we lost Karmen and our comrades that day, we lost a huge piece of our soul. It's been a long road back from that dark place for all of us. And that's what Karmen's legacy in Lean on Us is all about. We want to make that journey back to happiness and hope with our veterans. We want to provide our support to the wounded, to the families who've lost so much, to the children who sadly enough may end up as foster kids, to the men and women who return vastly changed from the young recruits they once were. At Lean on Us, we want to give back in the name of Karmen's sacrifice, in the name of her love and friendship."

He paused, his gaze roaming the room, taking in the crowd, and letting them think about why they were here beyond just a great party. "We want to thank Dane Harrington for hosting us, and we want to thank all of you for coming here tonight. Your donations will help us help so many. So please, find it within yourselves to dig even deeper. With your support, there are so many ways in which Lean on Us can do even more to help."

Lyssa was deeply touched by Gideon's words. He'd never wanted to be the money man, asking people to step up. Yet here he was, doing just that. Because it mattered.

Nestled close to Cal, she murmured, "I really think he's healing."

Cal pulled her in, his wonderful hug saying so much.

Beside her, Rosie was smiling, one of the most beautiful, loving smiles she'd ever seen. It was how Lyssa herself looked at Cal, because it was exactly how she felt.

In the spotlight, Gideon said, "It's my honor to introduce to you a very special woman." He held out a hand, and an elegantly dressed woman in her sixties walked to him across the dance floor. "Please give a round of applause for Karmen's mother, Ernestina Sanchez, without whom none of this would be possible."

She stepped onto the dais, where Gideon kissed her cheek, said a few words to her, then returned to Rosie's side.

Mrs. Sanchez adjusted the microphone, then looked up at the crowd. "It started with a painting my mother loved. She taught my daughter to love this painting as much as she did, taught her to appreciate its magic. Because it *is* magic."

The back wall lit up with an image of the Miguel Fernando Correa painting. Two angels, light and dark, touching fingertips in solidarity. The room reverberated with *oohs* and *aahs* of appreciation.

"When my beloved Karmen gave that painting to

Gideon Jones, she knew its destiny would one day lead to this." Her eloquent voice carried across the ballroom as she waved a hand over the crowd. "Karmen saw the goodness that would come. And I am so honored—" She put her hand to her chest. "—that the Lean on Us Foundation will forever carry on her memory. She worked fearlessly and tirelessly for the greater good. She lost her cousin in the Twin Towers, and all she ever wanted to do was serve her country, to help make a better world, to save lives." She looked directly at Dane Harrington. "It's wonderful knowing that the person with whom the painting now resides will use its power to do even more good. Thank you all."

The balloons on the ceiling drifted on the waves of cheers and clapping as Ernestina Sanchez stepped down.

Gideon hugged Mrs. Sanchez as they passed, and he returned to the lectern. "Thank you, Ernestina." He gave her a fond gaze. "We appreciate everything you've done for us." Then he turned to the sea of faces before him. "Ralph Esterhausen was a soldier. He always did more than his duty, always worked above one hundred and ten percent. He was my friend, my confidant, my brother. I mourn him to this day. As I mourn Johnny Danzi and Hank Garrett and Karmen Sanchez. I mourn these comrades who fell on the same day in the same godforsaken desert. With us tonight is a family that Lean on Us is all about. Ralph Esterhausen's family. We can never replace their loss, never understand their pain, but they can lean on us when they have no one else."

Rosie, Ari, and Lyssa reached into their bags for tissues. Cal soothed Lyssa with a caress down her arm.

Gideon went on. "Crystal Esterhausen and her sons are with us tonight. And she would like to say a few words."

He held out his hand. Mrs. Esterhausen's dress hung on her frame as if the years and the grief had stripped her down to the bone. Two teenagers trailed her, the eldest close to college age, both dressed in new suits, their hair combed back.

She stepped gingerly onto the dais, her sons only a couple of steps behind her as she stood at the lectern. "I miss my husband." Her voice was raspy with emotion. "My boys miss their father. We always will. It hasn't been easy, and sometimes I wish I hadn't—" She stopped, breathed in, let it out, her nostrils flaring. "There are people I wish I hadn't blamed," she rushed the words. "I think if I'd had a place to go like Gideon Jones's foundation, maybe I wouldn't have acted the way I did." She reached into her dress pocket for a lace-trimmed handkerchief, and the rest of the audience dabbed their eyes too. "My boys have scholarships. Now I can see their future when, for a long time, I couldn't." She paused again before adding, "I want to say thank you for letting me lean on you."

She turned quickly, and together she and her sons walked out of the limelight.

The applause was thunderous, and as it died down, Cal leaned close to Lyssa's ear. "Gideon helped her get some counseling. I think she did it for her kids, but it seems to have made a world of difference."

Lyssa knew that Mrs. Esterhausen's forgiving words must be another major healing for Gideon.

Gideon was about to head over to the podium again when his friend Zach put his hand on his arm. "Let me take care of this, buddy."

Zach took command of the microphone. "I don't need an introduction. This guy—" he hooked a thumb at Gideon. "—might have trouble finding nice things to say about me. And none of them would have been true anyway. My name's Zach Smith, and once we shipped over there, me and Gid were Alias Smith and Jones." Laughter rose up. Zach laughed too. "Yeah, at least some of you are old enough to remember that TV show. Good on you. But that was us. Alias Smith and Jones. And let me tell you, Gid was the biggest prankster over there. Why, I remember the time he put—"

"Wrong audience," Gideon called out.

Zach grinned. "Well, maybe I better not tell you that one. At least not until later tonight." Laughter filled the room. "What I will tell you is that Gideon Jones helped make all our lives bearable. So it doesn't surprise me that now he's working to make life bearable for soldiers coming back. Gideon sees a need, and he jumps in—now all we need is for the full lot of you to jump in with him. Soldiers need you, veterans need you, families need you, foster kids need you. Let's get cracking." He raised a fist in the air and belted out a resounding, "Huzzah." All the Mavericks joined him, until the room took up the cheer.

In that moment, Lyssa understood that the foundation had truly come to life. They were going to help so many people.

She turned, wrapping her arms around Cal, wanting to share the moment with him.

"I knew there were some sparks flying between you two." Dane was grinning as they drew apart. "Even if you tried to deny it that day in the office, Lyssa." Then he shook Cal's hand. "Great job with the speeches. They were short and sweet, and the donations are already pouring in."

"We can't thank you enough." Cal's words were heartfelt.

Then it became a melee of Mavericks and Harringtons, a chorus of *great* and *fabulous* and *amazing* and *well done.*

Lyssa had met all the family and talked a bit with Dane's sister Ava. She was a compelling combination of sweet and sharp, with a ready smile and a keen intelligence in her eyes, her hair a glossy red. The two brothers were Troy and Clay, who were a bit like Dane with the same short dark hair, blue eyes, and handsome, bad-boy looks. Gabby was the youngest, her long blond hair falling like silk to the middle of her back.

Then Matt grabbed Gideon with an arm around his shoulders and said in a loud voice to their gathering of friends and family, "We've got an announcement."

Lyssa spied Rosie and Ari holding hands. And she absolutely knew, her heart about to burst.

Her mom knew, too, her hands already to her mouth and tears of joy filling her eyes as Lyssa's dad wrapped an arm around her, his share of tears blurring his eyes too.

Then Gideon and Matt shouted out together, "We're pregnant!"

Dane said, laughing, "Isn't that an anatomical impossibility?"

But everyone knew what they meant, and it became the world's biggest hugfest. There weren't enough tissues to go round.

But there was certainly more than enough love.

Finally, Lyssa found herself enveloped in the arms of Ari and Rosie and Paige. "This is so great! All of our babies will be the same age."

"Noah and Jorge can babysit them like big brothers should," Ari said.

It was the most wonderful thing she could ever imagine.

Except for Cal.

When she turned, he was right there. He would always be right there. Supporting her. Making her laugh. Inspiring her.

Loving her.

She threw her arms around him, tears blurring her vision. "I love you so much."

"I love you just as much." His kiss tasted of joy and family.

Soldiers and veterans and foster kids would always have Lean on Us.

And she and Cal would always have each other.

★ ★ ★

"Four pregnant women," Dane's brother Troy said as the Harrington siblings gathered. "Am I the only one who finds that terrifying?"

"I heard someone say Paige Collins is having twins," Clay put in.

Ava's eyes went wide. "That makes five!" Then she smiled as she looked over at the Maverick matriarch. "I bet Susan Spencer is in heaven."

"She is," Dane said softly, watching Susan hug and kiss the cheeks of each family member.

The gala was a rousing fundraising success. Each person had spoken straight from the heart, especially Gideon. Dane had respect for the man and what he wanted to accomplish. He had respect for Cal, who he knew damn well was running the foundation without a cent of recompense.

This spirit seemed to be what the Mavericks were all about. They weren't just brilliant billionaires who worked together, they were a true family.

More than once, he'd found himself wishing he were a Maverick. He had a feeling his siblings would feel the same way. He admired what each and every Maverick had accomplished. And he admired Bob and Susan Spencer for how they'd raised them all.

He was happy for all of them. Cal, with his arm around Lyssa's shoulders, holding her close, as if he were afraid she might disappear. Matt starry-eyed for Ari. Gideon, who would have been floating up among the balloons without Rosie to keep him grounded. Evan with his hand on Paige's belly, thrilled that he would soon be a father.

Dane had spent his entire adult life keeping his brothers and sisters together after the deaths of their parents. Even before that, he'd all but raised them when their parents hadn't been around that much. Now that they'd all found their own paths and were doing well, his life had become about business, the resorts, expansion.

He had no complaints...but lately, not complaining didn't seem quite good enough.

Dane thought about the painting he now owned, about the magic Ernestina Sanchez had talked about, and found himself wondering if there was any chance the magic might rub off on him...

★ ★ ★

ABOUT THE AUTHORS

Having sold more than 10 million books, Bella Andre's novels have been #1 bestsellers around the world and have appeared on the *New York Times* and *USA Today* bestseller lists 93 times. She has been the #1 Ranked Author on a top 10 list that included Nora Roberts, JK Rowling, James Patterson and Steven King.

Known for "sensual, empowered stories enveloped in heady romance" (Publishers Weekly), her books have been Cosmopolitan Magazine "Red Hot Reads" twice and have been translated into ten languages. She is a graduate of Stanford University and has won the Award of Excellence in romantic fiction. The Washington Post called her "One of the top writers in America" and she has been featured by Entertainment Weekly, NPR, USA Today, Forbes, The Wall Street Journal, and TIME Magazine.

Bella also writes the *New York Times* bestselling "Four Weddings and a Fiasco" series as Lucy Kevin. Her sweet contemporary romances also include the USA Today bestselling "Walker Island" and "Married in Malibu" series.

If not behind her computer, you can find her reading her favorite authors, hiking, swimming or laughing. Married with two children, Bella splits her time between the Northern California wine country, a log cabin in the Adirondack mountains of upstate New York, and a flat in London overlooking the Thames.

Sign up for Bella's New Release newsletter:
BellaAndre.com/Newsletter

Join Bella Andre on Facebook:
facebook.com/bellaandrefans

Join Bella Andre's reader group:
bellaandre.com/readergroup

Follow Bella Andre on Instagram:
instagram.com/bellaandrebooks

Follow Bella Andre on Twitter:
twitter.com/bellaandre

Visit Bella's website for her complete booklist:
www.BellaAndre.com

NY Times and *USA Today* bestselling author Jennifer Skully is a lover of contemporary romance, bringing you poignant tales peopled with characters that will make you laugh and make you cry. Look for *The Maverick Billionaires* written with Bella Andre, starting with *Breathless in Love*, along with Jennifer's new later-in-life holiday romance series, *Once Again*, where readers can travel to fabulous faraway locales. Up first is a trip to Provence in *Dreaming of Provence*. Writing as Jasmine Haynes, Jennifer authors classy, sensual romance tales about real issues such as growing older, facing divorce, starting over. Her books have passion and heart and humor and happy endings, even if they aren't always traditional. She also writes gritty, paranormal mysteries in the Max Starr series. Having penned stories since the moment she learned to write, Jennifer now lives in the Redwoods of Northern California with her husband and their adorable nuisance of a cat who totally runs the household.

Newsletter signup:

http://bit.ly/SkullyNews

Jennifer's Website:

www.jenniferskully.com

Blog:

www.jasminehaynes.blogspot.com

Facebook:

facebook.com/jasminehaynesauthor

Twitter:

twitter.com/jasminehaynes1

Printed in Great Britain
by Amazon

78432146R00219